THE POR[

By $

A DI Ruth Hunter Crime Thriller
Book 13

THE PORTMEIRION KILLINGS

DI Ruth Hunter Crime Thriller #13

SIMON MCCLEAVE

STAMFORD
PUBLISHING

No part of this publication may be reproduced, stored, or transmitted in any form or by any means, electronic, mechanical, photocopying, recording, scanning, or otherwise without written permission from the publisher. It is illegal to copy this book, post it to a website, or distribute it by any other means without permission.

Names, characters, businesses, places, events, and incidents are either the products of the author's imagination or used in a purely fictitious manner. Any resemblance to actual persons, living or dead, or actual events is purely coincidental.

First published by Stamford Publishing Ltd in 2022

Copyright © Simon McCleave, 2022
All rights reserved

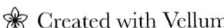 Created with Vellum

Your FREE book is waiting for you now!

Get your FREE copy of the prequel to
the DI Ruth Hunter Series NOW
http://www.simonmccleave.com/vip-email-club
and join my VIP Email Club

Also by Simon McCleave

THE DI RUTH HUNTER SERIES

#1 *The Snowdonia Killings*
#2. *The Harlech Beach Killings*
#3. *The Dee Valley Killings*
#4. *The Devil's Cliff Killings*
#5. *The Berwyn River Killings*
#6. *The White Forest Killings*
#7. *The Solace Farm Killings*
#8. *The Menai Bridge Killings*
#9. *The Conway Bridge Killings*
#10. *The River Seine Killings*
#11. *The Lake Vyrnwy Killings*
#12 *The Chirk Castle Killings*
#13 *The Portmeirion Killings*

THE DC RUTH HUNTER MURDER CASE SERIES

#1. *Diary of a War Crime*
#2. *The Razor Gang Murder*
#3. *An Imitation of Darkness*
#4. *This is London, SE15*

THE ANGLESEY SERIES - DI LAURA HART
(Harper Collins / AVON Publishing)

#1. *The Dark Tide*

#2. In Too Deep

#3. Blood on the Shore

The courage in journalism is sticking up for the unpopular, not the popular.
Geraldo Rivera

Capitalism is against the things that we say we believe in - democracy, freedom of choice, fairness. It's not about any of those things now. It's about protecting the wealthy and legalizing greed.
Michael Moore

Siblings are our partners and rivals, our first friends, and our first enemies.
Erica Goldblatt Hyatt

For Emma and Luca x

Chapter 1

March 2021
HMP Rhoswen
6.32pm

It was 48 hours since Detective Sergeant Nick Evans of the North Wales Police had been arrested on his doorstep for the murder of Paul Thurrock. The last two days had been a confusing and distressing whirlwind of interviews, holding cells, a magistrates' court – and now prison.

Taking a step forward, the young, awkward-looking prison officer, with shaved ginger hair and a splash of freckles across the bridge of his nose, gestured for him to come forward. Despite the confidence of his motioning arm, his roaming and slightly twitching eyes revealed his nerves.

Nick thought that the officer didn't even look old enough to shave. He then took a step forward and stood, feeling somewhat exposed in just his boxer shorts. Nick was starting his induction onto the VP wing of HMP Rhoswen, North Wales' newest 'Super Prison'. VP stood for Vulnerable Prisoners and was where rapists, paedophiles and any sex offenders were kept apart from the main population for their own safety. The VP wing also housed informants, witnesses, police officers and anyone else who might be targeted within the prison.

'Nicholas Evans,' the prison officer said, gesturing to him again. He had an old-fashioned gold pinkie ring on his little finger. 'Need you to strip,' he mumbled.

Taking down his boxers, Nick stood there naked.

Well this is nice, he thought sardonically. He consoled himself that at least he was in a new warm prison rather than some draughty, freezing Victorian jail that you found in Britain's major cities. He'd been a police officer long enough to know the drill of arriving in prison, but it still felt very degrading.

'Open your mouth,' the officer snapped in an unfriendly tone. Nick knew the type. Young and inexperienced – he was trying to overcompensate by being hostile. He didn't blame him. There were some right scumbags in UK prisons who would pounce on the first sign of weakness in 'a screw.'

Nick opened his mouth and the officer took a closer than comfortable look inside. In fact, he was so close that Nick could smell his breath - chewing gum and stewed tea.

'Lift your tongue,' the officer commanded.

Nick lifted his tongue, still trying to get his head around the fact that this was actually happening. It felt surreal. He knew all the cliches about being in a nightmare and that at some point he was going to wake up from it. But that's exactly how it felt.

The Portmeirion Killings

The officer gestured. 'Arms out and legs apart.'

Nick complied.

The officer checked him all over, lifted his scrotum for inspection and then said, 'Squat.'

Lowering himself down, Nick obliged feeling even more humiliated. The fact that he was completely innocent of the crime he had been charged with made it seem so much worse.

'Cough,' the officer said.

Nick coughed while still squatting down. It was to make sure that he was not carrying anything inside his rectum – drugs, a weapon or a small mobile phone.

The officer handed him the regulation grey sweatshirt, jogging trousers and white socks with a sour expression. 'Put these on and follow me.'

As he got dressed, Nick replayed the events leading up to his arrest yet again.

The previous week, Amanda's daughter, Fran, had gone out in Llancastell for a few drinks after work. Paul Thurrock, her manager, had sexually assaulted her in an alleyway in the middle of town. Even though Fran had been adamant she didn't want to press charges against Thurrock, Nick had had *a quiet word* with him to make sure he never went near Fran again. In fact, Nick had promised Thurrock that if he did, Nick would take him out to the middle of Snowdonia and bury him in a hole. It wasn't the smartest thing that Nick had ever done and it went against all the principles he had learnt as a recovering alcoholic who was following a 12-step programme.

Two days later, someone had assaulted Thurrock, who, for some reason, had pinned the blame on Nick. Taking it upon himself to follow Thurrock, Nick watched as he parked at the top of Llancastell's central multi-storey car park. Thurrock had exchanged drugs or money with someone sitting inside a nearby Range Rover. A quick PNC check had revealed, to Nick's utter shock, that the Range Rover belonged to an old adversary of Nick's - Curtis Blake.

That was a major development.

Nick and Curtis Blake had a history of bad blood going back nearly twenty years. Then, two days ago, someone had murdered Paul Thurrock and set up Nick to take the fall. Nick knew it was Blake.

Curtis Blake was the head of a notorious Merseyside OCG, the Croxteth Park Boyz. Essentially he was a psychotic gangster who still ran a sizeable chunk of Liverpool's drug trade. Blake used to have contacts in the Netherlands where he owned drug factories. He had used violence and intimidation to seize the supply of class-A drugs within Scotland's major cities, in particular Glasgow, where he had cousins who helped him out.

Nick hated everything about Blake. His creepy grin during arrests and questioning. His perma-tan and expensive veneers. His cars, Mediterranean villa and yacht. His fondness for starving his massive American Bully dogs – originally bred from American pit bulls and Staffordshire terriers – and then locking his enemies and rivals in a room with them, laughing at the screams as they were torn to pieces. Nick thought he was a disgusting excuse for a human being.

Nick also had a more personal reason for hating Curtis Blake. An ex-girlfriend of his from school, Laura Foley, had got hooked on drugs while at Liverpool University. She quickly became a heroin user. On a beautiful August evening in 2003, Laura had overdosed and died in the house she shared in Toxteth with three other smackheads.

Nick couldn't bear to think of her like that. Even though Nick was only a uniformed PC on the beat at that time, he did some digging around the investigation into Laura's death. It was clear that Curtis Blake had supplied the heroin that had killed her. So, if he was honest, Nick had been obsessed with getting his revenge on Blake ever since.

In 2019, Blake was convicted of intent to supply, but charges of being a member of an OCG and conspiracy to murder were dropped. He was transferred from HMP Wakefield to Rhoswen for his own protection. There was then a turf war in Merseyside as gangs tried to divvy up Blake's empire, but intel suggested that he had managed to keep hold of most of his drug business. However, a few weeks ago, Blake had been released from prison on appeal.

'CID officers are here to interview you before you go up onto the wing,' the prison officer said, breaking Nick's train of thought as he pointed to an interview room further down the corridor.

Nick nodded as his heart sank. He had spoken to the CID officers from St Asaph twice. For obvious reasons, Ruth and the CID team from Llancastell weren't authorised to investigate Thurrock's murder. It was a conflict of interest. If St Asaph wanted to talk to him again, it might suggest they had new evidence. And that was bad news.

'Follow me, Evans,' the officer barked.

Wandering down the corridor on the ground floor of HMP Rhoswen, Nick spotted several other interview rooms. They were used for applications for bail, appeals, meetings with solicitors, as well as ongoing investigations.

'In here,' the officer pointed as he opened the dark navy door.

As Nick went in, he saw the familiar faces of DS Carter and DC Reagan from St Asaph CID sitting at the interview table. They had an array of folders and documents in front of them.

'Take a seat, Nick,' Reagan said in a deadpan tone.

Pulling out a chair, Nick spotted Reagan looking up at him. He was in his 20s, with sharp features and beady eyes.

Don't judge me, you twat. I didn't do this.

Chapter 2

Ruth walked along the landing and then poked her head into the spare bedroom. Daniel was standing on his bed while attaching a poster of a Chelsea footballer to his wall. Daniel was ten-years-old and he'd been living with her under a temporary foster care licence for a week now after the death of his father Vincent. She hoped to make it permanent at some point.

'Hey, do you need any help with that?' she asked.

'I'm fine thanks,' Daniel replied and turned to her with a smile that melted her heart. 'Did you know that Mason Mount has been at Chelsea since he was six-years-old?' He was referring to the footballer on his poster.

Ruth shook her head. 'I didn't know that but it seems very young.'

'No.' Daniel shook his head. 'Reece James joined when he was six and Tammy Abraham when he was seven.'

'Oh right,' Ruth replied. 'Well there you are then.' She then frowned. 'Are you putting Blu Tack all over my walls?'

'Yes,' Daniel replied with a shrug. 'But I can repaint the wall when I take the posters down.'

'Good idea.' Ruth smiled. 'I'll leave you to it then.'

With a little chortle to herself, Ruth turned and padded along the thick carpet of the landing towards the stairs. Her only child Ella was in her early 20s now and she had moved away. It was lovely to have Daniel, with his wonderfully innocent view of life, in the house.

Walking down the stairs, Ruth adjusted a few of the pictures that weren't straight. There was a photo of Ruth and her partner Sarah that had been taken a few months ago. There were still times when Ruth couldn't believe that she had Sarah back in her life after all that had happened.

Back in November 2013, Ruth and Sarah had been living together as a couple in their flat in Crystal Palace, South-East London. Sarah boarded a train to London Victoria one morning and simply disappeared. No contact, no note, no clue as to where she had gone. As a copper, Ruth had made sure the CCTV footage from that day had been scoured. Every station on that line had been searched. There had been television appeals and articles in the press. There had been sightings of Sarah from all around the world. Ruth had even followed women who she thought looked like Sarah, but she had simply vanished.

Little did Ruth know that Sarah had become secretly embroiled in the seedy world of elite sex parties in London through a man named Jamie Parsons. A few days before she had disappeared, Sarah had witnessed Lord David Weaver raping and then 'accidentally' killing a teenage girl in a bedroom at one of these *Secret Garden* sex parties. Lord Weaver was a life peer who had served as both Foreign Secretary and Chief Whip in the late 1980s. He was a very visible member of the House of Lords, often photographed with the great and the good, the rich and famous. His wife Olivia moved in social circles with lesser members of the royal family.

To make matters worse, Sarah's presence in the room had been spotted by Jamie Parsons and three others. Jurgen Kessler, a German banker and close friend of Parsons, who was wanted by Berlin Police for questioning in connection with the murder of two young women. Patrice Le Bon, the multi-millionaire owner of several Paris model agencies, who was under investigation for human trafficking. And Sergei Saratov, a Russian billionaire, who had gone underground when police investigated his extensive use of escorts and sex workers in hotels that he owned in an exclusive European ski resort. These men were very rich, very powerful – and therefore very dangerous. And Sarah was an eyewitness. She was taken away to France and was forced to move around Europe working as a high-class escort.

Several months ago, Ruth had travelled to Paris and rescued Sarah, who was now living under Witness Protection while the Crown Prosecution Service constructed their case against Lord Weaver.

Getting to the bottom of the stairs, Ruth walked along the hallway and stuck her head into the living room where Sarah was intently watching the news.

'Wine?' Ruth asked.

'Stupid question,' Sarah laughed.

Ruth ambled to the kitchen, opened the fridge and grabbed a cold bottle of Sauvignon Blanc. She twisted off the top, remembering that when she was younger any wine with a twist top was foul and cheap. Twist tops were the preserve of fizzy wines such as *Lambrusco*.

Taking out two glasses that resembled fish bowls, she poured out two generous glasses that equated to half the bottle already and returned to the living room.

She handed Sarah one of the glasses. 'Here you go, mush.'

'Thanks,' Sarah said, but she had an anxious expression on her face.

Ruth raised an eyebrow. Sarah had seemed fine a few seconds ago. 'You okay?'

'Not really,' Sarah admitted as she gestured to the news on the television. 'They've called off the search for Gabriella's body in Wiltshire.'

Gabriella Cardoso was the seventeen-year-old Portuguese au pair that Sarah had seen Lord Weaver strangle in November 2013. Gabriella had told the family she was working for that she was going out with friends in Notting Hill on Friday November 1st 2013, but never came home. There was a police investigation but there was a suggestion that she might have travelled to Australia to meet up with backpacker friends from Portugal out there. However, there was no record of her travelling out of the country in the days after her disappearance. It wasn't until Sarah gave her testimony that there had been any suggestion of foul play regarding Gabriella's disappearance.

Ruth and Sarah had hoped that if police had found Gabriella's body, then the case against Lord Weaver would be far stronger. The fact that the police had now stopped searching an area where they had previously thought Gabriella's body might have been buried meant that they were back to square one again. And that meant Sarah was in the frustrating limbo of Witness Protection with no end in sight.

Ruth sat down next to Sarah on the sofa and put a reassuring hand on her shoulder. 'I'm really sorry.'

Chapter 3

'Okay if we start now?' Carter asked.

Nick looked around the prison interview room and then nodded. 'Yeah.'

A long electronic beep sounded as Reagan pushed the button on the recording machine. They both opened files and Carter gave Nick a quick look of acknowledgement.

'Interview conducted with Nick Evans, HMP Rhoswen. Present are Detective Sergeant Reagan, Nick Evans and myself, Detective Sergeant Carter.' He then glanced over. 'Nick, you understand that you have been arrested and charged with the murder of Paul Thurrock? Our interview today is in relation to that offence.'

Nick stared down at the table. He had slightly zoned out. He just couldn't believe that he was sitting on the other side of the table in an interview room. It didn't feel real.

'Nick?' Carter asked.

Nick slowly looked up and met Carter's eyes. 'Yes, I understand.'

'I just want to run through a few things with you to

start with,' Carter explained, looking down at one of the folders in front of him. 'Can you tell us where you went when you left Llancastell Police Station the night Paul Thurrock was murdered?'

Nick sighed. 'We've been through this three or four times now. I went home. I went straight home. That's it.'

Reagan fixed him with a stare. 'But you didn't, did you?'

Nick closed his eyes in frustration momentarily. Then he looked over and nodded. 'Yeah, I did. I'm not lying to you.'

Carter sat forward with an understanding expression. 'Listen, Nick, I get it. Paul Thurrock was a scumbag. He sexually assaulted your stepdaughter and then blamed her. If that was my daughter, I'd want to kill him too.'

Nick was aware that there was some kind of good cop/bad cop routine going on here.

'I didn't kill Paul Thurrock,' Nick said quietly. 'I don't know what else to tell you.'

'Come on.' Reagan rolled his eyes and then snapped, 'We've got overwhelming evidence that you did. Don't waste our time here.'

There was an awkward silence.

Nick already knew the evidence against him. His motive was clear – the sexual assault on Fran. There had been several witnesses to Nick's threatening conversation with Thurrock in the industrial estate car park. Even though he had merely grabbed Thurrock by the balls, it was also technically *assault*. Thurrock had also told his brother Stu that Nick had threatened to drive him out to Snowdonia and *put him in a hole*. Added to Thurrock's testimony that Nick had assaulted and broken his jaw two days later, the evidence was stacking up against him.

However, the prosecution didn't have anything linking

Nick to the scene of the crime, Thurrock's flat, the night he was murdered. No forensics, no eyewitness, no weapon. Nick's barrister felt that the prosecution's case was flimsy. There was also a decent chance of Nick being granted bail. Between 15-20% of those charged with murder in the UK were granted bail if the judge believed there was a good chance the defendant was very unlikely to commit any offence or tamper with witnesses while waiting for trial. Nick was a Detective Sergeant with a spotless record and he had no criminal offences of any note. He just wanted to see Amanda and Megan. It was killing him just being away from them for 48 hours.

Carter interlaced his fingers as his arms rested on the table. 'You just need to tell us what happened, Nick. If you went over to Thurrock's flat to have another *quiet word* and things got out of hand, no one's going to blame you.'

Nick narrowed his eyes. 'I wasn't there. I'm not going to admit to doing something when I wasn't there and I didn't do it.'

'Jesus.' Reagan gave a frustrated grunt. Reaching into a folder, he pulled out a photograph of Nick's car. 'For the purposes of the tape, I am showing the suspect a photograph, Item Reference 8EH. Do you recognise this car?'

Nick started to feel uneasy. Why was there a picture of his car?

'Yes,' he confirmed.

'And can you confirm that you are the registered owner of this black Vauxhall Astra, licence plate Lima Delta one nine, Tango Oscar Sierra?' Reagan asked, pointing at the photo.

'Yes.'

Carter nodded, looked over and gestured. 'And this was the car that you drove home the night that Paul Thurrock was murdered.'

'Yes.'

Where the hell are they going with this?

Reagan pulled out another photo. 'For the purposes of the tape, I am showing the suspect a photograph, Item Reference 9DS. This is a photograph taken of the footwell in the back of your car. Can you see this tiny black spot on the carpet that has been circled?'

Nick nodded but his stomach lurched. He knew what it was. He knew it was a speck of blood and he knew that it belonged to Thurrock. He just had no idea how it got there.

'Would it surprise you to know that that spot is in fact blood?' Reagan explained dryly.

Nick gave an almost imperceptible shrug. Whoever had set him up had done a professional job so far.

'Nick,' Carter said in a friendlier tone. 'DNA tests show that the blood belongs to Paul Thurrock. Is there anything you can tell us about that?'

'No,' Nick said in a whisper. He was fucked.

Chapter 4

DI Ruth Hunter and DC Georgie Wild walked along Llancastell High Street. A group of teenagers were milling around outside McDonald's, flirting, laughing and shouting. There was little in their clothing to differentiate the genders. Hoodies, trackies and trainers. A couple of girls wore tight tops that exposed their midriffs under a zipped down hoodie but that was it.

As they passed them, a boy with a vape spat on the pavement a few feet from where they were walking.

Georgie glared at him. 'Oi, don't do that!'

Even though the boy was only about thirteen, he sneered at her. 'Who the fuck are you? Fuck off, bitch.'

The teenagers all laughed as the boy gave them a cocky, victorious look.

Georgie moved her jacket so he could see the cuffs attached to her belt. 'You want to come with me to the station, nobhead?'

The boy smirked but he did now look worried. 'What, for spitting?'

Ruth gave her a look as if to say *Leave it.*

'Use of foul and abusive language. Public order offence,' Georgie snapped. 'Take your pick.'

The boy ignored her and went back to the group, muttering under his breath.

'Little bastard,' Georgie growled.

'Get out of bed on the wrong side today?' Ruth asked, teasing her.

'No, boss,' Georgie protested. 'I just think stuff like that is getting worse.'

Ruth shrugged. 'We used to say that when I joined the Met thirty years ago. Teenagers are teenagers. He was just showing off.' Ruth pointed to the car. 'Come on, we'll go through that new drive-thru coffee place. My treat.'

Georgie smiled. 'You're on.'

They had just interviewed the owner of a local jewellery shop that had been raided the day before by a gang wearing balaclavas and carrying hammers.

As they approached the car, Georgie's phone rang and she answered it.

Pulling out a cigarette, Ruth cupped her hand against the breeze, lit it and took a deep drag.

That's better, she thought.

Her head had been in a continual whirl ever since Nick's arrest for murder. She knew Nick was innocent and that he'd been set up. She was also certain that it had something to do with Paul Thurrock's relationship with Curtis Blake. Her instinct told her that Blake had murdered Thurrock and made it look like Nick, therefore *killing two birds with one stone.*

The problem was that Llancastell CID were prevented from going anywhere near the investigation into Thurrock's murder, for obvious reasons. However, the CID team were pulling in every favour they could to covertly keep up to speed with the case which was being run out of CID in St Asaph.

Even though Nick was being housed on the VP wing, she knew he would be a target. There were no guarantees of his safety and, if rumours were to be believed, there were several prison officers on the take at Rhoswen.

'Boss,' Georgie called over now she had finished her call. 'That was Dan.' She was referring to Detective Sergeant Dan French from Llancastell CID. From the look on Georgie's face, Ruth could see it wasn't good news.

'What's wrong?'

'They've found a trace of Thurrock's blood in Nick's car,' Georgie explained.

Ruth's stomach tightened. 'Jesus Christ.'

'Do we know if they're looking at Blake?' Georgie asked.

'I gave them everything that Nick had discovered,' Ruth said. 'But we have to tread very carefully.'

'A mate of mine reckons CID at St Asaph are a bunch of jobsworth twats,' Georgie growled. 'If they knew Nick, they'd be doing everything in their power to look elsewhere for Thurrock's killer.'

'I know,' Ruth said quietly. 'Drake said he'd go to their Super but it has to be seen to be impartial. And if we tread on any toes, we'll get the IOPC coming down on us like a ton of bricks.'

IOPC was the Independent Office for Police Conduct which investigated serious allegations against UK police officers. They were working closely with St Asaph and if they had any suspicion that officers from Llancastell CID were interfering, there would be disciplinary proceedings and people could lose their jobs.

Georgie shook her head as she opened the car door. 'I can't believe this is happening.'

Ruth knew that Georgie and Nick were close. In fact, at times they had been a little too close for comfort but Georgie clearly cared for him. Looking at her watch, Ruth saw that it was time to get a coffee, go back to the office, grab her things and go home.

'Do you think he'll get bail?' Georgie asked.

Ruth shrugged. 'Apparently Rhoswen is full to bursting. Any sensible judge would see that Nick isn't going to be a risk on bail. He has a young family and he's a DS with not a single blemish on his record.'

'Georgie!' said a voice out of nowhere.

A good-looking mixed-race man in his early 30s approached. He had a broad smile and was fashionably dressed with a smart, leather laptop bag slung over his shoulder.

He doesn't look like he comes from round here, Ruth thought as he came over and gave Georgie a hug.

'Jake,' Georgie exclaimed with a grin and then looked over at Ruth. 'Boss, this is a really old friend of mine, Jake.'

'Hi Jake,' Ruth said with a smile. 'I'm Ruth. I work with Georgie.'

'Jake managed to escape this dump.' Georgie gestured to him. 'He's a big shot journalist from London.'

'Hardly.' Jake looked slightly embarrassed. 'You got time for a drink and a catch up?'

Georgie glanced over at Ruth. Technically she needed to go back to Llancastell nick and officially sign out.

'Go on,' Ruth said with a smile. She had already picked up on some kind of attraction between them. 'I'll sign you out.'

'Thanks, boss.'

Chapter 5

Wandering along the first floor walkway to his cell, Nick could feel the anxious knot in his stomach. He hadn't felt like this for a long time. Despite being sober for several years now, for a moment his mind contemplated what he could get to lessen the anxiety or make him feel calmer. The irony was that he could get anything he wanted in prison – spice, crack, weed, diazepam. Anything. He could also get *prison hooch*. It was an alcoholic drink made by mixing rotting fruit – usually oranges – with crumbled bread for the yeast. It was mixed with hot water and, after a few days of fermenting, you had *hooch*. Putting this out of his mind, Nick knew he had to find out when and where the prison meeting of Alcoholics Anonymous was.

As he approached his cell, Nick saw that a man was lying on the other bed reading a newspaper. It had been empty earlier.

The man was in his early 20s, scrawny with a long jaw and scruffy hair. 'All right?' he said in a thick Yorkshire accent as he looked over the paper.

'Yeah,' Nick nodded. 'I'm Nick.'

'Steve,' he replied as Nick went over and sat down on his bunk.

'Just arrived?' Nick asked as he looked over at Steve, trying to gauge why he might be on the VP wing. It wasn't something that Nick was going to ask.

'They've downgraded me to Cat B,' Steve mumbled, 'so I got transferred over from Wakefield. What about you?'

'Yeah, just arrived,' Nick said.

Steve peered over at him. 'You look like a copper.'

Nick shrugged. 'Do I?'

Steve pulled a face. 'I'm not sharing a cell with a copper.'

Nick couldn't work out if this was a joke or a threat.

'That's all right then.' Nick gave him a half-smile. 'Because I'm not.'

Steve gestured to the paper. 'Want this, when I've finished?'

'Why not,' Nick said.

Steve shook his head. 'Two hundred grand a week this idiot is getting just for playing football. Crazy money, isn't it?'

'Yeah,' Nick replied. 'It's a bloody fortune for kicking a ball around.'

Steve took a second or two to process what Nick had said and then nodded as if Nick had said something incredibly profound. 'You're not wrong there. I was a decent footballer when I was a kid. Had trials for Halifax and Leeds.'

Nick looked at him. 'Right. That's impressive. Where did you play?'

'I was a nippy little winger,' Steve replied and then pointed. 'Left-footed too. Bit of a rarity when I was young.

Now they all reckon they're two-footed, but they're bloody not. Not even Messi.'

'No,' Nick said, not sure how to reply.

'You got a team then Nick?' Steve asked, looking relieved. Nick assumed that Steve was thankful that he wasn't sharing a cell with a psychopath.

'Not really,' Nick replied. 'Rugby's more my game.'

Steve laughed. 'Oh yeah. Course. You're a taff.' He then rolled up his shirt to reveal a *Leeds United Forever* tattoo on his arm. 'This is my lot. Bloody rubbish at the moment, mind.'

Nick nodded as he went to move the pillow on his bed so he could lie back. Hidden under the blanket was a razor blade. It was a message from someone inside the prison that he should kill himself while he had the chance.

Welcome to Rhoswen, Nick thought darkly to himself. He just prayed that at his bail hearing the next morning, the judge would see sense and send him home on bail and with a curfew.

Suddenly the wing exploded with noise. Something was kicking off somewhere. There were shouts of 'bastard' and 'scum' as the screws hurried down the corridor, slamming the cell doors shut and locking them. That was policy when violence broke out in prison. Get everyone locked up safely and out of the way.

Steve looked at him and grinned. 'Thank fuck for that.' He pulled out a large pre-rolled spliff and lit it. He took a big pull, exhaled and filled the cell with marijuana smoke. He then offered it to Nick. 'Want some?'

Nick shook his head. 'No, ta.'

'You don't smoke?' Steve asked as if this was amusing.

'No, not my thing,' Nick admitted. He'd tried weed a couple of times in his late teens but it left him feeling agitated and uncomfortable.

'Really?' Steve snorted as he took another long drag. 'Chills me out. I've got ADHD so I think it helps with that.' He then looked over. 'Ever tried spice?'

Nick shook his head. 'No.'

'Yeah, well don't,' Steve advised him. 'You never know what you're getting. Some bloke in Wakefield got some spice soaked into a drawing that his daughter had done for him at school. He smoked it, hallucinated and jumped over the balcony. Lucky there was a net or he'd be dead. Fucker thought he could fly.'

Nick got up and poured himself some water from the tap in the small sink. The cup was thin and plastic, the water was warm and metallic. He pulled a face.

'Not bloody Evian, is it?' Steve laughed.

'No,' Nick mumbled.

'Word of advice, mate,' Steve said. 'If you tell them you're a junkie and withdrawing, they'll give you a daily dose of methadone. That takes the edge right off. Better than weed, that stuff.'

'Thanks,' Nick said politely as he sat back down on his bed and noticed how it was bolted to the wall. 'But I'll take my chances.'

'Fair enough,' Steve said as he blew more marijuana smoke into the cell as he read his paper.

Nick lay back on his bed as the faces of Amanda and Megan came into his mind's eye. However he did it, he was going to clear his name and get back to them somehow.

Chapter 6

'It's nearly lights out time, Daniel,' Ruth said gently as she poked her head into his bedroom.

Daniel pulled a face. 'Can I just read this interview with Declan Rice?'

Ruth smiled. 'Of course.'

'I hope he goes to Chelsea,' Daniel said, gesturing to the magazine.

'Sorry?'

'Declan Rice,' Daniel explained. 'Best CDM in the country. He was at Chelsea's Academy but they let him go when he was sixteen, so now he plays for West Ham. But his dad is a Chelsea season ticket holder and his best mate is Mason Mount, so I hope that persuades him to move back.'

'Right,' Ruth said with a nod, pretending she understood what he had said. She went over and kissed his forehead. 'Night. Sleep well.'

'Night, Ruth,' Daniel replied, still engrossed in his magazine.

Padding along the landing, Ruth took a breath as a

feeling of affection welled inside. She knew that taking on Daniel was a big responsibility but when she saw his face, so full of contentment and happiness, she knew she had done the right thing.

Ruth went downstairs and saw that Sarah was sitting in the living room watching TV.

'Is he all right?' Sarah asked.

'Yeah,' Ruth replied with a smile as she slumped down next to her. 'Yeah, he is.'

For a few seconds they sat in a comfortable silence with some television quiz show blaring.

A famous actress was one of the contestants. Ruth looked at her on the television screen. She had to be about fifty but she looked incredible.

Ruth turned to Sarah. 'Do I look old?'

Sarah grinned as she peered at Ruth's face as if inspecting an oil painting. 'Yes.'

'Oh piss off!' Ruth laughed, giving her a playful hit on the arm.

'Do I look my age though?' Ruth enquired.

'Yes, I suppose so,' Sarah replied with a shrug.

'Bloody hell, you could at least do me the courtesy of lying, you muppet,' Ruth sighed. '*No Ruth, you look good for your age actually.*'

Sarah smirked and raised an eyebrow. 'You want me to lie?'

'I actually hate you,' Ruth said. 'I'm serious.'

'Why are you being so bloody vain and needy tonight?'

'I don't know,' Ruth replied. 'I just feel old. Do you think I should have Botox?'

Sarah shrugged. 'I don't know. If you want to.'

'It's quite normal for women my age to have Botox and stuff like that these days, isn't it?' Ruth said.

'Yeah,' Sarah replied with a bemused smile. 'Of course

you could stop smoking and drink less. That would take years off you.'

'Ah, but if I did that,' Ruth joked, 'there wouldn't be any point in living at all.'

'You're not even joking, are you?'

'No ... How's your mum?' Ruth asked as she sat back on the sofa, kicked off her shoes and stretched out her toes.

'I left her dozing,' Sarah explained. Her mother, Doreen, had cancer and was receiving chemotherapy at the University Hospital at Llancastell. The cancer was advanced and Ruth suspected that Doreen might not make it through to the new year.

Sarah looked over with a curious expression. 'Actually, she says that she wants to speak to you about *something* but she won't tell me what it is.'

'Eh?' Ruth frowned. 'Do you know what she's talking about?'

'No.' Sarah shook her head. 'Her exact words were, *I need to talk to Ruth about something before I'm gone.*' Sarah raised an eyebrow. 'I've no idea what she's talking about. Maybe the morphine is making her cranky.'

'Right'. Ruth laid back so her head was on Sarah's lap and her feet up on the arm of the sofa. 'Why can't she tell you?'

'I don't know,' Sarah sighed. 'Maybe she committed some terrible crime and she wants to make some deathbed confession.'

Ruth pulled a face and said, 'Oh, don't say that.'

There were a few seconds of silence.

'Maybe she's a serial killer and she's going to tell you where she's buried all the bodies,' Sarah joked.

'Ha ha.' Ruth rolled her eyes.

'I do have to get my head around the fact that mum is dying,' Sarah stated sadly.

'I know.' Ruth put out a comforting hand and held Sarah's and gave it a squeeze. She then looked at her. 'I'm really sorry. I know how close you've become since she moved over here.'

'We are,' Sarah admitted. 'And it makes me feel sick when I think about it. I think that's why I'm making jokes.'

'I can't remember what I felt when I lost my mum,' Ruth conceded as she tried to think back.

'No?' Sarah asked quietly.

'I can't remember if that's because my memory is bad,' Ruth admitted with a furrowed brow. 'Or because I didn't feel very much.'

Sarah looked at her and raised an eyebrow. 'That's a strange thing to say.'

'I know,' Ruth said with a slow nod of her head. 'My mum was a funny woman, and I don't mean amusing. Just not quite right.'

'How do you mean?'

'She just wasn't ever very present,' Ruth said, struggling to articulate exactly what she meant. 'She did all the things a mum was meant to do. Make us tea, wash and clean our clothes, take us to the swings. But there was a sense that her mind was always elsewhere.'

'Do you know why?' Sarah asked.

'She rarely talked about my grandparents or her childhood,' Ruth said. 'I know they were dirt poor and lived in a couple of rooms in Battersea … She just didn't ever say very much. I found out when I left home that she'd been taking Valium for years *for her nerves.*'

'Mummy's little helper,' Sarah said, quoting the 60s nickname for Valium.

'Maybe that's why she was so disconnected from everything?' Ruth pondered as the emotion of remembering began to get to her. She took a breath to steady herself. 'I think what made me sad was that I just never got to know her. I didn't know what she liked, or disliked. What she was interested in. How she felt about anything. She felt like a stranger even though we lived in the same house for sixteen years.'

'That's really sad,' Sarah said.

'Yeah, it is.'

Sarah looked at her. 'I love you, you know that?'

Ruth smiled. 'Yeah, I do know that. And it puts an extra skip in my step when I think about coming home at the end of the day.'

Chapter 7

A taxi pulled up outside Georgie's house on the outskirts of Llancastell. She and Jake tumbled out, giggling their heads off. Even though it was only 10pm, they were drunk.

Georgie handed the driver a ten-pound note. 'Keep the change.' She then frowned at Jake. 'I don't know why you're getting out, mush.'

'I'm staying in Portmeirion,' Jake protested.

Georgie pointed into the distance. 'Well off you go then.'

'It's miles away,' he protested.

'And you've got an expenses account,' Georgie said, teasing him.

Jake shrugged and took a few steps back towards the taxi. 'Okay. I'll see you around then, Georgie.'

I know he's calling my bluff, she thought to herself.

Georgie marched over and looked at the taxi driver. 'Looks like he's staying, I'm afraid.' She then slammed the door shut.

Jake gave her a grin.

'Don't be a smug twat.' Georgie then grinned at him as the taxi pulled away. 'And don't get any funny ideas, okay? You're on the sofa.'

'Hey, don't flatter yourself,' Jake joked, holding his hands up innocently. 'I don't fancy you anymore.'

'Yeah, obviously,' Georgie snorted as she opened the front door. She and Jake had been flirting all night and they both knew what was about to happen. They had gone out together during sixth form and were inseparable. However, Jake had gone off to do a journalism degree at the London School of Printing after school. Despite their promises to keep the relationship going, the inevitable breakup happened after about six months. They were too young and there were too many temptations for both of them.

Since then, Jake had worked his way from local London papers to freelance work on *The Times* and *The Guardian*. Georgie remembered a story he had written about corruption involving former government ministers lobbying 'old pals' after leaving office, and the ineffectiveness of the Advisory Committee on Business Appointments, which Jake had described as *feckless and woefully ineffective*.

As they got into the hallway, Georgie turned and looked at Jake in the half-light cast by the outside streetlights. He was tall, with sharp cheekbones and twinkly eyes.

'Are you going to kiss me any time soon?' she asked, raising her eyebrow.

'Eh?' Jake gave her a wry smile. 'You just said ...'

'Shut up.'

'You do understand what the term *mixed message* means, right?'

Georgie moved forward, put her arms around his waist

and looked into his big, brown eyes. 'Jesus, don't play hard to get. You're not that cute.'

Jake grinned. 'No?'

Georgie held his gaze. 'No.'

Jake leaned in, kissed her softly on the mouth and pulled her hard towards him.

That's better, Georgie thought.

Running his hand through her hair, Jake pushed her gently back against the wall as they continued to kiss.

He then stopped for a moment and looked at her. 'Am I still on the sofa?' he whispered.

Georgie rolled her eyes. 'Don't be a nob, Jake. I didn't invite you back here for you to sleep on the sofa,' she replied quietly.

'Oh good,' he laughed.

'But now you're drunk,' she said, 'you can tell me what you're doing back in North Wales.'

'No chance.'

'Why not?' she asked. 'Is it *top secret?*'

'I've already warned you,' he laughed. 'I could tell you what I'm up to, but then I'd have to kill you.'

They kissed again and moved over to the sofa.

Chapter 8

'Did I wake you coming in?' Ruth said in a virtual whisper as she peered into Doreen's bedroom. It had tasteful floral wallpaper and cream curtains. On the far side was a small dresser where Doreen kept her make-up, perfume and jewellery.

Doreen had her glasses on and was engrossed in reading a book on her Kindle.

I don't think she heard me, Ruth thought.

'Doreen?' Ruth said a little louder.

Doreen looked over and smiled. 'Ruth.'

'I'm not disturbing you, am I?' Ruth asked.

'Don't be daft,' Doreen snorted and then gestured to the book she was reading on the screen. 'There's some lunatic roaming Norfolk, cutting people up and sending the body parts to this detective called James with cryptic notes carved into the flesh.'

'Lovely,' Ruth said with a wry smile.

'It's not lovely, Ruth,' Doreen protested, getting carried away. 'I think it's this bloke called Roger who was bullied at school and he's going around murdering everyone that used to bully him.'

'Right,' Ruth nodded. 'Well, revenge is definitely a powerful motive.'

'Yeah, well my advice is never go and work in the police in Norfolk, Ruth,' Doreen said with a stern tone. 'In the last book, this woman serial killer targeted police officers and sacrificed them in graveyards. It was horrible.'

'Don't worry, Doreen,' Ruth laughed. 'I have no intention of going to work in Norfolk.'

'Good,' Doreen said, now reassured as she took off her reading glasses and then peered over at her. 'How's Daniel doing?'

'Settling in well.'

'Such a lovely boy,' Doreen said. Her face lit up every time she saw Daniel or even mentioned him. 'I never had a son but if I had, I'd have liked him to be just like Daniel.'

Ruth nodded in agreement. 'Me too.'

Doreen patted the bed and smiled. 'You going to sit down then, or is this a flying visit?'

'Sarah seems to think that you want to talk to me about something?' Ruth said, not beating about the bush.

'Oh, that,' Doreen said, but her expression had changed.

'Ironically, she wondered if you wanted to confess to me that *you* were a serial killer?' Ruth laughed.

Doreen gave her a forced smile.

Oh, this is not good.

There were a few tense seconds as Ruth wondered quite what Doreen was going to tell her.

'I'm not quite sure how to put this,' Doreen said very quietly.

Ruth looked at her with a soft, benign expression. 'It's fine. Take your time.'

Doreen took a long, visible breath and then a tear came to her eye. 'Sorry …'

'Don't be sorry,' Ruth said as she reached over and put a reassuring hand on Doreen's arm. 'Whatever it is, we can work it out. And I promise you, you're going to feel a lot better talking about it, whatever it is.'

'Yeah, you're right.' Doreen nodded as she wiped the tear from her face with the cuff of her nightie. 'It's just … I'm not Sarah's actual mother.'

What? Jesus! I didn't see that coming! Ruth thought, trying desperately not to show that she was shocked.

'Okay…' Ruth said in a steady voice. 'How do you mean?'

'My sister, Alice, was a junkie. Heroin,' Doreen explained. 'She was Sarah's mother. But Alice was in no fit state to look after Sarah when she was born, so me and my husband took her in. And sadly, Alice passed away about a year later from an overdose.'

'And you've never told Sarah any of this?' Ruth asked.

Doreen shook her head as the tears came again. 'No. We always meant to but it never seemed to be the right time. And now time is running out, I'm not sure what to do.'

Chapter 9

It was 6am and Jake was driving back to where he was staying at Castell Deudraeth, which was a four star hotel on the grounds of Portmeirion, North Wales. Gone were the days where he would search around for the cheapest, grottiest B&B he could find. He was on to a major news story and *The Times* was happy to foot the bill for him to stay a few nights in comfort.

Jake had won the admiration of the new editor the previous year with an article exposing the murky world of political lobbying. He had exposed one MP who had openly described himself as a *cab for hire* in his willingness to use his power and influence within Parliament. The disgraced MP had taken money from a well-known private equity company in return for his support of their bid for the Essex Thameside franchise on a Government Transport Select Committee. When they had won the franchise, the MP had been rewarded with a six-figure bonus.

Jake also exposed the willingness of former MPs and even members of the Cabinet to sell their influence, information and contacts for hard cash once they were out of office. Jake suggested that such MPs should be put on some kind of *gardening leave* or given *a cooling off period*, rather than offer paid services only months after sitting in the Cabinet Office with the Prime Minister. The Ministerial Code did require ex-ministers to *consult* with the ACBA – the Advisory Committee on Business Appointments – regarding any paid work or employment they entered into two years after leaving office. Jake scoffed at the advice from the ACBA, claiming that it was both absurd and naïve that there were no sanctions for those who chose not to follow that advice.

Jake's article concluded that the lobbying industry was a £2 billion-a-year business that was self-regulating. There were no requirements for lobbying companies to register their clients, which allowed former members of government to make fortunes selling the power, influence and information they had been entrusted with as public servants. It was scandalous and needed addressing with legislation.

Jake pulled off the main road. He didn't care that he felt tired from the night he'd spent in bed with Georgie. He found himself smiling to himself at the thought of it. If he was honest, he'd like to see her again. Even though they hadn't been together for over ten years, it felt so comfortable being with her. Jake had struggled to have any long-term relationships while he had lived in London. He worked long hours and found most of the women he met in Britain's capital city to be pretentious, humourless or tediously earnest.

As Jake cornered a long bend in the road, he saw the tiny village of Portmeirion down to his left. It had been built between 1925 and 1975 in an Italian Baroque style that made it a unique curiosity for tourists. The village had been used by films and television shows, most notably *The*

Prisoner in the 1960s, as well as being a favourite of The Beatles – George Harrison loved it so much he celebrated his 50th birthday there.

Jake glanced in his rear view mirror and saw that a dark red car was behind him and getting closer. The road was virtually a single track so there was no way the car could overtake him.

He'll just have to wait, Jake thought to himself, trying not to get irritated. He'd had far too good an evening with Georgie to let an impatient moron in a car rattle him.

Looking at the road in front of him, Jake planned the day ahead. He'd have breakfast and a quick sleep, before heading out for the day. He had a series of people he needed to interview for the article he was writing.

Glancing back into his rear view mirror, he saw that the car was now right up behind him to the point where he couldn't even see the number plate.

'For fuck's sake!' Jake growled under his breath. 'Where the hell do you want me to go?'

Suddenly, the dark red vehicle smashed into the back of Jake's car. He felt his car swerve on the road.

'Jesus!' Jake cried as he grabbed the steering wheel and got control of the car back. 'What the hell are you doing?'

His pulse started to race.

What's going on?

Pushing the accelerator flat to the floor, he hurtled around another bend, trying to comprehend why he was being chased.

Feeling the back wheels of his car slip, Jake steered into the skid and tried to get control of the car again. He took a nervous breath. Was this really happening? Was he really being chased?

Glancing back in the rear view mirror, he tried to get a look at the driver.

'What the fuck do you want?' he yelled.

This time the car hurtled into the back of his car, jolting it forward with a loud bang.

'Jesus!' Jake shouted, now terrified for his life.

He gripped the steering wheel but he had lost complete control of the car as he fought to stay on the road.

It was no use. He veered off the road at speed.

As if out of nowhere, a huge tree seemed to appear, looming down on him.

SMASH!

Everything went black.

Chapter 10

Nick had managed to find the early morning meeting of AA in HMP Rhoswen. It was being held in the large rec room over by the Chaplaincy and Education Block. The room was lined with sofas that were neatly arranged in a rectangle. With a dozen men in attendance, Nick had been pleased to see fellow alcoholics and addicts.

'Would anyone else like to share?' asked Lee, the middle-aged member of AA who had come in to run the meeting for the prison.

There were a few seconds of silence.

'Yeah, I'll share back with you, Lee,' Nick said. He had plenty to get off his chest, and sharing in AA meetings always made him feel better. 'Hi, I'm Nick and I'm an alcoholic.'

'Hi Nick,' replied the others.

'I haven't been in here long at all,' Nick explained. 'But I knew that I needed to get to a meeting and share. My head is all over the place at the moment. And I always used to drink when I felt anxious or nervous. I actually remember my first ever drink. I was fourteen and I went to this youth group with a mate of mine, Aled Mackay. Afterwards, a few of us went down to the woods where Aled had hidden three big bottles of Strongbow cider. And we passed it around and after a few gulps I remember feeling this warmth come over me. And this knot of anxiety that seemed to have been in the pit of my stomach just disappeared. I felt relaxed and more confident. I even told a joke. And I thought, this stuff is bloody amazing. I realised that alcohol could take away my anxiety and I could be the person I'd always wanted to be. And if I'd had a drink, I could go to a party and talk to girls, and be a bit lairy. If I had a few beers, I was the life and soul of the party. And I know that's what most teenagers experience, but for me, alcohol became my best friend. The most important thing in my life. Without it, I was emotionally crippled and an anxious mess. I guess I took that into adulthood. I used booze to regulate all my emotions. If I felt nervous, angry, lonely or sad, I'd drink on it and it would make me feel better. It would anaesthetise me from feeling anything. But then I got to the point where I drank all the time just to get through the day. I didn't want to feel anything. I wanted to be permanently numb. And when I realised I'd lost control of my drinking, it was a terrifying idea that I'd have to experience life without the comfort of drinking.'

The door opened and a stocky man in his 30s with a shaved head came in. He looked over at Lee and mumbled in a Scouse accent, 'Sorry I'm late, Lee. I was with Probation.' The man had a thick Liverpudlian accent.

'Come and sit down,' Lee said quietly, gesturing to a space on a sofa opposite Nick.

There was something familiar about the man that had just walked in. Nick thought he knew him from somewhere. Then Nick spotted a thick scar that ran from the corner of his mouth and around to the point of his chin. He definitely knew him from somewhere, he just couldn't place him.

Lee looked over and smiled, 'Do you want to carry on, Nick?'

'Yeah,' Nick nodded, trying to remember what he had been saying. 'And obviously being in here is a bit of a shock to the system. And when I feel this anxious, this rattled, my instant reaction is a need to change the way I feel. I don't want to sit with my head and with my emotions. And I know that alcohol will take that away in a few minutes. But the repercussions of picking up that one drink are catastrophic. I won't be able to stop. So, I have to work my 12-step programme and I have to get myself to a meeting. And that's why I'm so grateful to be sitting here this morning because I'm in a room of people who think the same as me ... And I'll leave it at that.'

'Thanks Nick,' Lee said along with some of the others.

As a man in his 60s on the far side of the room began to share, Nick realised that the man with the scar was staring over at him.

Where the hell do I know him from? Nick wondered, starting to feel a little uneasy under the man's intense glare.

Then it came to him.

Sean Keegan.

Nick's stomach tightened. Keegan was a member of the Croxteth Park Boyz and a known associate of Curtis Blake.

Shit. This is not good.

Nick looked up and met his gaze. Keegan stared back for a few seconds before scratching his nose and looking away.

Was it coincidence that a member of Blake's gang had

just walked into the AA meeting? Had Keegan recognised him?

Either way, Nick knew he needed to be granted bail and get out of Rhoswen before Keegan remembered how he knew Nick. If he hadn't already.

Chapter 11

Sitting at her desk, Ruth stretched out her back and yawned. She hadn't slept well. She wasn't sure what to do with Doreen's confession that she wasn't Sarah's biological mother. Ruth understood why Doreen felt she needed to get it off her chest – she was becoming increasingly aware of her own mortality. Ruth wondered what there was to be gained from Doreen sharing this information with Sarah. It might alienate Doreen from Sarah at a time when she needed her the most. Was it better to leave it as it was? Or was it important that the truth came out? Was it ever okay to bury the truth, even if a revelation might cause a lot of pain and hurt? Ruth wasn't sure what to advise Doreen to do. Maybe it was something they needed to talk about again.

Ruth was also wrestling with the thought of Nick in prison and Amanda sitting at home worrying. It was awful to think about. Looking at her watch, she saw that it was nearly 9am and time for the CID briefing. Nick's court hearing was up at Mold Crown Court at 11am and Ruth had promised him and Amanda she would be there.

The Portmeirion Killings

Despite putting out lots of feelers, Ruth had managed to get virtually no intel on what evidence the CPS had against Nick. She just hoped that the judge saw sense and allowed Nick to be released on bail. It would enable her and Nick to work on a strategy to find out what had really happened to Paul Thurrock and clear his name.

There was a knock at the door which broke Ruth's train of thought. Georgie appeared holding two cups of coffee.

'Morning, boss,' Georgie said as she came over and handed one to her. 'They didn't have flat white, so I went for cappuccino.'

Ruth gave her a smile. 'Perfect. You're a star, Georgie.' She then noticed Georgie stifling a yawn. Ruth gave her a knowing look. 'Late night was it?'

Georgie gave her a look of mock offence. 'I was in bed by ten.'

'On your own?' Ruth smirked.

Georgie forced a smile but didn't reply.

Ruth laughed. 'I don't blame you.'

Georgie frowned. 'Sorry?'

'Jake, your journalist friend,' Ruth explained. 'He's a good looking boy.'

Georgie smiled. 'I don't know what you're implying, boss.'

'Thirty years as a detective, Georgie,' Ruth said. 'I'm not implying anything.'

'Yeah, okay. Guilty as charged,' Georgie mumbled as she turned to go.

'Gonna see him again?'

Georgie shrugged. 'I hope so.'

Talking to Georgie, who was in her late 20s, about her love life had made her feel very old. Time really did march on at a relentless pace. It didn't seem five minutes ago since

Ruth was in her late 20s and working as a DC in Peckham in South London. How could the late 90s be a quarter of a century ago? It was scary.

Ruth sipped her coffee – *Perfect.* Although it would have been more perfect if she could have had a cigarette at the same time. The 90s. Those were the days, when you could smoke at work or in pubs. In fact, if she remembered correctly you could even smoke on aeroplanes – or maybe that was the 80s.

Yes, that was it. A girls' holiday to Majorca in 1986. She and her friends were only about seventeen. They had sat at the back of the cheap charter flight to Palma, smoking and drinking duty free Malibu, dreaming of meeting boys who looked like Wham, Spandau Ballet or Duran. Days were spent around the pool of the Hotel Victoria Gran Melia in Playa del Mallorca. They'd met a bunch of lads from Essex – all shell necklaces and highlighted mullets – who spent most of their time tossing Ruth and her friends into the pool to screams of flirty amusement. Ruth had eventually slept with one of them – Steve Bannister – whom she thought looked a little bit like Andrew Ridgeley from Wham. It was three minutes of fumbling, a grunt and then disappointment. Steve then refused to talk to her for the rest of the holiday, claiming she was *frigid.* Ruth had already begun to suspect that she might be gay and her experience with Steve Bannister did little to endear her to the opposite sex.

Bloody hell! And that was 35 years ago! How did I get to be so old?

Getting up from her chair with that depressing thought, Ruth grabbed a folder and headed out into the CID office where her team of detectives were waiting for her.

'Morning everyone,' Ruth said as she went to the front

of the room and perched on a table. 'We're still looking for any eyewitnesses for those jewellery shop robberies in town.'

DS Dan French looked over from where he was sitting. 'Boss, we've got a partial fingerprint from one of the cabinets in the shop, so we're going to run it through the national database.'

'Good,' Ruth said. 'Anything else I need to know about this morning?'

Detective Constable Jim Garrow motioned to show that he had something. 'Boss. RTA over at Portmeirion. Victim was pronounced dead at the scene.'

RTA stood for road traffic accident.

'Okay.' Ruth frowned. 'Why are we involved?' Usually, there was no need for CID to investigate, even if the crash had been fatal. It was only if there was anything criminal that they might be contacted.

'Uniformed officers noticed that the car had significant damage to its rear bumper and boot,' Garrow explained. 'Given that the car was found on a quiet stretch of road, and no other vehicle was involved, they weren't sure if the vehicle had been hit from behind.'

'Right,' Ruth nodded. If there was any suggestion of *foul play*, then it was definitely a matter for CID. 'Any ID on the victim?'

Garrow looked down at his notes. 'A Jake Neville.'

Ruth saw the blood drain from Georgie's face.

'Jake Neville?' Georgie asked in disbelief.

Ruth looked at her. Was it *the* Jake that she had met in Llancastell yesterday afternoon and the man Georgie had spent the previous night with?

'Your friend we met yesterday?' Ruth asked her quietly.

Georgie nodded, still looking utterly shocked.

There were a few seconds of quiet as the officers in CID realised that the death was personal to Georgie.

Garrow furrowed his brow. 'You knew the victim?'

'Yeah,' Georgie whispered. 'He was an old school friend. We went out for a drink last night.'

The CID office went silent.

'Sorry to hear that, Georgie,' French said with a sympathetic look.

'You going to be okay?' Ruth asked her.

'Yes, boss.' Georgie nodded but she had a tear in her eye. 'I'll be fine.'

Ruth gave her a concerned look. 'If you need some time off, Georgie …?'

'No.' Georgie wiped the tears from her face and shook her head emphatically. 'Thank you, boss, but no. I'm better off being here.'

Ruth wasn't convinced but she couldn't force Georgie to leave. 'Okay, if you're sure.'

Georgie nodded. 'I'll be fine. It's just a bit of a shock.'

'Of course,' Ruth said and then looked at her quizzically. 'Sorry to ask, but could Jake have been drunk when he crashed?'

'No.' Georgie shook her head. 'He left my house around 6am and he was definitely sober.'

Garrow glanced over. 'The vehicle was found just before 7am.'

'He was staying at a hotel in Portmeirion,' Georgie stated. The emotion seemed to have gone from her voice and she had gone into detective mode. 'Sounds like he was driving back there when he crashed.'

'Right. I have to go to Nick's court hearing,' Ruth said, looking down at her watch. She glanced at French. 'Dan, you and Jim get to the crash site and I'll see you down there.'

Georgie raised an eyebrow. 'Let me go, boss.'

Ruth frowned. 'I don't think that's a good idea, Georgie. You're still in shock.'

'Please,' Georgie implored her. 'It's going to help me to go down there. And I owe it to Jake and his parents to find out what happened.'

Ruth thought for a moment. Was Georgie too close to be investigating the accident? Or did she owe it to her to let her look into the death of her friend?

'Okay,' Ruth said to Georgie. 'But at the first sign that you're getting too involved or losing perspective, I'm pulling you off the case.'

Georgie gave her an emphatic nod. 'Thank you, boss.'

Chapter 12

Nick sat in the dock in Court 1 flanked by two prison officers. There was a Perspex glass screen in front of where he was sitting. They had been in court for around twenty minutes and the cuffs Nick was wearing were chafing on his wrists. The prison officer sitting next to him was in his 60s and smelt of stale cigarettes. Nick could hear him wheezing even as they sat there. Looking down, Nick spotted that the prison officer's shoes were immaculately polished so that the black leather shone like a mirror. *Ex-military*, Nick deduced immediately. He remembered reading somewhere that a third of UK prison officers had served in the armed forces so it was a fair bet.

Glancing up to the public gallery, he saw that Amanda was sitting with Ruth. He tried to give her a reassuring nod but he could see the stress in her face. It was painful to see the look of desperation and anxiety in her eyes as she looked at him and forced a smile. He just wanted to go up there and give her a comforting hug. His eyes then met Ruth's and she gave him a calm, supportive nod.

The Portmeirion Killings

Nick's solicitor, Rahid Jeffries, sat over to the left, shuffling through papers. He was young, with short neat hair and a smart navy suit. Jeffries had spent ten minutes before the hearing outlining their application for bail. Even though Nick had been charged with murder, Jeffries thought they had a good chance.

For a moment, Nick allowed himself to imagine walking out of the courtroom in half an hour and returning home. He could feel his heart swell with excitement just thinking about it. Picking up Megan, holding her tight and whirling her around. Laying with Amanda on the sofa and holding her. The painful truth was that he had taken those things for granted most of the time.

Nick tried to put those thoughts out of his mind. The sensible thing to do was to prepare himself for the worst. After all, he had spent the last fifteen minutes listening to Helen Christie, the solicitor for the CPS, summarising all her reasons for Nick to be turned down for bail.

Christie was tall, uber confident and spoke with the faintest of Manchester accents. She had concentrated mainly on the severity of the charge and the brutality of the attack on Thurrock. Nick had found it difficult to listen to, as he watched the elderly judge like a hawk to see his reaction. Every time the judge nodded in agreement, Nick's stomach tightened with sickening anxiety.

Jeffries got up from his seat and looked over to the judge. 'Good morning, your honour. Rahid Jeffries, I'm appearing before you on behalf of the defendant, Nicholas Evans, to make an application for bail as outlined in Section 4 of The Bail Act, 1976. The accused has been charged with one count of murder. My client is alleged to have murdered Mr Paul Thurrock between 6pm and 7pm on the 23rd March. However, your honour, I would like to point out there are no eyewitnesses to the alleged offence. I would also like to take this opportunity to draw your attention to the fact that the prosecution has not provided any clear evidence linking my client to the crime scene. I understand that the police investigation into Mr Thurrock's murder is still ongoing and that the circumstances around his death are unclear. At the moment, the evidence against my client is entirely circumstantial and in my opinion, unconvincing. Despite the serious nature of the alleged crime, my client is a respected police officer in Llancastell with over seventeen years' experience. He is also married with a young family and therefore he doesn't pose any kind of flight risk. I have listened carefully to the prosecution's application to refuse my client bail, but as I've already established, there are no grounds to believe that my client will either abscond, commit another violent crime, or interfere with witnesses. Unless your honour requires me to clarify any of these points, that concludes my application for bail.'

Jeffries sat down, took a sip of water from a glass and then looked over at Nick with a confident expression.

Nick took a breath. Surely the judge would be swayed by his record as a police officer.

The judge, Gerald Seymour, nodded and then looked down at the papers in front of him for a few seconds. 'Thank you for your presentations, Mrs Christie and Mr Jeffries … Mr Jeffries, I understand everything you have said about the prosecution's evidence, the current police investigation into Mr Thurrock's murder, and your client's character. However, it is my opinion that given the serious nature of the crime, and the extreme violence of the attack against Mr Thurrock, my only option is to refuse bail for your client at this time.'

What? God, no!

Nick felt his stomach lurch and he took a breath. He felt like the wind had been knocked out of him.

For a few seconds, he just had to process the fact that his application for bail had been refused and that he was going to spend months locked away in Rhoswen on remand.

Glancing back to where Amanda was sitting, he saw that she was sobbing and being comforted by Ruth. Then Amanda looked down at him, her face streaked with tears. She put her hand out towards him.

Nick tried to give her a reassuring look. He gritted his teeth in fury. Whatever happened, he was going to find out who killed Thurrock and clear his name.

Chapter 13

Georgie and Garrow had been driving across Snowdonia from Llancastell in virtual silence. Georgie was still in shock at Jake's death. Before they had left, she had gone into the female locker room to cry. She didn't want anyone to see just how upset she was, especially Ruth. Her thoughts turned to Pam and Bill Neville, Jake's parents. They lived on the outskirts of Llangollen. She felt compelled to go and see them as soon as possible. She knew that uniformed officers would already have been to their house to break the devastating news.

In her late teens, Georgie had been very close to Pam and Bill. Pam was a bit of an old hippy, wearing kaftans, and told tales of going to the Isle of White Festival as a teenager to see Jimi Hendrix. Bill was a Brummie and second generation West Indian. He laughed like a drain and smoked marijuana at the weekends. Georgie loved the completely relaxed, carefree atmosphere at their home when she stayed over. They thought nothing of her and Jake sharing a bed. In fact, Pam would bring them tea and toast in bed on a Sunday morning and sit on the end of the bed chatting away and making them laugh. It was a refreshing contrast to the traditional and often tense atmosphere in her own home.

'I'm so sorry to hear about your friend,' Garrow said gently after a while, breaking her train of thought.

Georgie gave him a half-smile. When she thought about it, it felt so raw and surreal. 'Thanks.'

'Were you very close?' Garrow asked.

'Yes,' Georgie replied quietly.

Georgie and Garrow's relationship had flourished since they had been partnered together in CID. There was no doubting they were chalk and cheese. Garrow was from a wealthy, middle-class background and university educated. She soon realised that what Garrow lacked in street wise nouse, he more than made up for with a sharp, analytical mind and instinct.

'We went out together when we were in sixth form at school,' she explained.

'Oh right,' Garrow said, nodding sympathetically. 'Had you kept in touch?'

'Not really,' Georgie stated. 'He went to university in London. London School of Printing, I think it was. We promised to keep the relationship going but we drifted apart.'

Georgie wasn't going to divulge that she had actually slept with a friend of Jake's in Llancastell. Racked with guilt, she had finished with him, claiming that it was just too difficult to keep a long-distance relationship going. Jake had been devastated. Six months later, Georgie's infidelity had come out. Jake had written her a five-page letter full of hurt and anger. Six years later, they bumped into each other at a mutual friend's wedding and laughed about what had happened. By then, Jake was living with someone in London and they had both moved on with their lives.

After a few more seconds of silence, Georgie looked over. 'But we went out last night, got a bit drunk and spent the night together. He left my house this morning to go back to his hotel.'

'Oh God,' Garrow said after a moment. 'Are you going to be okay? No one would blame you if you stepped away from this or took some compassionate leave.'

'No.' Georgie shook her head adamantly. 'I want to do this. It feels like the right thing to do.'

As the pastel colours of the classical turrets and towers of Portmeirion loomed into view, Garrow turned left onto a single-track road.

The sky was a clear blue with almost perfect cumulus clouds. A flock of birds appeared, creating an excited pattern as they headed for the lofty branches of nearby trees. Georgie couldn't watch them. It didn't seem fair that on the day that Jake had died the weather could be so perfect or that birds were going about their lives as if nothing had happened. She knew that didn't make any logical sense but it was how she felt. She wanted everything to stop so as to mark the significance of what had happened. Like that famous poem she had seen in a film once. She seemed to remember that one of the lines was *Pack up the moon and dismantle the sun.* That's exactly how she felt.

Trying to put these thoughts out of her mind, Georgie spotted several yellow police signs up ahead which had been erected to signal that the road was closed due to an accident. Beyond that, two patrol cars, marked with *HEDDLU* in black lettering, were parked across the road itself.

Then Georgie saw Jake's Audi which had smashed into a tree on the left hand side of the road. The sight of it made her catch her breath. Emotion swept through her. It was both a sickening and unreal sight. She could feel her stomach tighten as she looked at the twisted metal of the wreck.

As Garrow parked their car, she took a deep breath to steady herself.

'All right?' Garrow asked, sensing her unease.

'Fine,' she replied a little too impatiently as she unclipped her seatbelt and got out. She didn't want Garrow to be constantly checking on her wellbeing throughout the investigation, even though she knew he meant well.

The wind picked up and rattled the nearby hedgerows. A uniformed officer stood to one side beside the blue and white police evidence tape.

Georgie pulled out her warrant card as she and Garrow approached. She needed to snap into detective mode or she was going to totally lose it. 'DC Wild and DC Garrow, Llancastell CID. Were you first on scene, officer?'

'Yes,' the middle-aged female constable replied. 'There was nothing we could do for the victim I'm afraid.'

Garrow raised an eyebrow. 'But you think there's some damage to the vehicle that's suspicious?'

'Actually it was my sarge who thought something wasn't right,' the constable replied, pointing to a slim, younger man in his 30s.

'Okay, thanks,' Georgie said as they ducked under the tape and headed towards the sergeant and showed their warrant cards.

'Morning,' the sergeant said with an expressionless face.

'You called this in?' Garrow asked.

'Yes,' he said as he led them over to the crumpled car. He then gestured to the hatchback and rear bumper. 'Significant damage to the back of the car. It's not consistent with the accident. I thought it looked suspicious.'

For a moment, Georgie couldn't help but look at the front of the car. The driver's door and roof had been crushed beyond recognition. They had taken the full force of the impact. She pursed her lips together tightly as she thought about Jake's last moments. It looked like he might well have been killed outright on impact. She took a dry, uneasy gulp to prevent the tears from coming.

Come on, Georgie. Pull yourself together, she told herself in frustration.

Georgie crouched down on her haunches then to assess the damage. Garrow joined her.

'Someone has definitely driven into the back of this car,' Garrow said immediately. 'The question is whether this damage was caused before the crash, or if it was the actual cause.'

Georgie spotted something. Fishing a biro from her jacket pocket, she carefully flicked what had caught her eye. It was a tiny flake of something that had been trapped in the dented paintwork of the hatchback. She knew exactly what it was.

'We've got a dark red flake of paint here,' she said, taking out an evidence bag and slowly using the biro to transfer the paint into the bag.

Garrow looked at her and pointed. 'Yeah, there's more over here.'

Georgie frowned. 'It rained yesterday morning, didn't it?'

'Yeah,' he replied. 'Heavy downpour mid-morning I think.'

Georgie pointed to the crushed metal. 'Which means these tiny flakes of paint would have been washed away by the rain.'

'So, the damage was done in the last twenty-four hours,' Garrow said, following her train of thought.

Georgie continued to look. 'We need to get SOCOs down here asap.'

'You think someone could have rammed him off the road?' Garrow asked.

'By the look of the impact,' Georgie replied, gesturing to the damage, 'it's definitely a possibility.'

Why the hell would someone have rammed Jake off the road? she thought to herself. Then she remembered their conversation from yesterday and Jake's refusal to tell her about the article he was investigating for *The Times*. Was that it? It seemed to be so far-fetched, didn't it?

As Garrow stood, he gazed around. Then she saw him take a few steps backwards and survey the crash site. Something had clearly occurred to him.

'What are you thinking?' she asked him.

'The bend in the road is two hundred yards down there,' he replied, pointing back the way they had come. 'If Jake had crashed because he'd taken the bend too fast, he would have gone into the hedgerow up there.'

Georgie nodded. 'Yeah, this is a straight stretch of road, isn't it? There's no reason to suggest why he would swerve off the road and into the tree.'

'Unless someone hit him.' Garrow moved onto the road, crouched down again and peered back down towards the bend. 'There's not a skid or a tyre mark in sight.'

'Which means that Jake didn't even have time to hit the brakes,' Georgie said, thinking out loud. Nothing about the scene they were looking at suggested that Jake's crash had been a mere accident.

Garrow walked down the road for about thirty yards and crouched again. 'Have you got an evidence bag, Georgie?'

'Erm, yeah. Why?' Georgie asked as she marched down the road to where he was crouched.

'There's signs of impact over here.' Garrow pointed to glass and plastic that lay on the road. 'This looks like broken glass from a car's lights. And maybe part of a bumper.'

Georgie looked at him. 'This is where someone rammed into the back of Jake's car, isn't it?'

'That would be my guess.' Garrow looked at her. 'Everything about this crash site is wrong.'

A car honed into view and pulled up next to where they had parked.

Ruth got out and Georgie's mind momentarily switched to Nick and his court hearing.

Taking out a cigarette, Ruth cupped her hands, lit it and took a deep drag as Georgie and Garrow approached. Everything about Ruth's demeanour suggested an uneasiness.

'What happened?' Garrow asked apprehensively.

Georgie looked at Ruth's face – her expression was sombre. 'Nick didn't get bail, did he?' she said under her breath.

'No.' Ruth took a moment and then shook her head. 'The judge turned him down for bail. He said the attack was violent and the CPS claimed that he was a flight risk.'

'Jesus Christ!' Georgie narrowed her eyes. 'He's got a wife and young daughter. How can he be a flight risk?'

'I don't know,' Ruth said quietly. She was clearly rattled.

'Can he appeal?' Garrow asked.

'I don't think there's any point,' Ruth shrugged. 'I've never seen a bail decision overturned in North Wales.' She then gestured over to the car. 'What have we got here?'

'Significant damage to the rear of the vehicle, flecks of

paint from another car, no skid marks and a straight piece of road,' Georgie explained. 'Glass and plastic on the road just up there from some kind of collision.'

Ruth raised an eyebrow. 'You think he was rammed off the road?'

Georgie nodded with a sombre expression. 'Yes.'

Ruth took a moment and then said, 'In that case, this is a murder investigation.'

Chapter 14

As Georgie and Garrow headed back to Llancastell CID from Portmeirion, Georgie had decided they should visit Jake's parents over in Llangollen. She knew that uniformed officers would have already visited them to break the terrible news. However, she recalled that Jake had mentioned he'd been to see them when he first arrived in North Wales. Not only did she want to pass on her condolences, she also wanted to see if they had any idea why Jake was in North Wales. She wondered if whatever story he had been researching had anything to do with his death.

As Georgie gazed out of the window at the passing countryside, she had a sudden recollection of being with Jake the night before. The look on his face as he smiled and kissed her. Then his phrase, *I could tell you what I'm up to, but then I'd have to kill you.* What did that mean? Was he implying that he was working on something dangerous? Had someone run him off the road because of that?

Georgie buzzed down the window to get a blast of cold air and try to clear her head. Letting the icy wind numb her face, she closed her eyes. The shock and grief of Jake's death came to her in waves. It still felt unreal.

Turning left, they cut across the middle of Snowdonia. Mount Snowdon dominated the skyline to the north. She remembered the first time she had climbed the mountain on a school trip when she was at secondary school, and her sense of awe at the great mountain as it loomed up before her over 3,500 feet above sea level. Her geography teacher, Mr Peters, or *Paedo Peters* as he was called for no other reason than he looked a bit odd, told them that the name *Snowdon* came from the Old English for Snow Hill but the Welsh preferred to call it *Yr Wyddfa*, meaning burial place. Then she remembered that Jake had been on that very trip before she had ever known him. In fact, she recalled being jealous that Jake's attention was solely focussed on Sally Jenkins.

As Georgie looked up, she could see the mountain's grey, snow-filled crevices and dark tracks. They passed the mighty River Glaslyn which had forced itself through a narrow passage and cut a steep-sided valley, draining a large lake that had covered Beddgelert after the Ice Age. The surrounding wooded area was one of Wales' most famous beauty spots; the Welsh Highland Railway ran through the Aberglaslyn Pass and its spectacular scenery drew tourists from all over the world.

It took another thirty minutes before they pulled up outside Pam and Bill Neville's tiny cottage. Georgie's stomach tightened. Obviously she had dealt with grieving relatives as part of her job as a police officer on many occasions. However, this was personal. Between the ages of sixteen and eighteen, Pam and Bill had been her surrogate parents. She couldn't bear to think of the pain and grief they must be going through.

Walking down the windy garden path, Georgie felt she

was stepping back in time. The slightly overgrown, wild front garden that smelt of lavender. The dark wooden front door.

Georgie gave a tentative knock and looked at Garrow.

'Okay?' he asked under his breath.

'Yeah,' she replied with a nod. She needed to keep it together for Bill and Pam's sake.

The door opened and Pam looked at her. She looked drawn and tired. It took her a few seconds to recognise her and then her eyes brightened a little.

'Georgie?' she said in a whisper.

'Pam, I'm so sorry,' Georgie said, stepping forward and hugging her. She felt Pam shudder with emotion for a few seconds.

Pam took a step back and looked her up and down with a half-smile. 'Look at you. I always knew you'd do something amazing with your life. Me and Bob were so proud when we heard you'd become a police officer.'

'Thank you,' Georgie said, feeling a little choked with emotion. 'This is my colleague, DC Jim Garrow.'

'I'm so sorry for your loss,' Garrow said gently.

'Come in,' Pam said with a gesture. 'Bob's gone out with the dogs. He's taken it really hard as you can imagine. He'll be really disappointed not to have seen you.' She then beckoned for them to follow her to the kitchen. 'Come and sit down. Do you want tea?'

'Lapsang Souchong?' Georgie asked with a smile. She recalled how Pam loved different blends of tea but Lapsang Souchong was always her favourite.

Pam smiled back. 'You remembered?'

'Of course,' Georgie replied. 'How could I forget?' Then she gave Pam a meaningful look. 'I was with Jake just before he died. In fact, he was coming back from my house to Portmeirion when the crash happened.'

Pam looked confused. 'Was he? I didn't know you'd stayed in touch?'

'We hadn't,' Georgie admitted. 'But we bumped into each other yesterday afternoon. We went out for a drink and then he stayed over at my house.'

Pam nodded as she took a few seconds to take this in. 'Oh right ... Do you know what happened?'

'Not yet,' Georgie replied, wondering how much to divulge at this stage.

Pam clicked on the kettle and then stood over by the fridge. Georgie noticed there were several photographs of Jake as a child and teenager secured by a variety of fridge magnets.

'Was he drunk?' Pam asked.

'No, nothing like that.' Georgie shook her head. 'We had a few drinks last night but he was fine by the time he left me. We're not sure why he crashed.'

Pam narrowed her eyes. 'The officers that came earlier said the car had hit a tree? I don't understand. Did he swerve to avoid someone else?'

Garrow looked over. 'We're not sure why the car left the road, Mrs Neville.'

'Pam, please,' she said. 'Do you think he was speeding?'

Georgie shrugged. 'It's hard to tell, Pam.' She then gave her a meaningful look. 'I'm really sorry to have to tell you this, but we think another car might have been involved.'

Pam looked confused. 'So, did he have to swerve to avoid it?'

Georgie and Garrow shared a glance.

'No.' Georgie hesitated. How was she going to break this to her? 'We believe that someone might have run Jake off the road deliberately.'

'What?' Pam's eyes widened in horror. 'Why would anyone do that?'

'We're not sure yet,' Garrow replied.

'Do you know why Jake was up in North Wales?' Georgie asked.

'He was working on a story for *The Times*,' Pam replied with a confused look.

Georgie shifted forward on her seat. 'Any idea what that story was about?'

'Not really,' Pam replied as she began to make three cups of tea. Georgie looked over and spotted that Pam's hands were shaking. She got up and went over.

'I'll give you a hand, shall I?' Georgie said as she placed the cups in a neat row and popped a tea bag in each.

'Thank you dear,' Pam said as she put a hand on her shoulder.

'Is there anything you can tell us that might help?' Garrow enquired.

'No, I don't think so.' Pam then thought for a few seconds. 'Actually, Jake mentioned that he was going to talk to Brenda Williams over at Abbey Farm.'

Georgie took the kettle and poured water into the cups. 'Do you know why?' she asked Pam.

'No. No idea,' Pam said with a frown. 'I think he only mentioned it because Brenda is an old friend of ours.'

Georgie did vaguely remember the name Brenda Williams from when she was with Jake. She remembered something about Brenda having an identical twin brother.

'Is there anything about Brenda or Abbey Farm that might have interested Jake or *The Times?*' Georgie asked.

'I'm not sure. I do know that someone from some big American power company approached Brenda a while ago about buying a huge chunk of her land,' Pam explained.

Garrow looked up from his notepad on which he was writing. 'Why did they do that?'

Pam then looked at them as if something had occurred to her. 'Something to do with the area being the perfect place for building a new nuclear power plant. It's been in the local papers.'

Georgie nodded. 'What did she tell them?'

Pam snorted. 'She told them to piss off.' Then Pam narrowed her eyes. 'You don't think this has anything to do with what's happened to Jake, do you?'

Georgie gave her a kind smile. 'It's hard to say at this point.'

She then exchanged a look with Garrow – it was definitely a line of enquiry that needed looking into.

Chapter 15

As Georgie and Garrow approached Abbey Farm, she could see Horseshoe Pass in the distance. Its correct Welsh name was *Bwlch yr Oernant*, which meant *Pass of the Cold Stream*, which Georgie had always thought was far more romantic than the English 'Horseshoe Pass'. It separated Llantysilio Mountain which rose 1,854 feet to the west, and Cyrn-y-Brain to the east. The road itself had been built in the early 1800s and travelled in a horseshoe shape around the sides of the steep valley.

Five minutes later, Georgie and Garrow pulled up on the main yard at Abbey Farm. The main farmhouse looked a little dilapidated. It was flanked by some outbuildings, a mud-splattered John Deere tractor and some old farming equipment. A couple of black labradors started to bark to signal their arrival.

Getting out of the car, Georgie was instantly hit by the thick smell of silage. One of the labradors came closer, baring its teeth at her and growling.

'Bess! Bess! Get away!' shouted a loud, angry voice.

It was Brenda Williams. She was short, stout and in her

early 60s. She was wearing dark corduroy trousers that were tucked into filthy wellies and a blue Barbour wax coat.

Fishing her warrant card from her pocket, Georgie showed it to her. 'DC Wild and DC Garrow, Llancastell CID. We're looking for Brenda Williams.'

Brenda peered at her for a few seconds. 'Georgina Wild?'

Georgie gave her a half-smile. 'Yes. Hi Brenda.' She must have met Brenda when she was with Jake. Maybe a family party?

'I heard you'd become a copper,' Brenda said with a nod. 'Good for you. I suppose you've come about the sheep, have you?'

Georgie looked at Garrow with a frown. They didn't have a clue what she was talking about.

'Sheep?' Garrow asked politely.

'Someone's been poisoning my sheep,' Brenda explained. 'I've lost ten in the last two weeks. I reported it last week.'

'Sorry to hear that,' Georgie said. 'But that's not why we're here.'

'Really?' Brenda said, pulling a face. 'The blokes that came last week said there'd be a follow up.'

'Uniformed officers?' Garrow asked, trying to clarify what she meant by the word *blokes*.

'Aye, that's right,' Brenda said with a frown. 'So, why are you here then?'

'We've come about Jake Neville,' Georgie stated gently.

'Jake?' Brenda asked with a deep frown. 'I don't understand.'

Georgie looked at her. 'I'm afraid that Jake Neville was killed in a car crash early this morning.'

'Oh God, no.' Brenda looked rocked by the news.

'That's terrible.' She blinked and took a deep breath. 'Poor Pam and Bill. I need to call them.'

'We understand that Jake had been to see you?' Garrow said.

Brenda nodded but she was clearly still in shock. 'Yes. Day before yesterday.' She wiped a tear from her eye. 'I can't believe it. I remember when Bill brought Pam and Jake back from the hospital. He was premature so he was in there for a couple of months.'

There were a few seconds of silence. One of the labradors came over and sniffed at Georgie and Garrow before trotting away.

'Can you tell us why he came up here?' Georgie asked.

'He rang me a month ago to ask about Eastland Energy,' Brenda replied.

'Eastland Energy?' Garrow said with a frown.

'The American nuclear company,' she replied. 'They want to buy up some of my land to build a bloody power plant. When I told them to sod off, my sheep started to die.'

'And you thought the two were connected?' Georgie asked.

'Of course.' Brenda shrugged. 'Seemed obvious to me. If they couldn't persuade me to sell them the land, they'd ruin me and get the land that way. Bastards. You know what these bloody Americans are like. Don't take no for an answer, do they?'

Chapter 16

Nick was still reeling from the decision not to grant him bail as he waited outside the visitor area of HMP Rhoswen. There were a dozen prisoners all waiting in a line. Some chatted and laughed. Others slouched against the wall or looked lost in thought. At the end of the corridor was a huge image of the snow-capped mountains of Snowdonia. It provided momentary relief from the prison's sterile interior of thick concrete walls and black, wipe-clean floors and harsh white lighting.

Nick remembered the PR spin for North Wales' £250 million super prison when it was built just over a decade earlier. It was based on the Scandinavian penal system where the emphasis was on rehabilitation rather than punishment. Rhoswen was hailed as a 'game changer' in the UK penal system. Rates of violence, suicides and re-offending had dropped dramatically in countries such as Norway where such prisons had been described as 'miraculous.' However, HMP Rhoswen had proved to be a catastrophic disaster. It had some of the highest rates of violence against staff, drug use and suicides. Category C prisoners and those close to release had been housed alongside dangerous Category A prisoners and 'lifers', producing a volatile, toxic mix. Some of the new facilities had been left unfinished as the prison's budget soared out of control.

'Behind the yellow line,' said the young female prison officer, pointing to where the floor was marked out with thin yellow lines like a tennis court. The lines were there to indicate the sight lines of the CCTV cameras that were mounted up on the walls or the sensors for the internal doors. Prisoners needed to stay the right side of the lines so that they were always visible. Nick couldn't help but feel humiliated by being treated like this but he knew that if he was going to survive, he needed to find an acceptance quickly.

One of the male prisoners smirked at the prison officer. Even Nick could tell she was new and lacking in confidence. The staff turnover at Rhoswen was staggeringly high and morale was at an all-time low.

'Come and stand here, please,' the officer said to the smirking prisoner.

'How old are you, miss?' he asked her with a mocking grin.

'Just come and stand here, now,' she said, her voice quivering a little with nerves.

'Jesus, I've got pubic hair older than you, miss,' he mumbled under his breath.

'What did you say?' she asked.

'Danny, leave it, will you?' another prisoner said with a huff.

The prisoners glared at each other.

The tension began to mount and Nick worried that a fight was about to kick off.

Jesus, just what we need.

Another prison officer arrived and beckoned them towards the door that led into the visitors' area which looked more like a hall in a modern secondary school.

Nick immediately saw Amanda sitting at a table in the far corner. She smiled and stood up as he approached. Before he'd even arrived, he saw her eyes well with tears.

'Hey,' he said comfortingly as he gave her a hug.

'Hey,' she said, her voice breaking with emotion.

After a few seconds, they sat down at the low table on red padded chairs. They held hands and looked at each other.

'I don't understand why they wouldn't grant you bail,' she whispered as she wiped tears from her face. 'You're a police officer, for God's sake.'

Nick looked at her, put his finger to his lips and glanced around nervously. Even though Amanda had whispered, he didn't want anyone to know that he was a copper.

Amanda pulled a face. 'Sorry.'

'It's fine,' Nick said quietly. 'The attack on Thurrock was violent. It's fairly standard for suspects for that sort of crime to go on remand.'

Amanda looked at him. 'How do we prove you're being set up?'

'I don't know at the moment,' Nick admitted with a frustrated shake of his head. 'Ruth has said she'll try and do some digging around but I don't want her losing her job over it.'

'There must be something else we can do?' Amanda said, sounding distraught.

'Look, it's going to be months before I go to trial. If I can point my defence counsel in the right direction, I'm hoping they can find evidence that Blake is behind it,' Nick said, trying to reassure her.

'And if they don't?'

Nick looked at her. 'If I'm going to survive in here, I need to remain optimistic that we can find something to prove that I'm innocent.'

Amanda leaned forward and took his hand with both of hers. 'You only spoke to Thurrock that once?'

Nick didn't like the tone of her question. 'What do you mean?'

'I'm just checking,' she replied defensively.

Nick tried not to get angry. 'We've been through this. I went to where he worked. I told him that I knew that he'd attacked Fran. And then I told him that if he ever went near her again, or even looked at her, there would be trouble. That's it.'

Amanda nodded but Nick could see that she wasn't convinced. He leaned forward and looked at her. 'Mand, if I'm going to get through this, I need you to believe me.'

'I do believe you,' she whispered. 'I'm just trying to make sense of it.'

'I've told you about my history with Curtis Blake,' Nick said with a frown. He didn't understand what the issue was. 'Paul Thurrock was clearly involved with Blake and probably selling drugs for him in Llancastell. My guess is that Thurrock asked Blake if he knew who I was. He might have even mentioned our little chat. Blake had some reason for wanting to get rid of Thurrock. Maybe he was skimming off the top or cutting the drugs down even further. Blake saw an opportunity to kill Thurrock and put me in the frame at the same time, so he took it.'

'Of course,' Amanda nodded. She looked almost relieved at Nick's explanation.

Before they had time to continue, Sean Keegan, the man with the scar Nick had recognised in the AA meeting, walked past. As he passed, Keegan tossed something onto their table and continued to saunter over towards the entrance back into the prison.

Nick was slightly startled and then spotted that there was a small, folded piece of paper sitting on the table.

Amanda gestured. 'What the hell was that about?'

'Sean Keegan,' Nick replied with a dark look. 'He works for Blake.'

'What?' Amanda exclaimed under her breath, her eyes widening. 'And he's in here?'

'Yeah,' Nick nodded as he picked up the piece of paper. 'It's not great but he's not on the VP wing which is something at least.'

Amanda shook her head. 'I hate the thought of you being in this place.'

Unfolding the note, Nick saw that Keegan had written something – *If you want out of here, gym at 3pm.* He passed the note to Amanda who read it.

'What does that mean?' she asked.

'No idea,' Nick replied with a shrug. 'But there's only one way of finding out.'

Amanda looked anxious. 'You can't go and meet him. What if he attacks you?'

'He's not going to,' Nick reassured her, although the thought had crossed his mind. 'If Blake is making contact, he wants something from me. I need to go and find out what that is.'

Chapter 17

Sitting back from her desk, Ruth gave an audible sigh as she read an email from DI Will Nelson at the NWROCU – the North West Regional Organised Crime Unit. DI Nelson was based over in Liverpool and Ruth had met him on several occasions since moving to Llancastell and found him to be a decent bloke. She had reached out to him 'off the record' to see what intel they had on Curtis Blake and if there were any ongoing investigations. Although the case against Nick wasn't completely watertight, it had been solid enough to reach the CPS' requirements to go to trial – so they clearly believed they could secure a conviction.

Ruth had seen Nelson's name in the papers recently after the conviction of three men from a Merseyside OCG for a total of 78 years for murder and conspiracy to supply. However, his email suggested there was little he could do to help. She didn't know if Nelson was unwilling to speak to her 'off the record' about Blake or if there genuinely wasn't any meaningful intel. His email to her was both disappointing and frustrating.

Ruth wondered how Nick was faring in HMP Rhoswen. Then her thoughts turned to Amanda and Megan. Ruth was Megan's godmother and she knew that she was too young to understand why Nick wasn't at home. Ruth made a note that she would go round to see how Amanda and Megan were coping after work in the next few days.

Glancing down at her watch, she saw it was 3pm and most of the CID team were back at Llancastell nick. Developments in the Jake Neville case had been filtering in to her throughout the day but she knew it was time to bring everyone up to speed.

Getting up from her chair, she noticed that she had started to make that tell-tale groan that older people made when they stood up or sat down.

Oh God, have I really become that person? she wondered.

Striding out into the CID office, she headed over to a new scene board that had just been created. They would need to move operations over to Incident Room 1 now this was a murder case.

At the centre of the scene board was a photograph of Jake Neville – handsome, smiling, carefree. Beside that were the basic details they knew so far.

'Right everyone, listen up,' Ruth said as she walked to the front of the room. 'We're going to need to move across to IR1 by tomorrow. I'll get Tech Support to set everything up in there overnight.' She pointed to the photograph of Jake and then looked over at Georgie to check on her. She was sitting at her desk, poised with a pen and paper. 'This is our victim. Jake Neville, aged twenty-nine. Jake left Georgie's home just after 6am and headed back to his hotel at Portmeirion. Travel time would have been just under an hour, so we think the accident occurred between six thirty and seven o'clock.' Ruth pointed to the detailed map of Portmeirion that had been attached to the scene board. There was a red pin to mark where the crash had taken place. 'This is the exact location where Jake's car collided at speed with a tree. Although there will be a PM in the next forty-eight hours, paramedics confirmed that Jake was dead by the time they arrived at 7.45am. It is likely that Jake died on impact.' Ruth spotted Georgie taking a visible breath as she sat forward on her seat. 'Jake's car had a substantial amount of damage to its rear. The road where the crash took place was straight. Officers found no evidence of skid marks on the road which indicates that Jake didn't have time to use his brakes. Flakes of paint from another vehicle were found within a damaged area on Jake's car so we believe that his car was hit from behind and rammed off the road.' Ruth looked out at the team. 'So, we are treating Jake's death as a murder. This was a young man, a talented journalist, who was deliberately killed, so I want us to do our best work to bring those responsible for his death to justice. We owe that to his family and friends who are devastated by his loss. As most of us know, Jake was a friend of Georgie's, so we also owe it to her, as our colleague, to find out what happened and who is responsible.' Ruth let what she had said sink in and then looked around. 'Okay, what have we got?'

French gestured to a printout that he was holding. 'The Forensic Collision Investigators are at the scene now, boss. Their initial assessment is the same as ours – that Jake was deliberately run off the road. The car will be removed tonight and the investigators will examine it tomorrow.'

'Thanks, Dan,' Ruth said with a nod. She was glad that the FCIs agreed with their initial suspicions about the crash.

Garrow looked over. 'Forensics are examining the flakes

of paint we found within the damage to the rear of the vehicle, boss. Initial test results by tomorrow morning.'

By narrowing down the exact colour and chemical composition of a particular paint fleck or chip, forensics were able to identify its manufacturer. From that, they could sometimes even narrow down the make of car.

'Thanks, Jim,' Ruth said. 'Anything else?'

Georgie pointed to her computer screen. 'We retrieved Jake's mobile phone, boss. There are some photos on his camera roll that are worth looking at.' Georgie clicked her mouse and the large monitor that was mounted on the CID office wall came on, mirroring Georgie's computer screen. The first image was from a local newspaper – *Anti-nuclear campaign group protest outside MP home.* 'According to this article, an American company, Eastland Energy, have been contracted by the Welsh Assembly to build a nuclear power plant in North Wales. Eastland identified a twenty-acre site close to a lake up by the Horseshoe Pass. However, the land is owned by Brenda Williams. The family has farmed sheep on that land for over two hundred years. When Eastland approached her, Brenda refused to sell them the land.'

French looked over. 'Can't they get the land through a compulsory purchase order?'

'They could,' Georgie nodded, 'but that needs to be agreed directly by the Secretary of State. Plus, this local campaign group have got the backing of some fairly wealthy residents. They've threatened to tie the CPO up in appeals and that could prolong the development by years.'

Garrow nodded. 'Brenda claims that since she turned down Eastland, ten sheep on her land have been poisoned.'

'Has anyone confirmed that?' Ruth asked.

'No.' Garrow shook his head. 'I don't think so, boss. Maybe we should get a toxicology report?'

'Good idea,' Ruth said. 'We're assuming that Jake was poking around to see if Eastland Energy was deliberately trying to drive Brenda Williams off her land.'

'That's my thinking, boss.' Georgie nodded as she clicked her mouse to show images of countryside and a lake. 'If you look at these, Jake took photographs of what I'm guessing is the intended site for the nuclear plant. He was an investigative journalist so it makes sense that he was snooping around to see what he could find.'

French raised an eyebrow. 'Are we suggesting that someone from Eastland Energy ran Jake off the road because he was digging around in their business?'

Ruth shrugged. 'I know it might sound a bit far-fetched but it's the only motive we've got at the moment.'

French signalled he had something. 'Boss, Eastland Energy are holding a public planning meeting and a presentation at Llangollen Town Hall tonight. I guess it's a PR exercise for any worried locals.'

Ruth nodded. 'Might be worth checking out.'

Georgie clicked to show an image of a building. 'Eastland Energy have temporary UK offices just outside Mold. I guess they're dealing with plans for their proposed plant.'

'In that case,' Ruth said, looking at Georgie. 'Let's go and have a word, shall we?'

Chapter 18

Wandering along the VP wing, Nick made his way towards one of the large communal gyms at the far end. The air smelt of prison food and disinfectant from where the floors had been recently cleaned. Except for the odd shout and boom of laughter, the wing was relatively quiet.

As he got to the doors, Nick checked his watch. 3pm on the dot. Opening the double doors, he saw five treadmills, a cross-trainer and four bikes on the far side. To the right were some mats on the floor and a rack of free weights. A scrawny-looking prisoner with a thick beard was doing stretches. To the left, a prison officer sat reading a newspaper. The heavy gym equipment was dangerous and Nick had heard of prisoners using free weights against each other as weapons. The prison officer was there to make sure people could train in relative safety and that none of the weights or equipment *went walkies*.

Nick strolled inside and nodded at the prison officer who looked thoroughly disinterested. He went and sat on one of the padded weights benches – he assumed that

Keegan had meant the gym on the VP wing. Nick didn't have access to the other wings in the prison. Technically, Keegan shouldn't be able to move freely from where he was being held into the VP wing either. However, Keegan was part of Blake's crew and they were a powerful OCG. They effectively ran parts of Rhoswen. They controlled the distribution of drugs, mobile phones, hooch, and any other contraband. Keegan would also have access to restricted areas of the prison. Officers were unlikely to challenge a gang like the Croxteth Park Boyz. Threats of violence or bribery usually ensured that a decent amount of prison officers either looked the other way or were even complicit in helping make life as easy and comfortable as they could inside the jail.

'Get out,' said a voice with a thick Scouse accent.

It was Keegan.

The man who was doing stretches looked at Keegan and wisely decided to scuttle away.

Keegan sauntered in and glared at the prison officer. 'Piss off, screw.'

The prison officer bristled, folded up his newspaper and walked over to the doors. 'I'll be just out here.'

Keegan ignored him and closed the doors behind him.

Nick's stomach tightened. He was now incredibly vulnerable. Keegan was stocky and about 6' 2". If he decided to attack Nick, then he wouldn't stand much of a chance.

Keegan ambled slowly back as if he didn't have a care in the world and then sat on the weights bench next to Nick.

Nick looked at him. He'd had enough of all the 'dick swinging' swagger. 'What do you want, Keegan?'

'Mr Blake says to say hello,' he replied with a cocky grin.

'You're not going to make it stick, you do know that?' Nick said, trying to sound as calm as he could.

'Really?' Keegan growled as he leaned forward. 'We'll see about that.'

Nick waited for a few seconds before repeating his question. 'You going to tell me what you want?'

Keegan smiled. 'Why? You got something more important to be doing, like?' he asked sarcastically.

Nick looked at him for a moment.

Reaching into the pocket of his navy blue trackies, Keegan pulled out a decent-looking smart phone. Most mobile phones that were smuggled into prisons were tiny burner phones, often carried inside prisoners' rectums, dropped by drones or brought in by corrupt prison officers.

'I've got someone who wants a quick word with you,' Keegan said as he passed the phone over to Nick.

Looking down at the screen, Nick could see that someone was on FaceTime. He instantly saw Curtis Blake appear on the screen. His face was podgy, sunbed brown and his teeth gleamed like they were ultra-violet. He wore his trademark cocky grin.

'Detective Sergeant Nicholas Evans,' Blake said into the camera. 'You've been a very naughty boy, haven't you? Bet you didn't think you'd ever be sitting in HMP Rhoswen next to me mate there Sean? Bet your wife and daughter are starting to miss you, eh lad? Amanda and Megan isn't it?'

Nick bristled but didn't want Keegan to see just how angry he was.

'At some point, one of you clowns is going to tell me what you want,' Nick growled. 'But if you go anywhere near my wife or daughter, I'll make it my life's mission to ensure you have a very slow painful death.'

Blake laughed and then tutted. 'Well that's not very

nice, Nicholas. And just when I was about to offer to help you out.'

'I don't need your help thanks,' Nick snapped.

'That's where you're wrong,' Blake said. 'Eh, I've got a couple of things to show you. You might find this very interesting.'

Blake moved the camera around what looked like an industrial warehouse. He then walked over to a long workbench. Nick could see two transparent plastic bags laying on the worktop but at first he couldn't see what they were.

A shaven-headed man in his 20s moved into shot. Just behind him, Nick could make out words on a sign on a back wall – *Murphy's Met...* – the rest of the sign wasn't visible. Was that any kind of clue as to Blake's location?

'Davie, Davie, say hello to our Nicholas, would you?' Blake said off camera.

Davie gave a smiley wave, reached over and picked up one of the transparent bags. Inside was a large, bloodstained kitchen knife.

'Do you wanna have a guess at what that is?' Blake asked.

'Not really,' Nick murmured – but he had a decent idea.

'I'm surprised. Clever bizzie like you,' Blake scoffed. 'Well, I'm a bit pressed for time, so I'll tell you, shall I? It's the knife that killed Paul Thurrock. Show him what else we've got, Davie, will ya?'

Davie put down the bag containing the knife and picked up another, larger, transparent bag which he waved at the phone's camera.

Nick peered at the screen and then saw that the bag contained a white Adidas hoodie that was covered in blood stains.

'Paul Thurrock was wearing that hoodie when we went

The Portmeirion Killings

round there the other night,' Blake explained in an amused tone.

Nick felt sick. He had already been 99% certain that Blake was behind Thurrock's murder but now he knew for certain. However, the fact that Blake had kept hold of the murder weapon and the hoodie made him feel incredibly uneasy.

Blake's face appeared again on the screen. 'Now, I need you to listen to me very carefully, because this is a once in a lifetime offer. You have a choice to make. Davie here can pop round to your house and bury these in your garden. CID might then get an anonymous tip-off that they are there. Then I reckon you're bang to rights for shanking Paul Thurrock. And I also reckon you're gonna get twenty-five years. If you serve half that, that sweet little girl of yours is going to be about fifteen by the time you get out. And you're gonna miss out on seeing her grow up.'

There were a few seconds of silence as Blake smirked at the camera. Nick could hear something in the background. A deep, rumbling noise. It sounded like a train passing nearby.

'Or?' Nick asked, but he was pretty sure he knew what was coming next.

'See? I knew you'd be interested. Clever man like you,' Blake said. 'In my line of work, I come across nasty little scumbags who want to take me on. Who want to rip me off. And there's someone just like that in Llancastell right now. So, if you're interested, Davie is going to pop round, chuck that hoodie in his bin and make a phone call. This toerag is going to get nicked and get sent down for murdering Thurrock. And you're going to walk out of there a free man.'

Nick took a few seconds to take in what he had said. His head was whirling.

'What about the knife?' Nick asked.

'We gonna need to keep that as a little bit of insurance,' Blake explained. 'If you know what I mean?'

Nick took a breath. 'And what do you want in return?'

'Once you're a free man, Nicholas, I think you would owe me,' Blake said. 'So, I might need you to do a few things to help me out. Keep your eyes and ears open. That kind of thing.'

Nick couldn't believe that he had managed to find himself in this position. Curtis Blake was the person who he hated more than anyone else on earth. And now he was being backed into a corner where Blake controlled his liberty.

'You want me to be your informant?' Nick asked.

'I don't like the word *informant*,' Blake said. 'Think of it as the beginning of a beautiful working relationship. You never know. Going forward, I think you'd find that being an associate of mine could also be very lucrative for you. Take that wife and little girl of yours on a decent foreign holiday every year, that kind of thing, eh? … Tell you what I'll do, I'll give you a couple of days to think it over. But don't think about it for too long or I'll assume that you want Davie to do your gardening for you.'

Chapter 19

Claudia Berllucci was Media and Communications Director of Eastland Energy. She was late 30s, with blonde bobbed hair and sharp, intelligent eyes.

'Jake Neville was up here about three days ago,' Claudia explained. She spoke with an American accent.

Ruth and Georgie sat on the opposite side of her neatly arranged desk. To one side, there was a framed photograph of Claudia in her late teens with an older man who had his arm around her. Ruth assumed it was her father. There were no other photos anywhere else in the office, which made Ruth wonder about Claudia's mother for a second.

'Can you tell us what Jake wanted?' Ruth asked, regaining her focus on why they were sitting there.

Claudia sat back at her desk, interlaced her fingers and gave them what could only be described as a frosty look. 'I think that's between me and Jake Neville, isn't it? ... But he did promise to pop back in a day or two if that helps?'

Claudia gave a slight smirk. 'We're going out for dinner actually.'

God this woman is incredibly irritating, Ruth thought.

'That's unlikely,' Georgie said as she visibly bristled and fixed Claudia with a steely stare. 'Jake died earlier today and we're treating his death as murder.'

'What?' Claudia exclaimed, sitting forward on her chair. Then she composed herself, taking in what Georgie had told her. 'Oh my God, that's horrible … What happened?'

Ruth ignored her question. 'We're going to need you to tell us everything you talked about with Jake Neville.'

Claudia blinked and looked flustered. 'Erm, I think I'm going to need to talk to our lawyers before I talk to you.'

'Okay. Your choice,' Georgie growled. 'You can call your *lawyers* from Llancastell Police Station when you get there.'

Ruth and Georgie got up from their seats.

'What?' Claudia exclaimed.

'Don't worry,' Ruth said in a dry, reassuring tone. 'We can drop you back here once we've finished with you.'

'You can't arrest me!' Claudia snapped nervously.

'We're not arresting you,' Ruth explained. 'But you spoke to a murder victim, so we're going to interview you at Llancastell Police Station under caution. However, if you continue to refuse to help with our enquiries, I will arrest you for obstruction and you'll have to spend the night in a holding cell until you appear before a magistrate in the morning.'

Ruth knew that her dislike of Claudia had influenced her decision to go in hard but she didn't care. She knew that Claudia's little comment about having dinner with Jake had upset Georgie and she was feeling protective.

There were a few tense seconds.

Claudia could see they weren't joking. 'Okay,' she conceded, shaking her head as if there was something amusing. 'Please, sit down. I can tell you what we talked about.'

Ruth glanced at Georgie as they sat back down again – it wasn't the first time this kind of threat had worked. Most people panicked at the thought of being hauled off to a police station, let alone a night in a holding cell. It was only seasoned criminals that took this type of thing in their stride.

'Jake wanted to know about the tendering process for our plans to build the nuclear power plant in North Wales. I gave him the details of our bid, when it was made, and why I felt it had been the successful bid and won the contract with the Welsh Assembly. He wanted to know if we had used a lobbying firm and who they were. I gave him those details too. I made it clear that Eastland Energy were happy to be completely transparent about everything to do with how and when we secured that contract.'

Ruth frowned. 'Did he say why he wanted all this information?'

'No,' Claudia replied. 'But he was a journalist. He wasn't about to share anything that he was investigating. If we did have anything to hide, which we don't, it would have given us time to cover our tracks. But I can assure you, our tender, our use of a lobbying firm, and our dealings with the Welsh Assembly were all legal and ethical. There was no reason for me not to cooperate.'

Georgie looked over at her. 'How many people work for Eastland Energy here in North Wales?'

'We have a skeleton staff of ten,' Claudia replied. 'Obviously when we finally start the build, it will be a lot more.'

'We're going to need contact details of everyone that works here,' Ruth informed her.

Claudia frowned. 'Why? That feels like an invasion of their privacy.'

Georgie gave an audible sigh to let Claudia know that she was getting on her nerves. 'Jake Neville was researching an article about your company. My guess is that it was going to be less than flattering. Now he's dead.'

Ruth looked over at her and said calmly, 'If you don't supply the information that we request from you, we will execute a search warrant and rip this place apart.'

'Okay, I will get you those details,' Claudia replied reluctantly.

Georgie looked over at her. 'We understand there's been a lot of local opposition to the planned construction?'

'There always is with anything to do with nuclear power,' Claudia replied with a shrug. 'People are paranoid but also ill-informed. They still bring up Chernobyl but that was thirty-five years ago. These days, nuclear power is as environmentally friendly as wind turbines. In fact, using fossil fuels is far more dangerous.'

'What do you know about Brenda Williams?' Ruth asked. She was getting bored of Claudia's well-rehearsed spin on the benefits and advances in nuclear power. They were there to solve a murder.

Claudia blinked as she thought carefully about her answer for a moment. 'We've been negotiating with Miss Williams for the past few months.'

Georgie raised an eyebrow. 'Really? We understand there hasn't been any negotiation. Brenda Williams told me that she had flatly refused to sell you the land you've identified for building the plant.'

Claudia gave them a half-smile. 'I'm sure she tells that to everyone.'

'Sorry.' Ruth narrowed her eyes. 'Are you saying that Brenda is willing to sell you her land?' Ruth wanted to have the details of any discussions between Brenda and Eastland Energy as it might have a bearing on what had happened to Jake.

'All I'm saying is that I've been in this business for a long time,' Claudia stated in a slightly pompous tone. 'I've found that everyone has a price eventually. We just have to find out what that is. In the US, we'd term what Miss Williams is doing as *playing hardball*.'

Georgie sat forward in her seat. 'As ridiculous as this might sound, were you aware that Abbey Farm has lost ten sheep in the past few weeks?'

'Sorry,' Claudia said with a faintly bemused expression. 'Sheep?'

'Miss Williams runs a sheep farm. It's been in the family for generations,' Georgie snapped. 'She thinks someone is poisoning her sheep to put her out of business.'

Claudia frowned. 'And she thinks that Eastland is somehow responsible? I think that's slanderous, isn't it?'

'You can see how suspicious it looks,' Ruth explained. 'She refuses to sell her land to you. And now her sheep are dying for no apparent reason.'

Claudia looked angry. 'I can categorically tell you that we would have nothing to do with anything like that. We are a reputable and ethical company and I resent what you are insinuating. And unless there's anything else, I'd like you to leave, please.'

'Thank you for your help,' Ruth replied calmly as she got up.

Garrow and French had parked at Portmeirion and made their way across the colourful Italian styled village. They knew that Jake had been staying in the hotel and they needed to check his room to see if there was anything there that might be useful to the investigation.

They walked past the ice cream parlour. Its mint-green façade and old fashioned signs made it look like it was from the set of a film from the 1950s. The village opened up into a series of vibrant, labyrinth-like paths and walkways. Buildings were an array of bright colours – blues, oranges, soft pinks and sunshine yellows. Small trees and neat hedges, arches and statues gave it a surreal Mediterranean look. Passing through an apricot archway under a tall building, Garrow glanced up to see that the roof of the arch had been evocatively painted in the style of Leonardo Da Vinci's Sistine Chapel.

'This place is mad,' French mumbled looking around with a bemused frown.

'You've never been here before?' Garrow asked incredulously.

'Nope,' French replied with shrug. 'Never had the inclination. I thought it's where tourists and pensioners came for an ice cream and to buy pottery.'

'It was used for that TV series *The Prisoner*, in the 60s.'

'Never heard of it,' French said. 'And I was born in 80s.'

To their left, the stunning sandy beach and estuary swept away towards the rugged landscape to the south.

'The Beatles used to come here,' Garrow explained. 'It was one of George Harrison's favourite places. In fact, he had his 40th birthday party here.'

They crossed a small square with a fountain and an ornate pool. The central piazza had a Gothic Pavilion and golden statues of Hercules and the goddess Friga.

French laughed. ' I can see why. I feel like I've taken acid just walking around. It's all very *Yellow Submarine*, isn't it?'

The hotel itself was at the end of the village. It was a large white Art Deco building overlooking the beach and the sea beyond.

Garrow and French showed their warrant cards to a receptionist and explained that they needed to see Jake Neville's room.

A young girl led them up to the first floor, opened the door and showed them inside.

'Thanks,' French said. 'I'll let you know when we're done.'

The girl left and Garrow surveyed the small room. It was fashionably decorated in muted shades of green with delicately patterned floral wallpaper.

French unzipped a black wheelie case at the centre of the bed. 'He hadn't even unpacked,' he remarked as he sifted through.

Garrow checked the wardrobe, the bedside tables and then the bathroom.

Nothing.

'Looks like he dumped his bag and left,' Garrow said with frustration. He then gestured to the case. 'Anything in there?'

French shook his head. 'Nothing but clothes and a washbag.'

They looked at each. It seemed their trip to Portmeirion had been a wasted journey.

Chapter 20

As they headed down to Llangollen, Ruth looked at the passing countryside. In the distance, a slope of old yew trees that bent sideways in the wind. To her left, a swathe of patchy grass which flattened out to a stone-strewn meadow. She reached into her jacket, pulled out a packet of cigarettes and fished one out. She looked over at Georgie.

'You don't smoke, do you?' Ruth asked, well aware that smoking was far less common in Georgie's generation.

'Nope,' Georgie replied.

'Never?'

Georgie shrugged. 'Oh you know. The odd cigarette when I was pissed and when I was younger. But never properly.'

Ruth nodded. 'Wise choice. I wish I could stop.'

Georgie shrugged. 'Then why don't you?'

'Good question.' Ruth gave her a quizzical look and then smiled. 'Because secretly I don't want to stop. I just say I do.'

Georgie laughed. 'Fair enough.'

Ruth frowned. 'Yeah, you Millennials have put us Generation Xers to shame with your healthy living, no smoking, less drinking.'

Georgie pulled a face and then grinned. 'There are always exceptions to the rule.'

'What are you talking about?' Ruth asked. 'You're always in the gym. And there isn't an inch of fat on you!'

'I just wear baggy tops.'

'Rubbish ... You are a Millennial, aren't you?' Ruth asked.

Georgie nodded. 'Yeah, by a year or two. I think Gen Z kicks in about 1996 or 1997.'

'Gen Z? Does it?' Ruth asked with a wry smile. 'We didn't have generations when I was younger. You were either a kid, a teenager, an adult, or an old git, end of.'

'Ah, it was a simpler time,' Georgie said sardonically.

Ruth laughed. 'Are you mocking me, DC Wild?'

'Me, boss? God, no,' Georgie replied with mock indignation.

'But it really was a much simpler time.' Ruth went to light her ciggie and then looked over. 'Mind if I smoke this out of the window?'

'Of course not,' Georgie replied. 'I know the deal. I drive, you smoke.'

Ruth chortled as she buzzed down the passenger window and lit her cigarette. She took a long drag and looked outside.

The road was narrow, with passing places at regular intervals. Sheep were dotted unevenly up the green hilllands that swept up to her left. Georgie slowed the car a little. It was the sort of place where sheep might wander aimlessly into the road or tractors might hurtle around a corner with no warning.

Ruth looked down at her phone, thinking she should

give Amanda a call to see how she was getting on. There was no signal, which wasn't a big surprise in a remote area like this. She remembered when she had first arrived in North Wales wondering how people lived in such remoteness. Roads that were no more than tracks. No mobile phone service. No flat white coffees on every corner. She was so used to it now, it no longer annoyed her. It was part of its charm.

Half an hour later, Ruth and Georgie were standing on Pam and Bill Neville's doorstep. They were there to update them on their investigation into Jake's death. The reluctant winter sunlight slanted along the front of the house, casting elongated rectangles of watery grey. To the left, the lawn descended to a long sturdy hedge of raspberry spiraea that bordered that side of the garden. There was an old thick powdery smell from the moss that had crept up and now shrouded a garden wall. For a moment, the air filled with the clear precise call of a wood pigeon high above.

Ruth looked at Georgie's intense expression. 'Are you okay?'

Georgie nodded distractedly. 'Yeah, I'm fine.'

'I know you're personally involved in this and you want to find out what happened to Jake,' Ruth said quietly. 'But if it gets too much for you at any point, I need you to let me know.'

'Okay. Thank you, boss,' Georgie replied. 'It's just weird. I virtually lived in this house between sixteen and eighteen. Every Sunday, Jake's dad Bill would make a huge breakfast. Bacon, sausages, mushrooms. He and Pam would be up early but they left ours in the warming oven.

We never got up until midday but it was always there for us when we eventually surfaced. Jake would attempt to make poached eggs. He claimed that adding vinegar to the boiling water helped but they ended up a stringy mess every time.' Georgie smiled sadly as she looked at Ruth. 'Silly bugger.'

The front door opened and Pam looked out. She attempted to look welcoming but Ruth could see she was broken. Her hair was a little unkempt and she wore a baggy burgundy cardigan that came down to just above her knees.

'Come in, please,' she said, beckoning them to come into the house.

'This is DI Ruth Hunter,' Georgie said quietly. 'She's going to be in charge of the investigation into what happened to Jake.'

Ruth looked at Pam. She didn't seem to have registered what Georgie had just said to her. 'I'm sorry for your loss. We're going to do everything we can to find out what happened to your son.'

Pam blinked and then gestured to a door and said, 'Shall we go in here?'

'Of course,' Ruth replied as they entered the living room. It was cluttered with books, Asian and African trinkets and a huge burgundy rug. There was a jade green oriental wall hanging over the sofa where Ruth and Georgie sat down. The sun shone through a big window that had a Victorian Gothic shape to it. Outside, the leaves and branches of some honeysuckle and wisteria blew and bobbed in the wind, occasionally scratching lightly on the glass.

Ruth sat back on the sofa that had seen better days. She sunk down a good six inches as the springs had finally given up. The sofa was covered in a navy-coloured throw and the arms were stained by faint coffee rings and a sprinkle of cake crumbs.

'If there's anything we can do in the meantime?' Georgie asked gently.

'I know that Bill and I would like to plan the funeral,' Pam explained in a virtual whisper.

Ruth gave her an empathetic look. 'I'm afraid there will be a delay in releasing Jake for a funeral at the moment. We're convinced that he was murdered so the coroner won't allow that to happen yet. And there will need to be a post-mortem.'

Pam nodded slowly as tears came to her eyes. 'Oh yes, I understand.'

Ruth knew that mentioning a *post-mortem* could be very unsettling. You were basically telling a relative that their loved one was going to be opened up, prodded, examined and tested.

The door opened and Bill Neville entered. He was thin, wiry and bald. He had a long thick beard that came down into a point like a jazz musician's.

Georgie got up immediately and went to him. 'Bill.'

'There she is,' Bill said in a Caribbean accent as he hugged her.

'I'm so sorry,' Georgie whispered as she hugged him back.

After a moment, Georgie stepped back and took his hands in hers. Just as she remembered, his fingers were covered in silver rings. 'We're going to find out what happened to Jake, I promise you.'

Bill nodded sadly as he looked at her and gave her hands a squeeze. 'I know you will, Georgie. It's *so* good to see you.'

'And you,' Georgie said gently. 'I just wish …' She didn't need to finish her sentence.

Bill nodded. He knew what she meant. He went over and slowly sat beside Pam on a smaller sofa on the other side of the room.

Ruth leaned forward and looked at them both. 'I know that Jake was investigating this proposed nuclear plant and Eastland Energy,' she said, 'but was there anyone else who might have wanted to harm Jake up here? Anything from his past?'

Pam shook her head. 'No, of course not. He hadn't lived up this way for years.'

Bill looked at his wife with a quizzical expression and then glanced over. 'Actually, there is something. I thought of it earlier.'

'Really?' Pam pulled a face at him. 'I'm sure the Langs don't have anything to do with what's happened.'

'Let me tell them what happened,' Bill said sternly.

Ruth nodded reassuringly. 'Please. Anything, however insignificant it might seem, might help us.'

'Jake went on a stag do about five years ago in Spain somewhere,' Bill explained. 'The groom was Adam Penhall.'

Georgie nodded. 'I was at school with Adam.'

'Yeah,' Bill said as he looked over at Georgie. 'Adam, Jake and a few others had kept in contact since leaving sixth form. Adam's best man was David Lang, who you probably knew too?'

'Yeah,' Georgie replied. 'He was a good sportsman. I think he played rugby for North Wales didn't he?'

'That's right,' Bill said. 'There was a terrible accident one night. The boys had all been drinking. Jake pushed David into a swimming pool as a joke. It was far shallower than Jake thought it was going to be. David hit his head, broke his neck and was paralysed from the waist down.'

'I'd lost touch with them all by then,' Georgie said, 'but I do remember hearing something about that at the time.'

'It was terrible. And Jake felt so guilty,' Pam explained, 'but David said he didn't blame Jake. It was just an accident and could have happened to anyone.'

Bill shook his head. 'But David's father, Eryl, didn't see it like that.'

'Why?' Georgie frowned. 'What did he say?'

'He said he could never forgive Jake for what he'd done to his son,' Bill said. 'I heard a few times in the pub that Eryl had got drunk and sworn that he wished that Jake was dead.'

Chapter 21

It was 7pm by the time Ruth and Georgie sat down at the back of Llangollen Town Hall. Built in the 1850s, it was designed in the Gothic Revival style. The main hall inside was large, and doubled as a venue for comedy and music events. Ruth estimated there were probably a hundred local residents in the audience. It smelt of wood and was slightly musty, like an old library.

Claudia Berllucci got up from where she had been sitting on the slightly raised stage, went over to the microphone and tapped it to make sure it was working. There wasn't the slightest hint of nerves or uncertainty as she began to address the meeting. Ruth wondered why most Americans she had ever met had been blessed with that kind of uber confidence.

'Good evening, everyone,' Claudia said with a half-smile that was neither too serious, nor too casual. She wore a dark navy trouser suit and court shoes. 'Firstly, on behalf of Eastland Energy I'd like to thank you for coming here this evening. I'm here to give you some information and answer any questions about our proposal for a new power plant in this area. We, at Eastland Energy, believe that safe nuclear energy is going to be the future of energy for the next century and beyond. The overall cost of nuclear power is comparable with any other forms of energy. In terms of safety, the International Atomic Energy Agency recently concluded that modern nuclear power plants are among the safest and most secure facilities in the world.'

As Claudia continued, Ruth spotted a young man in a wheelchair to one side of the room. He had an angular, intelligent face and a shaved head that looked like it was an attempt to hide early balding. It was a much better look than those men who endlessly styled their hair to cover receding hairlines or bald patches.

Georgie had clearly spotted who Ruth was looking at and said, 'That's David Lang. And that's his dad Eryl next to him.'

Eryl Lang was a gruff-looking a man in his late 50s with a patchy grey beard and a similar receding hairline to his son.

'I wonder what they're doing here?' Georgie said in a virtual whisper.

'Concerned locals, at a guess,' Ruth replied.

Claudia continued. 'I know there are many concerns about how environmentally friendly nuclear power is. Unlike fossil fuels, nuclear power does *not* produce greenhouse gases like carbon dioxide or methane.' Claudia then turned over a cue card. 'Although the estimated cost of a new plant in this area is between two and three billion pounds, remember that a huge amount of this money will go into the local economy. New jobs, new hotels, new infrastructure.' Claudia looked over at a man in his 50s with silver-grey hair and gestured. 'For example, we've already had a meeting with Kevin Matteo here who runs a local haulage firm. If we get the go-ahead, Kevin will be expanding his fleet of lorries and taking on dozens of extra drivers.'

David Lang looked over and shook his head incredulously. 'There are still nuclear accidents, however safe you say nuclear power is,' he said loudly.

Claudia took a moment and then gave him a reassuring smile. 'It's David, isn't it?'

'Yes,' he replied.

'Chernobyl was thirty-five years ago, David,' Claudia stated confidently. 'That type of nuclear power station doesn't exist anymore and hasn't for a long time.'

'But the area you build on is going to be uninhabitable for thousands of years,' David argued. 'What about the impact on local wildlife or the water table?'

There were some murmurs and claps of support.

Claudia held up a glossy brochure. 'We have addressed all these concerns in great detail in here. And you are welcome to take a copy from the back of the hall when you leave here.'

Eryl Lang stood up. 'We're not interested in your spin. The simple fact is that the energy you're creating with nuclear power can be created by renewable energies. Tidal or wind. We just don't need nuclear power in this area, with all the danger it poses to our families.'

There were more vociferous cheers and clapping.

'You're living in the bloody dark ages, Eryl,' shouted Kevin Matteo. 'The plant is going to regenerate this whole area and provide jobs for our kids and then our grandchildren.'

'Yeah, as long as they're not born with any mutations,' David snapped back.

The discussion descended into a slanging match, with everyone talking loudly over each other.

Confident that it wasn't going to escalate into anything

more than a heated debate, Ruth looked at Georgie. 'I think it's time for us to go.'

Georgie and Ruth left Llangollen Town Hall and headed over towards their car. As Georgie opened the door she spotted David Lang and his father coming out and heading down the pavement, deep in animated conversation.

'David?' Georgie shouted as she gave Ruth a look and then approached them.

'Georgie?' David enquired with a grin of recognition.

'Hey.' Georgie smiled. 'It's good to see you.'

David gestured to her and then to Ruth. 'I heard you'd become a copper. Good for you.'

Eryl, who was standing on the other side of the wheelchair, bristled.

Maybe Eryl isn't a big fan of coppers? Georgie wondered.

'Dad and I are involved in the campaign against this new nuclear plant,' David explained.

Georgie nodded and gestured. 'Yeah, we were sitting at the back until it got a bit lively.'

David frowned. 'Oh right. I guess you were there in case it all kicked off?'

'Not really.' Georgie gave him a dark look. 'We're actually investigating Jake Neville's death.'

'What?' David's eyes widened. 'Jake's dead?'

Eryl gave a snort but said nothing. He had clearly still held a huge resentment against Jake. Ruth guessed that would make him a suspect in Jake's murder.

'Yes. I'm afraid so,' Georgie replied quietly.

'God, that's terrible,' David said, narrowing his eyes and shaking his head. 'What happened?'

'He was in a car crash earlier today,' Georgie explained. She then took a moment. 'But we are treating his death as murder.'

David looked puzzled. 'I don't understand?'

Ruth looked at him. 'We believe that someone ran him off the road deliberately.'

'God, that's horrible,' David said.

'Yeah, well I'd like to give that person a medal,' Eryl muttered under his breath.

Ruth and Georgie exchanged a surreptitious look.

'Dad!' David protested.

Georgie stared at him but tried to remain calm. 'Can you tell us your whereabouts between 6 and 7am this morning, Eryl?'

Eryl fixed her with a contemptuous stare. 'Oh, like that is it?' he hissed.

Ruth frowned. 'It's a simple question. And you've made it very clear that there was no love lost between you and Jake Neville.'

'Do you blame me?' Eryl growled with gritted teeth. 'His idiotic antics put my son in this bloody wheelchair. How would you feel if someone did that to your child? David could have had a decent career playing rugby. Now look at him.'

'Dad! That's enough!' David said sternly. 'You need to calm down.'

'You still haven't answered the question, Eryl,' Georgie said, unable to fully hide her loathing for the man.

'Christ! I was tucked up and fast asleep next to my wife,' Eryl snapped. 'You can go and ask her.'

'Don't worry, we will,' Georgie assured him with an edge to her voice.

'Yeah, well we can't be talking to you all night,' Eryl said with a huff. 'Come on, David, we need to go.'

Eryl grabbed the handles of David's wheelchair and manoeuvred him around.

David caught Georgie's eye. 'Sorry.'

'No problem,' she replied.

Ruth watched them go for a few seconds. If Eryl Lang had been involved in Jake's death, would he have been so blatant and open about his feelings towards him? Or was that a clever ploy to remove any suspicion?

Chapter 22

It was 8pm and Nick had already been locked down in his cell for two hours. The doors wouldn't be opened again until 8am in the morning. It was virtually impossible to talk to a prison officer in those 14 hours unless it was an emergency.

Like any other prison, HMP Rhoswen worked on a rigid timetable. Doors were opened at 8am for prisoners to wash and have breakfast. Then prisoners would be taken to work or educational activities. Lunch was at noon with other activities taking place from 1pm to 5pm when they would have their evening meal. When prisoners didn't have either work or a specific activity, they would be locked back up in their cells.

Some cells have a *courtesy key* so that prisoners can lock their own cell and prevent anyone else going in there. However, Nick knew that neither Steve nor he had been at HMP Rhoswen long enough to warrant one of those yet. They just had to run the risk of scumbags riffling through their stuff – or worse.

Nick lay back on the olive green blanket that covered

his single bed. The small television on the cell wall was showing a programme about cars. Nick had placed his breakfast for the following morning, which was delivered at the same time as their evening meal, on the cabinet next to his bed. There was a small, single portion of cereal, a carton of UHT milk, two tea bags, a sachet of jam and a pat of butter.

Nick sensed his cell mate, Steve, looking over.

'I'd love an Aston Martin, wouldn't you?' Steve asked, gesturing to the television.

Nick shrugged. 'You know what, I don't know much about cars. I know James Bond drove an Aston Martin DB5. I wouldn't mind one of those.'

'Sean Connery had one of the original cars from the Bond films,' Steve explained. 'They reckon it's worth £1.5million. Imagine that?'

Nick snorted. 'I'd be scared to drive the bloody thing.'

Steve laughed a little too hard and then looked at the wall beside Nick's bed where he had stuck photos of Amanda and Megan.

'Wife and daughter?' Steve asked.

Nick felt uneasy. He didn't want to reveal anything too personal to Steve until he had fully sussed him out.

'Don't worry, I'm not a nonce,' Steve informed him.

Well you would say that wouldn't you? Nick thought to himself.

Steve looked over at him. 'It's all right, I know you're a copper,' he said quietly.

There was an uneasy tension in the cell for a few seconds.

Nick shook his head. 'You've got that wrong.'

Steve gave a half-smile. 'Don't worry, mate. I'm a customs officer. Not quite the same as you, but not far off.'

'What makes you think I'm a copper then?'

Steve tapped his nose. 'Word gets around … Don't worry, I'm not going to tell anyone. None of my business. To be honest, I was glad when I found out. I don't wanna be sharing a cell with some paedo nonce or a rapist.'

Nick nodded.

'Obviously I can't talk about my case as I'm going to appeal,' Steve explained. 'You probably read about it in the papers?'

'Sorry?'

'200kg of heroin from Pakistan came in via West Midlands airport two years ago?' Steve said.

'Yeah, I do remember it being on the news,' Nick said.

'They arrested all eleven customs officers who were working that night,' Steve explained. 'I didn't know anything about it but the other officers threw me under the bloody bus. Now I'm in here.'

Nick nodded again. That was the thing about being in prison. Inmates always claimed they were innocent of the crimes they had committed.

'What about you?' Steve asked.

Nick wasn't about to divulge the details of what he'd been charged with. He wasn't sure that he was happy to admit to being a copper, even though he was fairly certain that Steve was telling the truth about being a customs officer. Nick had developed a pretty good instinct over the years for when someone was lying.

'Mistaken identity,' Nick said. 'I'm on remand here at the moment.'

'That must be hard,' Steve said. 'My kids are all grown up and living their own lives now. My wife fucked off with some bloke she met at work a few years ago. I've got a couple of grandkids that I'm missing seeing but they live in Scotland anyway.'

Yeah, I'm not sure I need to hear your life story, mate, Nick thought to himself, wondering if he was going to now regret sharing a cell with Steve if he was going to chatter all day and all night. But he needed to console himself that it could be a lot worse.

'Yeah, Megan's only three so I'm not sure she knows exactly what's going on or why I'm away,' Nick explained.

'That's hard,' Steve said in a sympathetic tone. Then he frowned. 'So, you didn't get bail?'

'No,' Nick said, but he wasn't going to elaborate why. However, Steve would know that there were very few crimes serious enough for someone not to be granted bail.

'Why's that?' Steve asked in an innocent tone.

'Like you, I can't really discuss the details of my case,' Nick replied. 'I just wish I was at home right now with my wife and daughter.'

Steve gave him a half-smile. 'Of course you do, mate.'

Mate?

Nick had met people like Steve before. Slightly uncomfortable in their own skin and keen to ingratiate themselves with everyone. People pleasers. The good thing was that people like that were harmless, if a little annoying.

'Bet you'd give anything for that, wouldn't you?' Steve asked.

Nick raised an eyebrow. 'How do you mean?'

'To be sitting at home with your wife and daughter. Feet up. Watching the television,' Steve said in a way that suggested this was more than just a passing comment. 'How about ten grand?'

What did he just say?

Nick sat up on his bed, narrowed his eyes and looked over at him.

'Ten grand? I'm not following you,' Nick replied, feeling a little uneasy about the direction their conversation had just taken.

'I'm getting out of here,' Steve said in a virtual whisper as he looked nervously over towards the door to make sure that a screw wasn't about to walk in.

Nick's eyes widened. 'What do you mean?'

'I've got to know two screws in here,' Steve shrugged. 'Apparently there's a way out of here through the gym but the screws want ten grand between them.'

'How does that work?'

'I can't tell you anything else, can I?' Steve snorted. 'Worth thinking about though, isn't it? I'm gonna be out of here in about two weeks' time, mate.'

Nick thought of his conversation earlier in the day with Blake.

'Yeah, I think I'm in enough trouble as it is,' Nick said as he lay back on his bed again.

Chapter 23

Ruth drank her third coffee of the morning and it wasn't even nine o'clock. She was now ensconced in the temporary office at the far end of IR1. It wasn't ideal. It was far smaller than her usual DI office and it was windowless. The desk she worked at had an annoying wobble that no amount of adjusting would seem to fix.

Ruth stifled a yawn and stretched. She hadn't slept well but that was par for the course these days. She had assumed that now Sarah was back, her sleeping would improve. She also imagined that her terrible anxiety dreams would stop too. However, neither were true. In fact, Ruth had been plunged into a dark dream the previous night where she had relentlessly searched a busy school for Sarah. At one point Ruth had been naked and frantically trying to find clothes to cover her as she sprinted down the school corridors.

A noise from IR1 distracted her train of thought. It was time for morning briefing, so she grabbed the remnants of her coffee and headed out into IR1 where the CID team was waiting.

'Morning everyone,' she said in a positive tone as she headed over to the scene board. She glanced over at Georgie and was reassured that she looked a lot better than the previous day. Pointing to the photo of Jake, she looked out at the assembled detectives. 'Okay, our crash investigators have confirmed that Jake was shunted by another vehicle off the road and into a tree. It's what we assumed had happened but that's now confirmed. Any progress on tracking the other vehicle involved?'

French looked over. 'I checked all garages in a twenty-mile radius of Portmeirion. No one reported any vehicles being brought in with the kind of damage that would suggest they were involved in the collision with Jake's car.'

'Okay, thank you, Dan,' Ruth said. 'Either the vehicle involved is outside that radius or it's being hidden somehow, possibly until the heat dies down on this investigation. What about the colour or make?'

'We should hear back from forensics in the next twenty-four hours on that, boss,' French replied.

'Let's look at all the routes into Portmeirion and get onto Traffic,' Ruth said. 'Pull any CCTV from 5am onwards. Once we've got a colour match on those paint flecks, we can cross-match that with any cars in the area.' Ruth turned back to the board. 'As far as I can see, we have two lines of enquiry on Jake's murder. First, someone didn't want him poking around in the plans for this nuclear power plant that was going to be built in the area. Secondly, we have David Lang's accident on a stag do in Magaluf in 2016. For those of you who aren't up to speed, Jake attended a stag do. He pushed David Lang into a swimming pool and David was paralysed as a result of his injuries.'

Georgie looked over. 'David has always maintained that he didn't blame Jake for what had happened. He said that it was just a stupid accident. But his father Eryl never forgave Jake for what he had done to his son.'

Garrow frowned. 'Does Eryl Lang have an alibi?'

Ruth nodded. 'He claims that he was tucked up in bed with his wife at the time of the collision. I'd like you and Dan to go and confirm that with her please. And despite what David Lang says about not blaming Jake, I'd like us to confirm where he was at that time too.'

'Does David Lang drive or have a car?' Garrow asked.

Georgie nodded. 'Yeah. If I remember correctly, he's got a Golf that's been converted to allow him to drive.'

'Jim,' Ruth said. 'Get on to the DVLA. Let's get the reg for both David and Eryl Lang's cars. If we can run them through ANPR, we can see if we can get a hit.' Ruth then pointed at a photograph of Claudia Berllucci. 'We believe that Jake was researching an article on Eastland Energy, the American company behind the proposed nuclear plant. Claudia Berllucci was pretty open about what Jake had asked her about the tender, their use of a lobbying firm and their dealings with the Welsh Assembly. Georgie, can you have a dig around and see if there were any allegations of malpractice at the time. And can you have a look at Eastland in general and see if they have any track record of intimidation or bribery in the past.'

'Yes, boss,' Georgie said.

'And we need to have a look at all the Eastland employees on the list that Claudia gave us. See if anyone on there has any form of criminal record,' Ruth said. 'This proposed plant had a budget in the region of two and three billion pounds, which is definitely a viable motive for murder when it comes to an investigative journalist snooping around and possibly jeopardising its construction.'

Georgie nodded and looked over. 'Boss, I was thinking. There are several locals who stand to make millions if the plant gets built. If you remember, Kevin Matteo, who runs a local haulage firm, was a very vocal supporter of the proposal last night. If someone like that got wind that Jake was planning some kind of story, then he would have motive to harm Jake too.'

'Good point, Georgie,' Ruth said. It was moments like that when Ruth saw her younger self in Georgie. 'See what you can find.'

The doors to IR1 opened and a burly looking uniformed officer came in and looked over at Ruth.

'Can I help you Sergeant Jenkins?' Ruth asked. Jenkins was the station's principal duty sergeant and made it his business to know everything that was going on in Llancastell nick – whether people liked it or didn't.

'We've had a call from a Brenda Williams at Abbey Farm,' Jenkins said in a serious tone. 'Someone set fire to her car this morning and the local fire brigade are in attendance.'

Chapter 24

As Ruth and Georgie took the turning for Abbey Farm, the afternoon sky seemed empty - a pale colourless void. They slowed almost to a stop to drive over the steel tubes of a cattle grid. Glancing over, Ruth saw that Georgie was looking directly ahead and her eyes were full of tears.

'Hey,' Ruth said softly.

'It's fine,' Georgie said with a sniff. 'I don't want to be like this.' She then rubbed her face with the palm of her hand before placing it back on the steering wheel.

'It's okay to be upset,' Ruth assured her.

'It's not though, is it?' Georgie said, avoiding looking over at her as they continued down the bumpy track. 'If I'm like this, then you'll take me off Jake's investigation … and that's not okay. I have to do this for him.'

'I understand that,' Ruth said as she thought of all she had been through with Sarah in the past eight years. 'Remember, I know what it's like to be personally involved in an investigation. I get it.'

Georgie nodded. 'Thank you.'

The Portmeirion Killings

Looking up, Ruth's attention was taken by a thin, swirling plume of black smoke that seemed to cut the colourless sky in half. The car slowly filled with the acrid smells of burning and petrol.

As they turned left and then pulled into the main yard at Abbey Farm, they could see the black, smouldering shell of Brenda Williams' old Land Rover. A fire engine was parked over on the right and there were three fire officers dousing the car with water. The air was now thick with fumes. Brenda Williams watched on from outside her farmhouse in disbelief.

As they parked and then got out of the car, Ruth recognised the chief fire officer. She approached and fished out her warrant card. 'Morning. DI Hunter and DC Wild from Llancastell CID.'

The chief fire officer nodded. 'We've met before, haven't we?'

'A couple of times,' Ruth replied. 'What can you tell us?'

'We got a call about eight thirty,' he said. 'By the time we got here, the car was nearly burnt out.'

'Was it deliberate?' Georgie asked.

He nodded. 'That would be my guess. I'm yet to see a car spontaneously combust while parked. It normally takes an accident to cause a fire like this. So, yes, this is deliberate.'

'Thank you,' Ruth said, not sure if he was being deliberately sarcastic or just giving her his honest opinion. She then spotted that someone had come out of the farmhouse and had joined Brenda. It was David Lang. He moved his wheelchair so that it was fully out of the doorway.

Ruth and Georgie looked at each other with a modicum of surprise and then approached.

'About time!' Brenda snapped, her face full of thunder.

'First it's my sheep. Now this,' she growled. 'I told you. Eastland are going to try to drive me off this farm and they're not going to stop until they get their way. You need to do something!'

David put a comforting hand on Brenda's arm. 'It's okay. We're going to expose Eastland for what they are. Don't worry.'

'What time did you notice that your car was on fire?' Ruth asked calmly.

'Just before eight thirty.'

Georgie looked at her. 'Did you see anyone or anything out of the ordinary?'

'You mean apart from my car covered in flames?' Brenda sneered sardonically.

'I meant, did you see anyone or anything this morning that might have been suspicious?' Georgie asked, remaining composed.

Brenda shook her head. 'No.'

Ruth glanced over at Georgie. She was pleased to see that she had remained calm despite Brenda's provocation. Ruth then gestured to the door. 'Okay if we come in?'

'Yes, of course.' Brenda led the way as she and Ruth disappeared inside.

'I'm surprised to see you here,' Georgie admitted.

'Oh, right.' David looked up at Georgie. 'I've been helping Brenda out ever since she told me that Eastland were trying to bully her in to selling the land to them.' David then gestured over towards the sizzling wreck of the Land Rover. 'Can't you do something? Brenda's a defenceless woman living here on her own and you've got an American multi-national doing shit like that.'

Georgie gave him an empathetic smile. 'Until we can prove that a crime has been committed, there's nothing we can do. But we're analysing the sheep that died recently, and we'll be looking at what's happened this morning. If there's any suggestion of foul play on Eastland's part, we'll be down on them like a ton of bricks.'

'Thank you.' David said. 'No wonder Jake was poking around here. I don't know what else Eastland are up to, but they're not as community friendly and squeaky clean as they'd like everyone to believe. And they've got a *very* shady past.'

'What makes you say that?'

'In 2009, Eastland were taken to court for attempting to bribe city officials in Philadelphia for a housing regeneration project. Tenants claimed that they had been intimidated so that they agreed to the rehousing settlements. In 2010, Eastland were accused of then trying to bribe an official in the United States Department of Justice who was working on that case.'

'Bloody hell,' Georgie said, raising an eyebrow. 'So, they've got form?'

David nodded and gave her a meaningful look. 'Jake called me a few months ago to tell me that he was writing a piece about Eastland and the nuclear power plant.'

Georgie frowned. 'Was that out of the blue?'

'No.' David shook his head. 'Jake and I stayed in touch after my accident.'

'Really? I don't understand.'

David shrugged. 'That stag do was pretty messy. Lots of booze, drugs and reckless behaviour. We'd been pushing each other fully clothed into swimming pools for the whole week. At one point, a German tourist complained about our music, so a couple of the lads picked him up on his sun lounger and chucked him into the deep end. What happened to me was a silly accident. It could have happened to any one of us and it could have been anyone who pushed me. It wasn't malicious, so how could I blame Jake? In fact, he was probably the sanest, best-behaved bloke on that stag do.'

Georgie smiled. 'Yeah, Jake was never that laddy, was he?'

'No,' David replied with a smile. 'To be honest, I was angrier that he went out with you for the whole of sixth form.'

Georgie pulled a face. 'What? Why?'

'I had a bit of a crush on you, if I'm honest. I was really jealous of him,' David admitted.

Georgie smiled at him, trying to stifle a slight blush. 'I'm flattered.'

'I tried to find some kind of peace and acceptance of why I'm in this bloody thing,' David explained, pointing to his wheelchair. 'And I never blamed Jake for any of it.'

'But your dad didn't see it like that?' Georgie asked.

'No, he didn't,' David replied sadly. 'He was always so angry with Jake, ever since it happened. It's been eating him up for years.'

'You didn't tell your dad you were still in touch?'

David gave her a dark look. 'Actually, he found out that I had secretly met with Jake while he was up here last week. He went mental.'

'When exactly was this?' she asked.

'Three or four days ago,' David replied.

'I know that he's your dad, David, but he seemed almost happy that Jake had been killed last night.'

'I know.' David shook his head sadly. 'I was so embarrassed.'

Georgie gave him a meaningful look.

David frowned as his expression changed. 'But my dad

didn't have anything to do with Jake being run off the road, if that's what you're thinking.'

'Are you sure about that?'

'Yes.' David nodded. 'Of course. He's all mouth but he would never have done anything about it.' He then looked at her. 'Jake was murdered by someone at Eastland. I'm convinced of it.'

Chapter 25

Ruth and Georgie sped down the country roads of Snowdonia as they headed for Eryl Lang's home. In the distance, Llangollen loomed into view. It was a picturesque town situated on the River Dee and popular with tourists most of the year round. The River Dee marked the edge of the Berwyn Mountains, the Clywydian Range, as well as the Dee Valley itself. Towering above the town to the north was Castell Dinas Bran, a medieval castle which dominated a hilltop. The ruins dated back to the 1200s but there had been some kind of hilltop fortress there for much longer.

'Crow Castle,' Georgie said, pointing to the ruins as they turned the corner towards the Lang's home.

'I thought that's what the English called it?' Ruth asked. She vaguely remembered Nick commenting on it in a way that implied that the *bloody English* had once again mistranslated a notable landmark in Wales. Her mind turned to Nick as she wondered how he was getting on and when she might be able to find time to visit him at HMP Rhoswen.

'It's what my nain always called it,' Georgie replied with a shrug. 'And I'm pretty sure that *Bran* is Welsh for crow. I always liked the sound of *Crow Castle* when I was a kid because it sounded creepy.'

Ruth gave a half-smile. 'It definitely sounds creepy.'

Ten minutes later, they pulled up outside a four-bedroom detached house in a quiet residential street. A woman in her 50s was kneeling on a patterned cushion in the large, neat front garden weeding a flowerbed. She looked up when she saw Ruth and Georgie getting out of the car and heading for the garden gate.

'Hello?' the woman said with a slightly anxious frown. 'Can I help you?'

Ruth and Georgie got out their warrant cards. 'DI Hunter and DC Wild, Llancastell CID. We're looking for a Mrs Lang?'

The woman nodded but looked confused. 'Yes. I'm Wendy Lang.'

'If it's okay, we'd like to ask you a couple of routine questions as part of an ongoing investigation,' Ruth explained with a kind expression.

'Yes, of course,' Wendy said. With her straight dark hair tucked behind her ears, and her thin bloodless lips, she had the air of a Victorian governess. She glanced around anxiously to make sure the neighbours hadn't noticed. 'Maybe we should go inside.'

'Good idea,' Ruth said as they followed Wendy into her home. It was tastefully decorated and incredibly neat and tidy. It smelt of air freshener and coffee.

'Please come through,' Wendy said as she led them down into a beautiful open-plan kitchen with huge glass doors that led out onto a well-kept garden. The kitchen was high spec with black marble tops and a central island surrounded by aluminium stools. It was also military in its tidiness. No homely litter of books or papers. There was a slight coldness to the overall design with hard colours and shapes.

Wendy gestured for them to sit down on designer aluminium chairs. 'Would you like tea or coffee?'

'We're fine thanks,' Georgie said with a smile as she fished out her notebook.

Wendy peered at Georgie. 'Don't I recognise you from somewhere? It's Georgina Wild isn't it?'

'That's right,' Georgie replied. 'I went to school with David.'

'Yes,' Wendy nodded as she remembered. 'You, David and some others went to some festival together when you were in sixth form?'

'That's right. We went to the V Festival,' Georgie replied.

'Yes,' Wendy said with a half-smile. 'I remember dropping you back at your parents' house. I don't think any of you had had any sleep.'

Georgie returned her smile. 'I'm pretty sure we didn't, but I think that was part of the experience.'

Ruth sat forward. 'We spoke to your husband and son last night at the meeting at the town hall.'

'Oh right.' Wendy pulled a face. 'I know Eryl came back in a bit of a mood going on about *bloody Yanks.*'

'I understand that your husband and son are very passionate about preventing the building of this nuclear plant,' Ruth said.

'Oh yes.' Wendy nodded. 'Eryl's very proud of his roots. His family has lived in this area for centuries and he doesn't want anything spoiling it.'

'We're looking into the death of Jake Neville,' Ruth explained.

'Right.' Wendy reacted awkwardly at the sound of his

name. 'Yes, I'd heard that he'd been in some kind of accident.'

Georgie looked up from her notepad. 'Actually, we believe that Jake's collision wasn't an accident. In fact, we're treating his death as murder now.'

'Oh God.' Wendy's eyes widened. 'That's terrible.'

'Your husband had a very different reaction when he discovered that Jake Neville had died,' Ruth stated, watching Wendy carefully.

Wendy took a few seconds and then sighed. 'I'm afraid Eryl never forgave him for what happened to David.'

Ruth looked at her. 'What about you?'

'It was a terrible accident.' Wendy shook her head. 'And David said that it could have been any of them. He didn't blame Jake one bit, so I accepted that.'

Ruth frowned. 'You bore no animosity towards Jake Neville at all?'

'Not really,' Wendy replied. 'And Jake raised money by running the London Marathon.' She then gestured to the door. 'He gave us the money so we could adapt and build on our extension so that David had somewhere to live.'

'What did Eryl think of that?' Georgie asked.

'Oh, we didn't tell him,' Wendy explained. 'I'm pretty sure that Eryl would have refused to take the money, so David and I agreed to keep it secret. We just said it was an anonymous donation.'

'Did you know that Jake and David had kept in contact?' Georgie said.

Wendy gave a slow nod. 'I suspected as much. But I never asked.'

'Did your husband know?'

'God, no,' Wendy snorted. 'He would have gone mad if he thought David had kept in contact with Jake.'

Georgie frowned. 'I'm confused. David told me earlier

that his father had discovered that he and Jake had kept in contact and he was incredibly angry.'

'Really?' Wendy furrowed her brow. 'I'm sorry, but neither of them told me about that.'

'Were you aware that Jake had travelled to the area a few days ago to research an article on Eastland Energy and the proposed nuclear plant?' Georgie asked.

'No. I had no idea he was up here until I saw the news about his accident.'

'Okay, thank you for your help,' Ruth said as she shifted back on her chair. 'We might need to speak to you again at some point.'

Wendy nodded. 'Of course.'

Ruth then stopped and looked at her as if something had just occurred to her. It was a tactic that she sometimes used to throw people off guard.

'Oh, actually I forgot to ask,' Ruth said with a frown. 'Can you remember where Eryl was yesterday morning between 6am and 8am?'

Wendy shrugged. 'He was out walking the dogs. Part of his morning routine.' A second later, an uneasy look came over Wendy's face – maybe she had realised that what she had just said contradicted what her husband had told them.

Ruth and Georgie shared a look – Eryl Lang had lied to them about his whereabouts at the time of Jake's murder.

Chapter 26

Garrow and French sat in traffic as they made their way through Llangollen on their way to question Kevin Matteo. Garrow glanced out at the main high street which was busy with tourists.

'There's something special about Llangollen, isn't there?' French said as they inched forward towards the traffic lights.

Garrow raised an eyebrow and looked at him. 'Well you know why that is, don't you?'

'No,' French replied with a wry smile. 'But I'm sure you're about to tell me, Prof.'

'Llangollen is the resting place of the Holy Grail,' Garrow said with a nonchalant shrug.

'What?' French said with a dubious look.

'It's true.' Garrow shrugged. 'Rather than gallivanting around Paris and London, Tom Hanks trying to crack *The Da Vinci Code*, he should have been up here in North Wales.'

'Are you making this up?' French scoffed.

'Of course not,' Garrow laughed. 'There was a book

called *The Grail Romances* which was written in the 12th century by Cistercian monks in places such as Valle Crucis Abbey. The book details the journey of the Holy Grail, plus a box containing the cross that Jesus was crucified on, the crown of thorns he wore and, most shockingly, details of a child that Mary Magdelene had had with Jesus. According to the book, Jesus' uncle, St Joseph of Arimathea, travelled to North Wales with these items to get them out of the hands of the Roman Empire. At that time, Wales hadn't been invaded. Joseph travelled to Castle Corbenic where the Holy Grail was kept for safe keeping. The word *Corbenic* is an old French word for crow or raven. The Welsh for crow is *Bran*. As you know, the castle overlooking Llangollen is called *Dinas Bran*, so it's the Grail Castle where the Holy Grail was buried for safe keeping.'

'Okay.' French nodded slowly. 'That's all great, but when I said that Llangollen was *a special place*, it's because I went on a stag do here once and ended up in bed with two barmaids. It was the best night of my life.'

Garrow rolled his eyes before letting out a loud laugh. 'Bloody hell, Dan.'

'What?' French said with an innocent shrug. 'I'm pretty sure it's never going to happen again.'

'I don't know why I bother,' Garrow muttered with an amused expression.

The traffic lights changed to green and they turned right onto the A5.

A few minutes later, they pulled up at the Matteo Haulage Company depot on the A5 about three miles from Corwen.

Garrow looked around. The site was enormous with half a dozen or so large articulated lorries parked up. The dark red Matteo Haulage Company logo stretched across the side of each lorry. To the left of the site was a series of

The Portmeirion Killings

garages and workshops, presumably where the vehicles could be worked on. To the right, a long line of diesel pumps and behind that a line of Portakabins.

Garrow and French got out of the car. The air was thick with the smells of diesel and oil.

A man in a yellow high-vis jacket approached with a cheery smile. It was clear that Garrow and French looked out of place.

'Can I help you fellas?' the man asked in a thick North Wales accent.

They pulled out their warrant cards.

'DS French and DC Garrow, Llancastell CID,' French explained. 'We're looking for a Kevin Matteo.'

'Right you are,' the man replied with an anxious nod and then pointed to a large blue Portakabin at the far end of the site. 'You'll find him over there.'

'Thanks,' French said.

They made their way across the site. The ground was concrete and heavily stained with black patches of oil. Garrow made sure he avoided them – he didn't want to be walking thick oil into the car or the carpet of the CID office. He loosened his collar as the temperature was milder than it had been recently.

Getting to the Portakabin, French gave an authoritative knock on the flimsy-looking wooden door.

'Come in,' boomed a voice from inside.

French opened the door and they entered. The inside of the Portakabin was untidy. There were three desks laid out, a few plastic chairs and shelves full of files and paperwork.

'Can I help?' asked a man who was sitting with his feet up on a desk drinking a mug of tea.

French showed his warrant card. 'We're looking for a Kevin Matteo?'

The man gave him a smug look as he took his feet down from the desk and looked at them with an expression that bordered on confrontational.

'Well you've found him,' Matteo said with a smirk, as if this was humorous.

'We'd like to ask you a couple of routine questions in connection with an ongoing investigation,' Garrow explained.

'That journalist bloke that was killed over by Portmeirion, is it?' Matteo asked.

French nodded. 'Yes, that's right.'

Matteo pointed to two paint-stained red plastic chairs. 'Take a pew.'

Garrow didn't like Matteo's manner. He seemed keen to let them know that he wasn't remotely concerned by their presence. In fact, he wanted to show that he found it amusing. Garrow had met men like Matteo before. Arrogant, aggressive and controlling but deep down uncomfortable in their own skin and full of fear.

'Thanks,' French said as he and Garrow sat down.

Garrow pulled his notepad and pen from his jacket. 'Can I just check that you are the owner of Matteo Haulage?'

'Yes,' he replied as if this was funny.

French looked over at him. 'Am I right in thinking that your haulage company has already spoken to Eastland Energy about the construction of their nuclear plant?'

Matteo pulled a face. 'I'm pretty sure that's confidential information.'

'This is a murder enquiry, Mr Matteo,' French said in a stern tone. 'And if we believe that information is pertinent to our enquiries, then we can go down a legal route to obtain it. But it would save us a lot of time and trouble if you can just give us that information right now.'

Matteo narrowed his eyes. 'I'm not gonna lie. I don't like the police much. You've made my life difficult over the years. And now you want me to save you time and effort?' he snorted.

'Would it be safe to say that if the nuclear plant was built, your haulage company would benefit greatly from that construction?' Garrow asked.

'Yeah,' Matteo replied. 'That would be *safe to say.*'

Garrow nodded. 'How do you feel about the Stop The Nuclear Plant campaigners in the area?'

'If you want my honest opinion, they're a bunch of tree hugging, meddling hippy do-gooders who don't have the first clue about the jobs and money that will come into this area if this plant gets the full go ahead.'

French looked at him. 'You think they're naïve then?'

'Naïve,' Matteo nodded. 'Yeah, that's a good word. Or another way of putting it would be *a major pain in the backside.*'

'And I'm guessing it made you angry that they were planning to launch a legal challenge in the High Court against the plant?' French asked in a tone that implied no judgement.

'Too right,' Matteo growled. 'These idiots are standing in the way of progress.' Matteo looked over at them. 'North Wales is on its arse since the mines went. The building of the plant will inject millions, if not billions, into a deprived area.'

'And of course, you stand to make a lot of money too?' French said.

'Yeah,' Matteo replied defensively. 'But I'm not the only one round here.'

Garrow stopped writing and looked over. 'Did you know that the journalist Jake Neville had come up to North Wales to write a story for *The Times* about Eastland Energy, their dealings with the Welsh Assembly and the impact the plant would have on the local environment?'

Matteo gave a nonchalant shrug. 'I'd heard some busybody was up from London poking their nose in where it didn't belong. None of my business though, is it?'

French raised an eyebrow. 'If Jake Neville had found improprieties in Eastland Energy's dealing with the Welsh Assembly, or that the building of the plant would have major environmental issues on the area, that might jeopardise plans for its construction. And that might cost you a huge amount of money.'

'Hang on a second.' Matteo pulled an annoyed face. 'You think I had something to do with this journalist's death? Jesus Christ, you're barking up the wrong bloody tree, mate.'

'Can you tell us where you were between 6am and 8am yesterday morning?' Garrow asked.

Matteo gave a huge, ironic laugh. 'Bloody hell! At home. I made my wife a coffee at about 6.30am, as I always do. Then did some paperwork. Why don't you ask her?' he snapped angrily.

'Don't worry, we will,' Garrow reassured him. Matteo's attitude throughout the whole interview had got right up his nose.

'Thanks for your help,' French said as he got up. 'We'll see ourselves out.'

Chapter 27

Ruth sat down as she prepared to hold a North Wales Police press conference. She was already aware that several major UK newspapers were sniffing around to see if Jake Neville's murder was linked in any way to the story he was writing on Eastland Energy. *The Times* had already run an article plus a small obituary as Jake was a journalist at the paper. Ruth had also heard the news of Jake's death being a murder investigation reported on BBC 5 Live as she and Georgie had made their way back to Llancastell CID.

Looking out at the assembled reporters, Ruth took a moment. Despite media training and holding over a dozen press conferences, she still felt uncomfortable.

Sitting next to her was Kerry Mahoney, the Chief Corporate Communications Officer for North Wales Police, who had come up from the main press office in Colwyn Bay. Ruth had met her various times and found her to be a rather supercilious, judgemental woman.

Mahoney raised an eyebrow and then leaned over to show Ruth a tweet on Twitter.

'Looks like you've got your work cut out on this one, Ruth,' she said. 'The top brass are going to be looking for you to make an arrest in the next couple of days or they'll be breathing down your neck. Obviously, I'll do everything in my power to keep the media side of things as calm as I can.'

Ruth glanced at the text.

BBC Wales@BBC Wales Breaking News

Sources claim that North Wales Police are treating the death of 29-year-old investigative journalist Jake Neville as murder. Neville, who worked for The Times newspaper and lived in London, had travelled to North Wales to research a story about a proposed nuclear power plant north of the picturesque town of Llangollen, a well-known tourist destination.

On the table in front of Ruth was a row of microphones. She cleared her throat. 'Good afternoon, I'm Detective Inspector Ruth Hunter of North Wales Police, and I am the Senior Investigating Officer in the murder of Jake Neville.'

Chapter 28

As Ruth made her way through IR1, her mind turned to why Eryl Lang had lied to them about his whereabouts at the time of Jake Neville's murder. Was it a mere memory lapse or something far darker?

'Boss,' French said, pointing up to the monitor on the wall. The red logo showed that it was a news item on BBC Wales. 'This was on the BBC about half an hour ago.'

She immediately saw that David Lang was being interviewed in the studio.

'Let's have a look,' Ruth said, gesturing to the frozen image on the screen.

French clicked his mouse and the interview played out.

'We have in the studio David Lang, part of the campaign group Stop The Nuclear Plant. Good afternoon, David,' the news presenter said.

'Good afternoon,' David replied.

'I understand that your campaign against the proposed nuclear power plant in North Wales is mounting a legal challenge in the High

Court against the Welsh Assembly and Eastland Energy. Is that correct?'

'Yes,' David said, nodding earnestly. *'The building of a nuclear power plant will be an environmental disaster to the whole of North Wales. It will affect our water supplies, coastal erosion and will leave us having to deal with highly reactive waste for centuries to come.'*

'How do you respond to the Welsh Assembly's statement that nuclear power is now one of the safest ways of producing energy in the world?' the news presenter asked.

'That's nonsense,' David snapped. *'Eastland Energy have made promises about the water supply in North Wales that are at best deceptive and at worst criminally negligent. The Welsh Assembly seems to have a fixation with nuclear power rather than renewable energy which has seen them grant the contract for this nuclear plant unlawfully. Friends of the Earth are aiding us in this legal challenge and it's our intention to delay the plant's building until we can launch a judicial review into how and why the contract was awarded.'*

'We understand that you knew the investigative journalist Jake Neville who was tragically killed two days ago?' the news presenter asked.

David nodded. 'We went to school together.'

'We understand that Mr Neville was writing a story for The Times newspaper looking at the bidding process for the nuclear plant and that North Wales Police are now treating his death as murder?'

David shook his head. 'I'm afraid that's something that I can't comment on at the moment.'

Ruth turned to French and raised an eyebrow. 'That's pretty strong stuff. Eastland's PR people must be pulling out their hair at the moment.' She looked around at the CID team. 'Has anyone checked through the list of Eastland employees yet?'

Garrow looked over. 'I've run all the names through the PNC database. Clean as a whistle boss. Not as much as a parking fine ... The only person I've been unable to do any kind of check on is Claudia Berllucci as she's American.'

Ruth nodded. 'Probably worth seeing if you can find out if she has any sort of criminal record in the US.'

Garrow nodded and scribbled something in his notebook.

French looked over with an office phone in his hand. 'Boss, there's been another arson attack at Abbey Farm.'

Chapter 29

It was mid-afternoon and it was 'Association' on the VP wing of HMP Rhoswen, which meant prisoners were allowed out for recreation and to socialise. Nick was still trying to work out what his next move should be. He couldn't allow himself to be *in the pocket* of someone like Curtis Blake. But Blake had the evidence that would see Nick spend the next fifteen years in prison. And then there was Steve's offer of escape from the prison gym. At first, Nick had dismissed Steve's offer as a ludicrous idea. He wasn't about to go on the run. However, it had occurred to him that being on the outside might be his only chance of finding the evidence that Blake was holding and either destroying it, or finding enough evidence to incriminate whoever actually did murder Paul Thurrock. The phrase *rock and a hard place* came to mind as he ambled down towards the recreation area where prisoners were playing pool and table tennis.

Suddenly, the air was splintered by ear-piercing screams of someone in the wing below. Going to the balcony, Nick looked down as a prisoner cowered and shook on the floor. The skin on his hands and face was bright red and heavily blistered. Nick knew he'd been *kettled*. It was a process where sugar and boiling water were mixed in a kettle and poured over another prisoner. The sugar made the boiling water stick to the skin, making it agonising.

As a roar of noise erupted from below, prison officers hurried over to help the prisoner and pull him away to receive medical help.

Nick spotted a familiar figure standing nonchalantly beside a wall with a hand in his pocket.

Sean Keegan.

Keegan glanced up and saw Nick looking down. He gave Nick a wink and gestured to the scolded prisoner, as if to indicate it was his handiwork.

'Fucking Sean Keegan,' said a voice. It was Steve, who was now next to Nick looking down at the chaos on the wing below. 'He virtually runs this place.'

'Yeah, I heard,' Nick said.

'Thought any more about our conversation?' Steve asked under his breath.

'Yeah,' Nick replied. 'We'll talk about it after bang up.' Nick then looked at Steve. 'Before that, I need a phone right now.'

Steve gestured to a cell further down the corridor. 'Irish guy called Patrick Maloney is your man. He can get most things in here. Just don't cross him because he's a mad bastard.'

'What's he doing on the VP wing then?'

'He's a political prisoner,' Steve explained. 'IRA informer.'

'Oh right.' Nick nodded. 'Thanks.'

Walking down the corridor, Nick felt almost dizzy as the anxious thoughts zipped around his head. Was he really about to set in motion a plan to escape from prison? How had he managed to get himself into a position where that was the only viable option open to him? Were there any clues from the FaceTime call he'd had with Blake that might help locate him? The only person he could ask to do something like that was Ruth.

Arriving at the cell, Nick noticed that it was nicely furnished with a larger flatscreen TV and satellite box on one side. The TV was showing horse racing. The cell smelt of fresh coffee and aftershave.

A thick-set man with wiry grey hair and piercing green eyes sat on a single bed rolling up a cigarette. Even though Nick knew the man was aware of his presence, he didn't look up.

Okay, here goes.

'I'm looking for Patrick,' Nick said in a flat tone.

The man continued to study the cigarette he was rolling. 'Are you?' he mumbled.

'Yes.'

'Go on then.'

'Steve said you might be able to help me out,' Nick said tentatively.

'Do I know Steve?' Maloney muttered as he licked the cigarette paper.

'Customs officer,' Nick explained. 'He's my cell mate.'

Maloney stopped for a few seconds, looked up and fixed Nick with an icy stare. 'And who the feck are you then?'

'Nick.'

'And what do you want, Nick?'

Nick glanced around to make sure that no one could hear him. 'A phone.'

'Why d'you think I've got a phone then?' Maloney growled at him.

Nick looked calmly back at him and then shrugged. 'My mistake. I'll go elsewhere.'

As Nick turned to go, Maloney got up from his bed. 'Come in and shut the door behind you,' he snapped.

Nick hesitated, then grasped the heavy, blue steel door and closed it.

Maloney looked him up and down for a few seconds. He then went to a side table, felt underneath it and retrieved a clear plastic bag. It was full of small mobile phones. He took one out and held it up for Nick to look at.

'You've got this until the morning,' Maloney explained. 'Four phone calls, £100. If you make more calls, I'll know and I will deal with you. If you try and keep the phone, you'll end up in the infirmary. If they toss your cell, it's your phone. If you tell the screws I gave you this phone, you'll be leaving this place in a box. Clear?'

Nick nodded uneasily. Maloney's manner was brusque and menacing and Nick had met enough criminals to know when someone meant what they said and could back it up.

'No problem,' Nick said, trying to sound as calm as he could. 'I'll get it back to you at breakfast.'

Maloney gave him a smile. 'I know you will.'

Chapter 30

Georgie gazed out of the car window as she and Ruth sped cross country towards Abbey Farm. They sat in a thoughtful, comfortable silence as they slowed around a bend and entered a tiny hamlet – a series of tumbledown cottages, a large meadow fringed by trees and a five-barred gate at its entrance. There were a set of temporary traffic lights and Georgie was forced to stop by oncoming traffic. She glanced left, spotting a little alleyway leading from the main road. A narrow fissure between two houses. A number of overflowing dustbins sat at its entrance, along with old cardboard boxes and an abandoned bicycle. A black cat sprang down from the top of a bin to the ground and wandered casually away.

'Cats or dogs?' Georgie said, breaking the silence.

Ruth frowned at her. 'Sorry?'

'Are you a cat or a dog person?' Georgie explained. 'You can tell a lot by which you choose.'

Ruth smiled. 'No pressure then?' she said dryly. 'Dogs. Always dogs. I don't have either, but if I did, it would have to be a dog.'

The Portmeirion Killings

'Really?' Georgie asked, raising an eyebrow.

Ruth shook her head. 'I take it you're a cat person then?'

Georgie smiled and shrugged. 'Of course. Dogs are lovely, but they're also stupid and needy. You're basically stuck with a toddler for over a decade. Cats fend for themselves.'

'So, you want a pet but you don't want to have to look after it?' Ruth laughed.

Georgie grinned. 'Pretty much.'

'Cats come and go as they please. They're selfish, self-absorbed and only appear when they want food. You're basically stuck with a teenager for a decade.'

'Touché,' Georgie snorted as the traffic lights turned to green and she pulled away. The more she got to know Ruth, the more she liked her. If she was honest, when Georgie had first met Ruth, she felt that she lacked a cutting edge. She wondered why someone who had worked as a copper for over thirty years had settled for being a detective inspector. Georgie had wondered why Ruth had never had the ambition to reach the upper echelons of the police force's highest ranks. Now it was clear that Ruth loved what she did and she was a natural at it. The right blend of gentle intuition, incisive analysis and an ability to make tough decisions when needed. Moving up the ranks would take her away from all that. In fact, the more time that Georgie spent with Ruth in Llancastell CID, the more she began to doubt her own ambitions of hitting those heights, where budgets, internal politics and spin were the order of the day.

As they turned the corner towards Abbey Farm, the sky filled with thick black smoke that had begun to drift across the road. Over to the left, they could see an enormous barn engulfed in bright orange flames. Two fire engines had pulled onto the field and great jets of water arced onto the flames to little effect. A police patrol car was parked nearby.

'Jesus!' Georgie muttered under her breath.

'Whoever is trying to drive Brenda Williams off this land is clearly happy to escalate this stuff,' Ruth said as Georgie pulled off the track and onto the bumpy surface of the field. 'We're going to need to provide Brenda with round the clock protection until we can find out who the hell is doing this.'

They got out of the car. The air was thick with acrid smoke which caught in Georgie's throat and she coughed until her eyes watered a little.

'You okay?' Ruth asked.

'Yeah, I'll be fine,' Georgie spluttered.

Before they had time to survey the scene, Brenda Williams came marching over, her face full of thunder.

'You need to do something about this, right now!' Brenda snapped. 'What are Eastland going to do next? Murder me?'

'I agree, Brenda,' Ruth said as she gave her a pacifying expression. 'I'm going to place a unit here around the clock for your protection.'

'Good,' Brenda huffed. 'At last.'

Ruth's comment seemed to have pacified Brenda a little.

'When did you first notice the fire?' Georgie asked as she pulled out her notebook and pen.

Brenda pointed over at a uniformed police officer who was using police tape to secure the area. 'I've told them everything and I haven't got the energy to go through it all again with you,' she growled.

'You didn't see anyone hanging around?' Ruth asked. 'Nothing out of the ordinary at all?'

The Portmeirion Killings

'No,' Brenda replied shaking her head.

Georgie began to cough once more as the smoke caught in her throat again. 'Sorry,' she spluttered.

'Why don't you go and get yourself a glass of water rather than coughing your lungs up,' Brenda suggested, pointing over to the nearby farmhouse.

'Yes, thank you,' Georgie said with a nod as she turned and headed across the field and then the main farm yard.

The farmhouse was whitewashed with black wooden beams but looked like it was in need of renovation. A large black door was half open so Georgie made her way inside. As far as she knew, Brenda lived alone.

The house smelt damp and as Georgie searched for the kitchen, she coughed again.

'Hello?' called a man's voice. 'Brenda, is that you?'

Georgie knew she recognised the voice as she followed it and found the kitchen.

Sitting at the enormous, oak kitchen table was David Lang in his wheelchair.

That's why I recognised the voice.

'Hi Georgie,' David said as she made her way to the sink.

'Sorry,' she croaked as she quickly filled a glass with water from the tap and then swigged it back. 'Smoke got in my throat. That's better.'

Georgie noticed that there was a laptop and various papers spread out on the kitchen table.

David gestured outside in the direction of the barn. 'It's terrible, isn't it? I can't believe they can get away with this.'

'And by *they*, I assume you mean Eastland Energy?' Georgie asked as she leaned against a work surface and finished her water.

David frowned. 'Of course! Who else would be trying to scare Brenda into selling up?'

'There are plenty of people who stand to make fortunes if Eastland build their plant,' Georgie pointed out.

'What, Kevin Matteo?' David snorted. 'I've known Kevin all my life and he's not going to start burning cars and barns to intimidate an old woman. He's just not like that.'

Georgie wandered over and spotted a photograph on the mantelpiece. It was of Brenda and a man in his 50s. He looked like her so she assumed it was her twin brother. 'This is Brenda's twin brother, isn't it?'

'Yeah,' David said with a nod. 'Frank. They really look alike, don't they?'

'Yes. It's uncanny,' Georgie said. 'So, where's Frank now?'

'When Brenda and Frank's father Aled died in 2004, he left them the farm. Except Frank wasn't interested in running it so he moved down to Cornwall. I think she said he now works as an art teacher in a school.'

Georgie frowned. 'But he hasn't come back since all this has happened?'

David shook his head. 'Severe arthritis so he's not very mobile. I know Brenda's been on the phone, keeping him up to date with everything.'

'I assume that Frank doesn't want to sell up to Eastland either?'

'I think he's happy to do whatever Brenda wants to do,' David explained.

Georgie went to the table and sat down. 'Were you here when Brenda discovered the fire?'

'Yeah, I've been here all day. I told Brenda that I'd help make sure all her paperwork is in order. All the deeds to the land for the farm. It's a right mess as she seems to have lost half of it. But if she has to go to court against Eastland, she's going to need to produce it all.'

Georgie did think it was strange that David had been at Abbey Farm both times she and Ruth had arrived faced with an arson attack.

'And you didn't see anything or anyone suspicious today?' Georgie asked him.

David tapped his wheelchair with a wry smile. 'I don't tend to roam around here in this thing. Abbey Farm isn't very wheelchair friendly.'

Georgie smiled back. 'No, I don't suppose it is.'

Chapter 31

Nick had been in his cell for over an hour with Steve. Neither of them had any work or activities that afternoon, so they were locked up. Steve was lying on his bed reading a newspaper while the television burbled some kind of home improvements show.

Taking out the burner phone he had *borrowed* from Maloney, Nick gestured to the area by the door which was the only place to get some semblance of privacy – in the broadest sense of the word.

'I'm gonna make a quick call,' Nick said.

Steve gave him a wink. 'Patrick sorted you out then?'

'Yeah, thanks,' Nick nodded as he got off his bed and took the four steps over towards the blue steel door. He then sent a text to Amanda – *I'm going to ring you from a mobile phone number in one minute, so pick it up. Don't text me back. Love Nick xx*. He didn't want any written communication from Amanda to be stored on Maloney's phone.

After waiting a few seconds, Nick rang Amanda's phone.

'Hello?' she said quietly.

'It's me,' Nick replied in a virtual whisper.

'How are you?' Amanda asked, sounding worried. 'Is everything all right?'

'Yeah, fine. I'm okay. Don't worry,' he said, trying to reassure her with the tone of his voice.

'Why are you ringing me from a mobile phone?' she asked.

'Long story,' Nick said. He wasn't about to explain what he was planning or why he had borrowed a burner phone from Maloney. 'How are you?'

'You know,' Amanda said. 'Worried about you but we're soldiering on.'

'How's Megan?' Nick asked. In his mind's eye, he saw her sitting up in her little pink bed – it broke his heart to think of her.

'She's started to ask where you are, but I've told her you're away with work,' Amanda replied, sounding a little choked. 'I'm not sure what I'm going to tell her in the long run.'

'I need you to do something for me,' Nick said in a serious tone.

'Okay.'

'I need you to go to our savings account and transfer the whole ten thousand over to the current account immediately,' Nick said.

Amanda didn't say anything for a few seconds. 'Why?' She sounded confused.

'It's to do with payments to my barrister if we appeal my bail hearing,' Nick explained, hating himself for lying to her.

'Really?' Amanda sounded suspicious. 'Does he think you've got a chance if you go to appeal?'

'Yes,' Nick replied. He had no intention of getting as

far as an appeal but telling Amanda something positive just seemed the right thing to do. 'He's being optimistic.'

'Right.' Amanda sounded relieved. 'I can go online tonight and sort it out.'

'Thanks,' Nick said and then took a deep breath. It was so hard hearing Amanda's voice at the other end of the phone. 'I really miss you both.'

'So do we,' Amanda whispered. 'I would give anything for you to be here right now.'

'I know,' Nick said. 'I'm so sorry all this has happened.'

'It's not your fault,' Amanda reassured him.

'I keep thinking if I hadn't gone to threaten Paul Thurrock that day, then maybe none of this would have happened.'

'You can't think like that,' Amanda said. 'You were looking out for Fran.'

'I know,' Nick sighed and then looked over at Steve, who was still engrossed in his newspaper while glancing at the television. 'I love you.'

'I love you too.'

'I'm going to need to get off this phone now,' Nick said. 'But you can visit me the day after tomorrow.'

'Yeah, I've booked it in already.'

'Great,' Nick said. 'I can't wait to see you.'

'Me too,' Amanda said sounding tearful. 'I love you. And be careful.'

'Love you too,' Nick said as he swallowed away a tear and ended the call.

Composing himself, he now needed to ring Ruth. He sent her a text similar to the one he had sent Amanda, warning her that he'd be ringing from a mobile phone number that she didn't recognise.

'Ruth?' Nick said under his breath as he checked that

Steve was still fully focussed on his paper and the television.

'Nick?' Ruth said, sounding confused. 'Why the hell are you ringing me from a mobile phone?'

'You're just going to have to trust me, and I can't say too much as I don't know who's listening in,' he explained in a whisper.

'Okay,' Ruth replied.

'Blake has made contact with me in here.' Nick looked over again at Steve. 'He's got two items in his possession. Both of them belonged to Thurrock. They're both very incriminating, so he's going to use them as leverage.'

'To force you to work for him?' Ruth asked.

'Yeah,' Nick replied. 'He seems to think he can manipulate things so that my case never reaches court.'

'How?'

'No idea,' Nick said. 'If I play ball, those items never see the light of day. I get released and Blake has me by the balls.'

'Shit,' Ruth growled. 'He's such a scumbag.'

'It's a long shot,' Nick said, 'but I might have some kind of clue as to where Blake called me from and where those items might be.'

'Anything is worth a try,' Ruth said.

'He was in an old warehouse,' Nick explained. 'I'm guessing it's in the Merseyside area. There was a sign behind one of the goons. It read 'Murphy's Met…' and then I couldn't see the rest. I'm thinking *Metals* or *Metallics*. And I heard a train passing by which means it's close to a railway line. I know it's not much to go on …'

'No, that's a good lead,' Ruth reassured him. 'Some of us will have a look tonight or first thing in the morning.'

'I've got this phone until 8.30am, and I don't want to call you on the main prison line.'

'No, that wouldn't be a good idea,' Ruth agreed. 'Call me at 8am and we'll see where we are with it.'

'Okay, thanks Ruth.'

'You don't need to thank me,' Ruth replied. 'I just want to help you sort this out.'

'Yeah,' Nick said. 'I'd better get off this phone now.'

'Of course,' Ruth said. 'You take care in there and I'll speak to you in the morning.'

Nick ended the call and puffed out his cheeks.

Steve looked over. 'Thought anymore about our little conversation from yesterday?'

Nick nodded. 'Yeah. Give me 24 hours and I'll have an answer for you.'

Chapter 32

It was 7pm and Ruth and Georgie had stayed late in the CID office. Ruth had told Georgie about her phone call with Nick and the warehouse where Blake had contacted him from. They were now scouring the Internet, looking for anything that fitted with what Nick had told them.

Hitting the search engine button again, Ruth noticed her hands in the glare of the desk lamp. They had started to look old. Old woman's hands. It was one of the tell-tale signs of a woman's age. That and a wrinkled neck. A face could be saved with good make-up or even Botox. Hair could be coloured or even added to. A body hidden with well-designed clothes. But hands and neck were a giveaway. She pinched the skin on the back of her hand. Someone had once told her that you could tell someone's age by the elasticity of the skin on the back of the hand. If the skin snapped back to its original position then that person was young and healthy. If the skin stayed in its pinched position, only to move slowly back, that was a sign that the ageing process was taking its toll.

'Murphy's, Liverpool,' Ruth said out loud, reading from her screen. 'I've got a gin distillery, a bar and a funeral directors.'

Georgie gave her a wry smile. 'That seems like the right order.'

Ruth laughed. 'It does. And at the risk of being prejudiced, the Irish do like their drink.'

'They do,' Georgie agreed. 'Stereotypes are stereotypes for a reason.'

Ruth sat back at the desk she was sitting at and let out an audible sigh. They'd now been searching for any kind of lead for over an hour.

'Anything useful, boss?' Georgie asked, looking over.

Ruth shook her head frustratedly. 'Nothing for the words *Murphy's Met...* We could be doing this all night.'

Georgie shrugged. 'I don't care. Anything that gives Nick a chance of clearing his name.'

Ruth suddenly thought of something. 'What if he read the sign wrong?' she suggested.

'How do you mean?'

'We're going on the assumption that Nick saw the letters '*Met...*' after the word *Murphy's*, so we've narrowed our search to companies with words beginning with '*Met*'. So, what if the 'M' was an 'N', just for argument's sake?'

'Okay, easy mistake to make.' Georgie nodded as she went back to her keyboard.

There were a few seconds of silence as they changed the focus of their research.

'Bingo!' Georgie exclaimed.

'What is it?'

Georgie looked over with a smile. '*Murphy's Network Solutions* on the Wirral Industrial Estate.'

'Close to a railway?'

The Portmeirion Killings

Georgie tapped again at her keyboard. 'By my reckoning, it's half a mile from the railway track.'

Ruth looked at her. 'Great work, Georgie.'

Georgie frowned. 'I'm pretty sure that was your idea.'

'Let's call it teamwork,' Ruth said with a shrug as she got up from her seat.

Georgie frowned. 'Where are you going, boss?'

'Wirral Industrial Estate.'

Georgie shook her head. 'Yeah, well I'm coming with you.'

'I can't ask you to do that,' Ruth said, narrowing her eyes. 'You could lose your job.'

Llancastell CID had been warned to stay out of St Asaph's investigation into Paul Thurrock's murder. It had been made very clear to Ruth that officers from Llancastell could face severe disciplinary proceedings if it was discovered that they had interfered in any way with that investigation.

'Why don't you go home?'

'Bollocks to that,' Georgie snorted. 'This is Nick we're talking about. And I'm not letting you go to a random warehouse on your own, boss. I'm coming with you and you can't stop me.'

Ruth nodded with a smile. She admired Georgie's loyalty. 'In that case, get your coat.'

Georgie got up from her desk and raised an eyebrow. 'I'm guessing I drive, you smoke?'

Ruth fished out her keys with a wry smile and tossed them over to her. 'Sounds good to me.'

Chapter 33

The Wirral Industrial Estate was virtually deserted when Georgie and Ruth parked up. It was dawn and the sky was a washed-out grey. As they got out of the car, the wind battered around them, flapping and swirling noisily.

Ruth glanced up at the warehouse that had a dark emerald-coloured sign outside – *Murphy's Network Solutions*. The building's bottom half was red brick and the top half vertical, corrugated metal that was a lighter olive green. To one side, a large metal shutter had been pulled down over the lorry entrance.

'Doesn't look much like a tech company office to me,' Georgie observed suspiciously.

'Which suggests it might be a front,' Ruth agreed, 'and we might be on the right track here.'

Ruth felt the tension in her stomach. Not only was she nervous about who or what they might find inside the building, she also knew that what she and Georgie were doing could lose them their jobs.

Taking a few steps forwards, Ruth scanned the front of

The Portmeirion Killings

the warehouse and then listened intently.

It was silent and still.

As she and Georgie walked towards a door, the stones crunched under their shoes - it seemed louder in the eerie stillness.

Ruth tried the door but it was locked.

A few more seconds of complete silence as Ruth walked over to a window and cupped her hands to look inside. The cavernous warehouse seemed to be deserted except for a couple of workbenches and a desk and computer.

'Anything?' Georgie asked in a whisper.

'Not really.' Ruth shook her head, wondering how they were going to get inside.

The wind picked up a little and rattled the metallic shutter that covered the lorry entrance.

Wandering over, Ruth could see that it was secured by a small padlock to an iron hoop on the ground. It gave her an idea. She looked over at Georgie and whispered, 'Back in a minute.'

Georgie frowned. 'Boss?'

Marching over to the car, Ruth snapped opened the boot, grabbed a heavy crowbar from the tyre repair well, and returned to the metallic shutter. She wedged the crowbar into the padlock and then, with a swift push, broke the padlock open.

'Impressive stuff,' Georgie said as she raised an eyebrow. 'And much better than a search warrant, eh?'

'Yeah, well technically we're not here,' Ruth said as she took the metallic shutter and pushed it up slowly in an effort to make as little noise as possible. However, the clattering sound it made seemed to reverberate around the shadowy interior of the warehouse.

Ruth winced, hoping that it hadn't attracted any

unwanted attention. Now that the shutter was open and above their heads, they slowly entered the warehouse.

Above them, the angular roof was held up by huge steel beams and girders. A streetlight from outside cast an orange hue inside through high windows, throwing sharp, angular shadows from the structure above. The air was dry and smelt of cement and chemicals.

'Right, let's look around and see what we can find,' Ruth said quietly as they snapped on purple forensic gloves and began their search. If she was honest, there wasn't much to look at.

Rummaging through the drawers of a workbench, Ruth quickly drew a blank. She then went to the computer but it was unplugged and looked old and dusty.

'Anything?' she asked, looking over at Georgie.

Georgie shook her head but their attention was suddenly drawn to a noise.

Footsteps which echoed loudly from somewhere.

A shadowy figure was approaching from a doorway on the far side of the warehouse. As it grew closer, Ruth could see that it was a man and he was carrying a baseball bat.

Oh shit, this isn't good, she thought with a nervous gulp.

'Who the fuck are you?' the man yelled in a thick Scouse accent. He had a shaved head, piercing blue eyes and was tall, thick-set, and his muscular arms were covered in tattoo sleeves.

Fishing out her warrant card, Ruth showed him in the hope that it would slow his approach. 'We're police officers.'

The man didn't break his stride as he marched menacingly towards them. 'Where's your search warrant then bizzy?' he snarled at her and then he spat aggressively on the floor.

Ruth could feel her pulse quicken. It was worrying that

The Portmeirion Killings

he hadn't hesitated even for a second when he'd seen her warrant card.

'I'm a detective inspector and I don't need a search warrant if I have reason to believe that a major crime has been committed or if someone's life is in danger,' Ruth said, trying to sound calm and confident even though her heart was thudding in her chest.

'Yeah? Well that's bullshit and you know it,' the man hissed as he slowed. He was only a few feet from where they were standing now.

Ruth's eyes glanced around, looking for some kind of weapon that she could use. There was a metal wrench but it was too far for her to reach without alerting the man.

Why the hell did I leave that bloody crowbar over by the shutter? she thought.

Georgie put up her hand. 'I'm gonna need you to stay there please. And you need to put that down right now.'

'And who are you, sweetheart?' The man grinned at her. 'I like the look of you. I think you and me could have some fun.'

Ruth took a breath and said in a steady voice, 'We have a uniformed patrol on its way and a CID forensic team with a search warrant.' She fixed him with a stare and gestured to the baseball bat. 'So, we need you to put that thing down and stay where you are.'

The man grinned and shook his head. His silver tooth gleamed for a moment in the light.

'I don't think so,' he growled as he stepped towards her aggressively. 'I've seen police ID before and that's a fake. Not the first time we've had fake bizzies snooping around here before we get raided by another gang. So, I'm going to beat the shit out of you two and then you can crawl back to wherever you've come from and tell them that no one fucks with the Croxteth Park Boyz. Understood?'

Ruth felt her stomach lurch.

'Don't be a twat,' Georgie snapped. 'You know how long you're going to serve for assaulting two coppers with a deadly weapon?'

The man shrugged and without warning swung the bat towards Ruth's body.

Shit!

Jerking back and ducking, she felt the bat miss her by millimetres.

He swung the other way and the bat caught Georgie across the upper arm and she cried out in pain.

With his teeth gritted, the man came for Ruth again. She backed away.

Oh God, this is not good. He's going to kill us.

Just as the man went to swing the bat into her ribs, Georgie appeared out of nowhere and cracked a wrench against the man's temple.

THWACK!

The man staggered and dropped the bat to the ground.

'You're nicked, you arsehole,' Georgie snarled as she kicked the bat hard so it spun across the concrete floor and came to rest twenty yards away.

The man's face was covered in blood which was pouring from the gash in his temple. He was stunned as he winced and put his hand to his bloody face.

'Jesus Christ!' he muttered, trying to shake his head clear.

Ruth glanced at Georgie who was breathing hard and holding the wrench. She pounced forward and smashed the wrench into the man's ribs. He gave a cry and doubled over. The blood was in his eyes and he could hardly see.

Georgie pulled out her cuffs but she was clearly in pain from where he'd hit her arm.

If we can wrestle him to the ground, we can cuff him, Ruth thought as she moved forward.

Before they'd had time to react, the man had turned and sprinted back down the warehouse from the direction that he had come.

Ruth looked at Georgie. 'You okay?'

Georgie clutched her right arm. 'I think he's broken my forearm. It kills.' Then she gestured. 'You need to go after him, boss. He might be our only link to the evidence Blake's got on Nick.'

Ruth nodded, knowing that they couldn't risk calling for backup. There would be no way of explaining what they were doing in a warehouse on the Wirral.

Ruth glanced up. The man was already thirty yards away.

She broke into a sprint down the warehouse even though she wasn't entirely sure what she was going to do if she did catch up with him. He might have been injured but he was still over 6ft tall and had youth on his side.

The man continued to run but he was clearly struggling as he clutched his side. He reached the door from where he had entered. He opened it and disappeared out of sight.

'Shit!' Ruth growled as she gasped for breath.

God, I'm so bloody unfit these days!

Crashing through the door, she spotted that the man had climbed on top of some industrial bins and was now limping across the flat roof of a series of garages.

Ruth had no choice but to follow. Crawling onto one of the bins, she got a waft of rotting rubbish from inside that took her breath away.

Jesus!

Balancing precariously on top of the steel, industrial bin, she tried to pull herself up onto the flat roof of the garage. She began to shake with the sheer effort.

I don't think I can do this.

She managed to secure a footing on the wall and clambered onto the garage roof, ripping the knees of her trousers and grazing the skin on her knees. It stung like hell but she had no time to think about it.

She jogged to the other side of the roof. Below was an open area of concrete, with half a dozen parked cars that backed on to two warehouses. A large white lorry was reversing up to some steel shutters, its siren bleeping. It looked like a builders' yard.

The man ran out of the yard through an opening in a brick wall and disappeared again.

Ruth hesitated. She was out of breath and feeling sick.

Fuck it, she thought as she leapt down and hit the concrete with flat feet. She felt a white-hot pain shoot up the outside of her right knee.

Beginning to run flat out, Ruth gritted her teeth and turned to follow the man.

As she got out onto the main road, she spotted that the man was now a hundred yards ahead.

Ruth was now sprinting, sucking in air as she went. Her chest felt increasingly tight.

I hope I don't have a bloody heart attack, she thought.

The man disappeared down a side street.

Ruth was starting to feel dizzy. She was running out of breath.

Slowing down, she glanced up the side street.

It was empty.

Shit!

Her pulse thundered loudly in her eardrums. It was making her feel disorientated.

She took a few steps into the side road and listened.

It was silent and still.

She had lost him.

Chapter 34

It was nearly ten o'clock by the time Ruth got home. Sarah's car was outside as she was 'baby-sitting' Daniel. Ruth felt physically drained as she pushed the key into the door. Her knees were throbbing and stung where she had ripped her trousers. Her whole body ached from the effort of chasing the suspect from the warehouse. And, more frustratingly, she and Georgie had drawn a blank in their search for the evidence that Curtis Blake held and was going to use to blackmail Nick.

Ruth just couldn't see a way out. If Nick agreed to Blake's terms, he would walk out of HMP Rhoswen a free man, but with the proviso that he was now working for Blake, passing him intel and God knows what else. If Nick refused Blake's offer, two items of Thurrock's were going to end up 'being discovered' that incriminated Nick. He would receive a life sentence and probably serve at least fifteen years. His life would be destroyed. She wasn't looking forward to telling Nick that even though they had tracked down the warehouse, they hadn't managed to find anything. Plus, her and Georgie's appearance at Murphy's

Network Solutions would have prompted Blake and his gang to be extra vigilant.

Opening the front door, Ruth tried to put those thoughts to one side until the morning.

'Hello?' Ruth called, feeling a tightness in her chest.

The house was warm with the familiar smell of something like oven chips.

God, it's so good to be home.

She poked her head into the living room and saw that Daniel was curled up on an armchair with his pyjamas and dressing gown on. He was watching football on the television. Sarah was sitting on the sofa, reading a magazine and drinking wine.

'Hey,' Ruth said quietly. 'And what are you doing up, young man?'

Daniel shrugged. 'Chelsea are playing in the Champions League.'

'Are they indeed,' Ruth said with a smile. She then looked over at Sarah and raised an eyebrow.

Sarah gave her an innocent gesture. 'How could I say no to that little face?'

Ruth laughed. 'Softie.'

'What happened to you?' Sarah said, pointing to her ripped trousers and scabbed knees.

'Long story, involving an industrial bin, a garage roof and an angry Liverpudlian,' Ruth explained, trying to make it sound as light-hearted as she could.

Daniel looked over. 'Was he a baddie?'

'Yes,' Ruth laughed, trying to hide the fact that this was the man who had actually tried to kill her with a baseball bat. 'He was a baddie.'

'Did you arrest him and put him in jail then?' Daniel asked.

'You know what,' Ruth replied. 'I didn't. He got away.

But we are going to find him and put him away for a long time, so don't you worry.'

Sarah put down her magazine and wine and then got up from the sofa. 'You look like you need a stiff drink.'

'I really do,' Ruth said as Sarah put her arms around her for a few seconds. 'A hot shower, a big glass of wine and a cuddle.'

Sarah took her arms from around Ruth and gestured to the kitchen. 'You get cleaned up and I'll get the wine.'

Ruth smiled at her. 'Thanks. Coming home to you two is a real life saver, you know.'

Sarah put her hand to Ruth's face for a moment. 'I know you made light of it, but I do worry when I hear you've been chasing scumbags over bins.'

'Perks of the job,' Ruth quipped.

'I'll go and get that wine,' Sarah said, rolling her eyes. 'You haven't even told me what you talked about with my mum a couple of nights ago.'

Ruth pointed to the stairs. 'I'll tell you when I come down, eh?'

Tonight is not the night to broach that subject, Ruth thought to herself. She would need to find a better time to have *that* conversation.

Chapter 35

Nick rolled over on his bed. He had hardly slept as his head was whirring. He checked his watch. It was 7.58am. There was the general sound of clanging and shouting as the prison started to spark into life. Someone somewhere was singing the Welsh National Anthem, *Hen Wlad Fy Nhadau*. In fact, they were booming it out in a deep Welsh voice that reverberated around the VP wing. Despite his tense mood, Nick couldn't help but smile to himself.

Sitting up in bed, he spotted that Steve was still fast asleep. The cell smelt of musty socks and urine from the toilet in the far corner. Due to falling numbers of prison officers and cuts to prison budgets, Nick had found that they were eating most of their meals inside their cells now. Contact time between prisoners was being kept to a minimum which was disastrous for everyone's mental health. No wonder so many resorted to numbing and self-medicating with prison *hooch* or the vast array of drugs available. As an alcoholic, Nick was worried that if he received a life sentence there would be part of him that would be tempted to blot out the emotional pain with prison-made booze. He knew that the results would be catastrophic. Once alcohol was in his system, the addictive craving would be set off which no amount of booze could ever satisfy. As the AA saying went, *one drink was too much and a thousand too little.*

Taking a deep breath, Nick looked up at the ceiling and said a prayer to whoever was up there that Ruth had managed to find something useful. He needed the knife and hoodie to be destroyed. He looked nervously at his watch again. It was now 8am and it was time to ring Ruth. The nerves in his stomach fluttered.

Here we go, he thought as he rang Ruth's number.

A few seconds later, Ruth answered the phone. 'Nick?'

'Hi. How did it go?' he asked hopefully.

'I'm really sorry, Nick,' Ruth replied quietly.

Nick processed what she had said for a few seconds. It had been a long shot.

'Don't worry,' Nick said as his whole being sank.

'We found the place,' Ruth explained. 'Murphy's Network Solutions on the Wirral. And we had an encounter with one of Blake's crew.'

'We?' Nick asked.

'Georgie came with me.'

'Did she?' Nick said, feeling guilty that Georgie had been dragged into his mess.

'Yeah,' Ruth replied. 'We're okay. Some neanderthal came at us with a baseball bat, so we know it was definitely the right place. But we searched it thoroughly and there was nothing there. Sorry.'

'Don't apologise,' Nick said, attempting to sound upbeat even though he knew that time was running out now and his hand was being forced. 'I'm grateful you guys went over there.'

'I'm wondering if I should bypass St Asaph CID and go and talk to the IOPC, even if it's off the record,' Ruth suggested.

'I don't think that's a good idea,' Nick said uneasily. 'Blake has got people on the take everywhere. One sniff that anyone is looking at him for Paul Thurrock's murder, they'll know I've been talking. And then that evidence ends up buried in my garden and an anonymous tip-off to St Asaph CID.'

'What are we going to do then?' Ruth asked. 'There has to be a way round this.'

'There is something else,' Nick whispered. 'But it's not something I can talk about, even on this phone.'

'Okay,' Ruth said in an uncertain tone. 'Just don't do anything stupid, okay?'

Nick knew that what he was about to do might be seen as incredibly *stupid* but he didn't think he had any other choice.

'I'll be fine, Ruth,' Nick said. 'I'll be in touch, okay?'

'Take care of yourself,' Ruth replied as she finished the call.

Nick exhaled an anxious breath as Steve stirred in his bed.

Okay, here we go.

'Steve,' Nick whispered.

'Yeah?' Steve said as he rolled over and looked at him. 'What's up?'

'That thing we talked about yesterday,' Nick said quietly.

Steve sat up in bed and looked at him. 'Go on.'

'I'm in,' Nick said. He couldn't believe that he was actually agreeing to join Steve's escape. It was a criminal offence, even if he was trying to clear his name, but he didn't have any other choice.

The Portmeirion Killings

'Good lad,' Steve said with a wink. 'Knew you'd see sense.'

Nick took a piece of paper and pen and then handed it to him. 'You're gonna need to give me the details of where you need that money paid.'

Steve smiled as he took the paper and pen. 'No problemo.'

'When are we going?' Nick asked quietly.

Steve stopped scribbling, handed him the sort code and account number details. Nick looked down at the paper. He now needed to ring Amanda and get her to transfer the ten grand without her becoming suspicious.

Steve looked at him and raised an eyebrow. 'Yeah, there's been a change to the plans.'

'How do you mean?' Nick asked, wondering what he was talking about.

'One of the screws I've been talking to is being transferred over to Birmingham in a week or two,' Steve explained. 'Not sure if they think he's bent or something, but let's say that our window of opportunity is now a lot smaller.'

Nick frowned. 'How small?'

Steve rubbed his chin and then said, 'We're going out tomorrow night.'

Chapter 36

Ruth rubbed her eyes as she looked out of her office into IR1 where the CID team were starting to prepare for their 9am briefing. The phone call with Nick was still nagging away at her. She knew that Nick was right. Curtis Blake had eyes and ears everywhere. The slightest suspicion that he, or a member of the Croxteth Park Boyz, was being looked at in relation to Paul Thurrock's murder and the incriminating pieces of evidence would *magically* appear and Nick would be sunk. It was a hard pill to swallow. Ruth also had Doreen's confession to deal with and how to handle that. To say that her head was feeling like a jumbled mess would have been an understatement.

'Boss,' said a voice breaking her train of thought.

It was Georgie.

'How's your arm?' Ruth asked with a concerned expression.

Georgie pulled a face. 'Really sore, if I'm honest.'

'Are you sure it's not broken?' Ruth enquired, feeling guilty that she'd allowed Georgie to come with her on something that wasn't official police business. It could have turned out a lot worse.

'Yes. I'm just going to have a lovely big bruise there,' Georgie reassured her as she shook her head. 'How did the phone call go with Nick?'

'Not great,' Ruth replied quietly. 'He was understandably disappointed.'

'What's our next move?'

Ruth let out an audible sigh. 'I just don't know yet. I'm working on it.' She then pointed out to IR1. 'But until then, we've got a murder case to run.'

Georgie nodded. 'Yeah, I know. I think that concentrating on Nick and what he's going through is a welcome distraction from what happened to Jake.'

Ruth gave her an empathetic nod as she got up from her seat and grabbed her bottle of water. 'Of course. This job is hard enough without having a personal stake in it. Come on.'

Striding out of the temporary DI's office, Ruth entered IR1 and headed for the front of the room. 'Morning everyone. If we can settle down, let's get on with this shall we?' She went over to the scene board. 'Okay. I have a phone call booked in with Reece Collins, the News Editor of *The Times*. Clearly Jake's death is now a national news story. I want to know what Jake had fed back to them about his research into Eastland Energy. Clearly Jake was writing some kind of expose on Eastland, looking at how the deal was won with the Welsh Assembly and if there were any irregularities in the tender, use of lobbyists or any hints of corruption. Jake had also been in touch with David Lang and was interested in the point of view of the campaign group *Stop The Nuclear Plant*. Jake would have been aware that there were grave misgivings about the environmental effect of the plant and that the campaign group were being funded by several local individuals to mount a legal challenge in the High Court.'

Garrow looked over. 'Which gives Eastland motive to do something to stop Jake writing that article.'

Ruth looked at Georgie. 'Anything come back on Claudia Berllucci?'

Georgie shook her head. 'Nothing yet. I've had to go through the American Embassy in London so I don't know how long that will take.'

Ruth looked out at her team. 'Can we find out if Eastland has any record of intimidation in its business dealings?'

French signalled to Ruth that he had something. 'Boss, I found an online article about Eastland Energy being taken to court by a labour union in Michigan in 2018. The article claimed that employees in the Eastland warehouse had been systematically bullied and threatened if they didn't meet Eastland's targets. When the employees joined a labour union en masse, Eastland tried to secretly intimidate new employees, claiming that belonging to a union was frowned upon by senior management and they wouldn't get promotion. The labour union hauled Eastland into court for malpractice. Also, two of the union delegates claimed they were being followed by employees of Eastland in the lead up to the trial. One of them thought someone from Eastland had tried to break into his home.'

Ruth nodded. 'Sounds like Eastland might have previous for intimidation then.' She thought for a second as she went to the board. 'Anything else?'

'Boss.' Garrow signalled he had something. 'Lab reports have come back on the fires at Brenda Williams' barn and her car.'

'Okay,' Ruth said. 'Anything interesting?'

'Yes,' Garrow replied. 'The tests show that both fires were started with paraffin.'

Georgie frowned. 'I just assumed it was diesel?'

'Actually paraffin is a much better accelerant,' Garrow explained. 'In fact, if you chucked a match into a puddle of diesel, it would just go out. It's actually very hard to get diesel fuel to ignite.'

'Thanks, Jim,' Ruth said with a nod.

'Yeah, thanks Prof,' Georgie quipped.

'What about the preliminary post-mortem?'

French shook his head. 'Nothing untoward, boss. The chief pathologist is pretty sure that Jake died on impact from severe internal injuries.' French looked over at Georgie with a sympathetic expression. 'For what it's worth Georgie, he wouldn't have known what happened.'

Georgie gave him a sad but grateful nod. 'Thanks, Dan.'

Ruth pointed to a photo on the scene board. 'What about Eryl Lang? He doesn't have an alibi and we know that he blames Jake for David being in a wheelchair.'

Georgie nodded. 'We know that Jake had been in contact with David over the campaign against the nuclear plant. And we know that Eryl was furious that they'd been in contact. Maybe that just tipped him over the edge?'

'Good point. It definitely works in terms of timing,' Ruth said in an encouraging tone.

Garrow suddenly pointed to his computer. 'Think we've got something here, boss.'

'What is it?' Ruth asked.

'Forensics have analysed the paint chips found at the scene of the accident. The chemical compound is specific to paint used in Japan between 2004 and 2015. So, effectively we're looking for any Japanese car manufactured within those years. Toyota, Honda, Nissan, Mitsubishi.'

Ruth nodded. 'Okay, that narrows it down a bit. Let's run that against any cars owned by Eastland Energy and …'

'Boss,' French said, interrupting her.

'What is it?' Ruth asked, slightly miffed at being interrupted mid-flow.

'DVLA have a dark red Toyota, 2014, registered to Eryl Lang at his home address.'

Chapter 37

An hour later, Ruth and Georgie pulled up outside the Langs' home. To the far side of the house, Eryl Lang's dark red Toyota was just about visible through the nearby trees that obscured the view to the driveway.

'Looks like Eryl might be in,' Ruth said, gesturing over to the car.

Georgie didn't answer – she was lost in thought.

'Georgie?' Ruth said.

'Sorry?'

Ruth pointed. 'The red Toyota?'

Georgie nodded as she looked. 'Yes, boss.'

Ruth glanced over at Georgie, who had been noticeably quiet on the journey out of Llancastell. 'You okay?' she asked.

Georgie looked at her and gave her a wry smile. 'You mean except for my throbbing arm?'

Ruth shrugged. 'Just that you've been away with the fairies since we left Llancastell nick.'

'I'm just trying to get my head around Eryl Lang,'

Georgie admitted. 'I can't believe he was still so angry after all these years that he lay in wait for Jake and rammed him off the road.'

Ruth shrugged. 'It happens. I worked a case in the 90s in South London. This bloke Terry Chard kidnapped an 8-year-old girl, Laura, in Streatham. He held her for two days and sexually assaulted her. We rescued Laura but, as you can imagine, the trauma of what had happened damaged her permanently. Her father, Christopher Till, was the headmaster of a local school. I went to Chard's trial. Christopher Till kept very quiet and never said a word. Chard was sentenced to life. He served fifteen years. On the day of his release in 2009, Christopher Till waited outside Wandsworth Prison. Before Chard had even got to the car that was taking him home, Till stabbed him in the chest and killed him on the spot.' Ruth looked over. 'Some people don't ever move on with their lives.'

'Yeah, I suppose so.' Georgie nodded and then pulled a face. 'I guess I'm blaming myself for Jake's death. If I hadn't taken him back to my house. If I hadn't told him to get going at 6am, he might still be alive.'

'You can't think like that,' Ruth said, shaking her head. 'Someone deliberately ran Jake off the road and killed him. That has absolutely nothing to do with you.'

'I know, but it keeps coming into my head,' Georgie confessed and then looked over at the house. 'You know what, when I saw Eryl Lang outside Llangollen Town Hall the other night, I knew something wasn't right. He made a right song and dance about being pleased that Jake had died.'

'You mean to throw us off thinking that he was guilty?' Ruth asked.

'Yeah, it's reverse psychology, isn't it? You don't make a big deal about being happy that someone has been killed in

The Portmeirion Killings

front of two police officers if you're guilty of their murder. My instinct was that he was making too much of it.'

'We don't know he's guilty yet,' Ruth said in a cautionary tone.

'I do,' Georgie said as she unbuckled the seatbelt.

Ruth didn't respond. Maybe having Georgie working on Jake Neville's case had been a mistake. Perhaps she was just too close to get perspective.

'Come on, let's have a look round,' Ruth said, getting out of the car. The temperature had dropped significantly since they'd left Llancastell and she buttoned up her coat against the wind.

Ruth marched down the garden path as curled leaves crunched under her feet. The trees to her left had smooth, grey bark that seemed to give off a thick, pungent smell. The flowerbeds were neat and precise with sharp edges.

They turned past the front of the house and headed over to the paved driveway which had recently been sandblasted and cleaned. Ruth immediately went to the front of the Toyota which had been recently washed and swept – it was immaculate, as if sitting in a showroom.

Ruth inspected the front of the car for signs of damage. Given the impact with Jake Neville's car, the front of the other car in the collision would have been severely damaged. However, there was not a scratch or a dent on it anywhere. It was a little disappointing as the car was exactly the same colour as the paint chips from the crime scene.

Ruth looked at Georgie as she peered at the gleaming paintwork and shook her head. 'There's nothing here that suggests this car has been in any kind of accident in the past two days.'

Georgie shrugged. 'Unless he's had it repaired since the accident.'

'Maybe,' Ruth said, but she wasn't convinced that a car with that amount of damage could have been repaired and returned as new in that timescale. 'I'd be amazed if anyone could turn something around that quickly.'

'We can always check his bank account or credit card to see if he's paid a garage in the past few days,' Georgie suggested.

Ruth could see that Georgie was unwavering in her conviction that Eryl Lang was guilty. Eryl had made his hatred for Jake very clear. Maybe this was clouding Georgie's judgement.

Ruth gestured over to the front door. 'Let's see what he's got to say for himself shall we?'

Georgie nodded as they marched down the garden path to the front door. However, it was open by about six inches.

Ruth gave Georgie a quizzical look, although she wasn't that surprised. When she first moved to North Wales, Ruth had been amazed at how many people in the countryside left doors open and houses and cars unlocked. It was a far cry from South London where sensible people secured their properties like a fortress.

Georgie pushed the front door open with a faint creak and went slowly inside. 'Hello? Anyone home?' she called out.

Nothing. The house was silent.

All Ruth could hear was the rhythmic ticking of the tall grandfather clock in the hallway. The air had the distinctive smell that you got when a house had been recently vacuumed and cleaned.

'Hello? Mr Lang?' Georgie called as she and Ruth moved quietly down the hallway to the kitchen. It was less out of suspicion and more out of not wanting to scare the life out of someone inside.

The Portmeirion Killings

'Hello? Anyone there?' Ruth asked as they entered the tidy kitchen.

'Boss,' Georgie said in an urgent tone as she pointed to an open door.

At first, Ruth couldn't see what Georgie was pointing to. Then she saw that there were smears of blood on the door frame at about shoulder height.

They went over and carefully entered the utility room. The white tiled floor was splattered with more blood and there were two smudged bloody handprints on the top of the washing machine and dryer.

This is not good, Ruth thought as her sense of unease grew.

'Jesus,' Georgie muttered under her breath.

They immediately snapped on forensic gloves as they went. This was beginning to look like a major crime scene.

The door on the far side of the utility room was open and led into a long, carpeted corridor. Ruth assumed this was the annexe that had been added and adapted for David's use.

Ruth could feel her pulse quicken as she spotted more blood. Someone had been badly injured and her immediate instinct was that they had been violently attacked. That posed two immediate questions. Where and who was the victim? And where was the attacker?

Ruth put her finger to her lips to signal to Georgie that they needed to be as quiet as possible as they went down the corridor. If the attacker was still on the premises, they might pose a serious threat.

Glancing down, Ruth saw that the beige carpet was spotted with more dark blood stains that ran down the corridor. As she made her way slowly into the annexe, she strained her hearing, listening for the faintest sound or movement.

Nothing.

All she could hear was the thumping of her heart in her chest.

As they passed what looked like a small office or study, she saw that it had been ransacked and turned upside down as though someone had been searching for something.

What the hell is going on? she wondered. She was beginning to feel tense.

As Ruth took another step forward, she could hear the slightest of sounds.

Is that someone talking somewhere?

Georgie looked over at her and signalled that she had heard it too.

Moving carefully down the corridor, the talking got louder as if someone was having an argument of some kind.

Ruth took a breath.

They got to the end of the corridor and the trail of blood stopped.

Entering what looked like a living room, Ruth could see it had also been ransacked. In the corner of the room, the television was showing a news programme. The talking they had heard had just been a heated political debate.

And there was still no sign of anyone anywhere.

Spotting a closed door to the right, Ruth signalled to Georgie. Ruth readied herself, took the metallic handle and pushed it down slowly.

She opened the door to reveal a small bedroom with a single bed. Again, drawers had been opened and the room turned upside down.

Was this a burglary that had gone wrong?

On the other side of the corridor was a kitchen.

The Portmeirion Killings

Drawers were open and utensils and cutlery flung across the work surfaces and floor.

Ruth looked at Georgie and said quietly, 'That's all the rooms this side isn't it?'

Georgie shrugged. 'It must be.'

Ruth frowned as she went into the kitchen. She clicked her Tetra radio. 'Three-six to Control, are you receiving, over?'

The Tetra radio crackled. 'Control receiving three-six, go ahead, over.'

'We have a possible crime scene at 45 Acre Lane, Llangollen,' Ruth explained. 'I'd like two uniformed patrols down here asap, over.'

'Three-six received, will advise.'

Ruth crouched down to look at what looked like a partial bloody footprint on the floor.

Georgie glanced down at her. 'There's a wooded area at the back here, boss. You think it's worth getting uniform to do a search there?'

'Good idea,' Ruth replied. 'If we find anything substantial, it might be an idea to get the Canine Unit out.'

Georgie nodded and then gestured. 'I'm going to do a sweep of this annexe again. Are we thinking it might be Eryl Lang who's been attacked?'

'His car was on the drive which would suggest he was at home. And now there's no one here, so possibly,' Ruth said as something metallic caught her eye. A small object had been taped to the underside of the kitchen table.

Ruth got up, reached under the table and pulled out whatever had been hidden there.

It was a computer memory stick.

Interesting, she thought.

The Tetra radio crackled again and Ruth naturally

assumed that it was Control giving her an ETA of when the uniformed patrols would be with her.

'Control to three-six, are you receiving, over?'

Ruth clicked the grey talk button on her radio. 'Three-six receiving, over.'

'Three six, we have a report of a body at a location approximately one mile north of your location. There is a uniformed patrol currently in attendance. I will text you the precise location now, over.'

Georgie appeared at the kitchen door. She had obviously heard the message from Control.

Ruth clicked the button as she processed the information. 'Control from three-six, we are on our way, out.'

Chapter 38

Ten minutes later, Ruth and Georgie spotted the turning to a field where the uniformed patrol was parked up. A young officer was already using evidence tape to seal off the area. Further up the track, an older female officer was standing over a body that had been covered with a grey blanket.

'I'm assuming that's Eryl Lang under there,' Georgie said as they got out of the car.

'That would be a fair assumption,' Ruth replied as she fished out her warrant card and approached the young officer who was unravelling the blue evidence tape.

'DI Hunter and DC Wild, Llancastell CID,' Ruth explained. 'What have we got Constable?'

The pale faced constable looked a bit shaken as he reached for his notebook.

Ruth gave him an empathetic look. 'First dead body, Constable?' she asked gently.

'No, ma'am,' he replied, 'but it is my first murder.'

'Right,' Ruth said with a nod. 'Take a few deep breaths.'

'Can you tell us what happened?' Georgie asked.

The constable looked down at his notepad again and then pointed. 'A motorist, Mary Patterson, stopped in that lay-by to answer her phone. She looked up here and saw the victim over there. So, she rang 999.'

Ruth frowned. 'Where is she now?'

'She was very shaken, ma'am,' the constable explained a little nervously. 'I checked her driving licence, got her address and then sent her home. I hope that's okay?'

'Yes, no problem.' Ruth nodded. 'Did she see anyone or anything?'

He shook his head. 'No, ma'am. She said there was no one else around.'

'Thank you, Constable. And take it easy. No one is going to blame you for being a bit wobbly at your first murder scene,' Ruth said. 'Can you set up a scene log for me? No one comes up this track without my say so.'

'Yes, of course, ma'am,' he replied.

Ruth and Georgie turned and headed up the track to where the other officer was standing, close to the body.

'No attempt to hide the body,' Georgie remarked with a frown.

'No,' Ruth said. 'And the body was possibly dumped in broad daylight which is pretty brazen.'

'Morning,' the female officer said. She was in her 40s with dyed blonde hair that was scraped back off her face.

'Morning, Sergeant,' Ruth replied, showing her warrant card again. 'CID at Llancastell.'

The sergeant frowned. 'You got here very quick.'

'We were just down the road,' Ruth explained.

Georgie pointed to the body. 'And we think we know who the victim is.'

'Right,' the sergeant said. 'Significant damage to the side and back of the victim's head.'

'Let's have a look,' Ruth said as she crouched down and slowly pulled back the grey blanket.

She could see that the victim was a man but his face was obscured by blood.

Then she recognised him.

It was David Lang.

Chapter 39

An hour later and the area where David Lang's body had been discovered was now a hive of activity. A white forensic tent had been erected over David's body and SOCOs were taking evidence to their van. Another SOCO was taking a series of photographs both of the body and the ground surrounding it.

Ruth pulled on a forensic suit. It was papery and made from highly dense polyethylene which meant that it made a strange crackling sound when she moved, and smelt of strong chemicals. She glanced over at Georgie who had put on her suit and was now pulling on her mask.

'I'm glad I'm not claustrophobic,' Georgie said, gesturing to her blue mask.

'I am,' Ruth replied. 'I hate them.'

Georgie raised an eyebrow. 'Not like the good old days then?'

'God, no,' Ruth snorted. 'We didn't even wear gloves when I joined the Met. There was a grumpy DS who used to tap his cigarette ash all over every crime scene.'

The Portmeirion Killings

Georgie shook her head in disbelief.

Ruth was still trying to process that it had been David Lang who had been under that blanket. It wasn't what she or Georgie had been expecting.

Georgie looked around. 'No wheelchair,' she observed.

'No,' Ruth said. 'My guess is that David was attacked and possibly killed at his home, put in some kind of vehicle and dumped here.'

Georgie gave her a dark look and nodded. 'It's got to be connected to the nuclear plant, hasn't it?'

'If we're looking for the same killer, then Eryl Lang didn't murder Jake,' Ruth said, thinking out loud. 'And given Eryl's involvement in the anti-nuclear plant campaign, I think that's going to be the focus of our investigation.

'Detective Inspector?' a voice called.

A woman in a full nitrile forensic suit and mask looked up from the body. It was the Chief Pathologist, Helen Rae. Ruth had only met her once before but she struck her as methodical and intelligent.

'What can you tell us?' Ruth said, heading towards her.

'Cause of death is a blunt force trauma,' Rae explained pointing to the head. 'Fractured skull. My guess is there was a severe intracranial haemorrhage. Your victim would have been unconscious and then dead in a matter of minutes, but we'll know more when I do my preliminary PM.'

'Any idea of time of death?' Georgie asked.

'No more than an hour,' Rae replied.

Ruth looked at Georgie, wondering whether they would have saved David's life and apprehended the killer if they had arrived at the Langs' home twenty minutes earlier.

Chapter 40

With another murder to investigate, Ruth had called an impromptu briefing of the CID team to bring them up to speed and allocate various lines of enquiry.

'Right everyone,' Ruth said as she pointed to a second scene board. 'Just to bring everyone up to speed. David Lang's body was found dumped on a track just north of Llangollen about two hours ago.'

There were a few mutterings of surprise from the assembled detectives as this was an unusual and serious turn of events.

'Any idea of how long the body had been there?' French asked.

'Only about an hour,' Ruth replied. 'Our estimation is that David was murdered at his home between 9am and 11.30am this morning and his body was taken from there and dumped soon after that. A motorist spotted David's body at 11.45am so that gives us a fairly narrow time frame.'

The Portmeirion Killings

'Are we thinking that whoever murdered Jake Neville also killed David?' Garrow asked.

'Look, Jake Neville was working on a story about the building of this local nuclear plant,' Ruth said. 'David was a leading member of a campaign group dedicated to stopping the building of that plant. And we know that Jake and David had been in contact in the days leading up to Jake's death. I don't believe in coincidences, so my instinct is that the same person killed them both.'

Garrow raised an eyebrow. 'And Eastland Energy would benefit from both their deaths.'

'Yes, that's true,' Ruth agreed. 'And whoever murdered David had ransacked the annexe that he lived in. They were looking for something but we don't know what that was or if they found it. We did find a computer memory stick hidden in the kitchen.' Ruth looked over at Georgie who was sitting at a computer looking intently at the screen. 'How are you getting on?'

Georgie pointed to the monitor. 'Technical Forensics have just sent over the encrypted files that they've managed to decode. I'm having a look now, boss.'

'Okay, let me know if you find anything,' Ruth said.

French pointed to a photo on the scene board. 'Kevin Matteo stands to make millions if the plant is built. And Jake and David were standing in the way of that.'

Georgie nodded. 'Matteo definitely has motive.'

'Jim and Dan, go and have a word with Matteo. Check where he was this morning. Also check his alibi for the time that Jake was killed. He claims he was working at his home. And have a dig around generally.' Ruth looked at the board.

'We still need to clarify why Eryl Lang lied about his whereabouts at the time of Jake's death.'

Garrow frowned. 'You don't think he had anything to do with his son's death though, do you?'

Ruth shook her head. 'No. I know he was annoyed that David had been in touch with Jake but that's not a motive for murder. And, from what I can see, they were working together on this campaign. I just want to tidy that up and have a chat about the car too. Georgie, we can go and talk to Eryl Lang about David and tie up those loose ends at the same time. Anything else?'

French looked over. 'Boss, toxicology report came back on the sheep that died on Brenda Williams' farm.'

'And?'

'They were definitely poisoned,' French replied looking at a computer printout. 'A highly lethal hydroxycoumarin anticoagulant called Brodifacoum.'

Ruth gave him a quizzical look. 'Does that help us?'

'It does.' French nodded. 'In layman's terms, the sheep were killed with rat poison.'

'Boss,' Georgie said looking over. 'Think we've got something.'

'What is it?'

Georgie clicked on the computer that synced her screen to the monitor mounted on the wall of IR1.

A newspaper article from the *Chicago Tribune* appeared. It was dated 2004.

The headline read *Woman receives three-year sentence for attacking journalist*. Beside the article was a photograph of a woman in her early 20s. It was Claudia Berllucci.

Ruth frowned. 'What are we looking at, Georgie?'

'Okay, so this article, along with several others, was on David Lang's encrypted memory stick,' Georgie started to explain. 'In 2003, Claudia Berllucci was still living at the family home in Chicago. Her father, Michael, was a renowned physics professor at the University of Chicago at the time. A female student made an allegation against Michael Berllucci, claiming he'd asked her for sex in return for better grades. Berllucci completely denied this but a local journalist, Sharon Kidman, ran with the story and did a complete hatchet job on Michael Berllucci. She basically hounded him in the press all the way to his trial. On the eve of his trial, Berllucci took his own life, protesting his innocence but claiming that Kidman's witch-hunt against him meant that he wouldn't receive a fair trial.'

'Jesus,' Ruth said, shaking her head.

'Claudia took it upon herself to make Kidman's life a misery in revenge for what she had done to her father. Kidman's cat was killed, her car was set alight and she had acid thrown over her right hand when leaving a restaurant. Kidman couldn't prove that it was Claudia who was responsible. However, at the beginning of 2004, Berllucci drove her car into Kidman's, causing her serious injuries. She went to prison for 18 months.

Chapter 41

Ruth and Georgie drew up outside the Langs' home. The road had been sealed off by police evidence tape that fluttered noisily in the wind. A couple of uniformed officers stood guard as neighbours gathered further down the road, talking amongst themselves. A SOCO van was parked outside with its back doors wide open. Ruth could see that SOCOs were coming and going from the house with evidence bags.

Getting out of their car, Ruth recognised the chief SOCO but she couldn't remember his name.

Colin? Chris? Jesus, my memory is definitely getting worse, she thought to herself. She would just have to wing it.

Taking out their warrant cards, Ruth and Georgie approached the SOCO.

'Afternoon,' Ruth said.

'Ah, Detective Inspector Hunter,' the man said with a jovial expression.

Ruth gestured to the Langs' home. 'What can you tell us?'

The Portmeirion Killings

At that moment, a female SOCO came over with an evidence form. 'Chris, can you just sign this for me?'

Christ! Yes, that's it. Chris Hutchins, Ruth thought.

'Of course,' Chris said as he scribbled on the form and the SOCO wandered away. He then looked at Ruth. 'We've got blood splatters in the utility room leading down into the annexe.'

Georgie nodded. 'Yeah, we saw them earlier.'

'We've got two used coffee mugs that were in the sink,' Chris explained. 'We'll try and get fingerprints and DNA off those.'

'Any sign of forced entry?' Ruth asked.

'None,' he replied. 'Your victim was definitely attacked in the utility room. That's where we can see the main blood pooling and splatter marks on the wall and the floor. My guess is that your victim tried to escape into the annexe but was pursued by his attacker. We understand that he was in a wheelchair so it would have been impossible for him to escape.'

'Is there any sign of the wheelchair?' Georgie asked.

'No. Not yet,' Chris replied. 'There is blood on the kitchen door and on the gravel out the back. I think your victim was probably carried outside, put into a vehicle and driven away.'

Ruth looked at him. 'What about a murder weapon?'

Chris shrugged. 'We haven't found anything but it would have been something heavy. Hammer or a mallet possibly.'

'Anything else?'

'Yes,' he said. 'We've got a decent footprint on the flowerbed beside the back door. Looks relatively fresh to us. We'll take a mould and get forensics to match it.'

'That's great. Okay, thanks Chris,' Ruth said with an

encouraging expression. 'Any idea where the victim's father, Eryl Lang, is?'

Chris pointed to the house to the right of the Langs' home. 'He's at the neighbours' house next door. Victim's mother is away visiting relatives in Chester but she has been contacted and is making her way back now.'

'Thanks,' Georgie said as she and Ruth headed down along the pavement towards the next house.

The wind seemed fresher than earlier. Ruth enjoyed the coldness pressing against her face and the little shove of the wind against her back. It had been a long day and she needed what help she could get. Across the road, a chimney puffed out blue-grey smoke into the woollen sky and somewhere, further along the road, a dog barked loudly in an unending, rhythmic chorus.

They went up the path, Ruth knocked at the door and they waited.

A few seconds later, a young female constable opened the door. They showed their warrant cards and explained who they were.

'Are you the FLO, Constable?' Ruth asked.

FLO stood for Family Liaison Officer, who was an officer appointed to stay with the bereaved family during a crime like this and keep them updated on the investigation.

'Yes, ma'am,' she replied. She was chewing gum which Ruth thought was unprofessional but she wasn't about to tell her that while they were in the neighbours' home and could be overheard.

'We'd like to talk to Eryl Lang,' Georgie explained.

'Of course,' the FLO replied and gestured. 'If you'd like to follow me.'

She showed them into a small living room that had patterned wallpaper and a dark green three-piece suite.

The Portmeirion Killings

There was an unmistakable lingering hint of must and mothballs.

Eryl was sitting on an armchair staring into space – he looked utterly broken. The constable left them, and Ruth and Georgie came into the room and sat down on the sofa.

'I'm so sorry, Eryl,' Georgie said gently.

He looked at her blankly. 'Are you?'

'Of course,' Georgie insisted quietly. 'I was very fond of David.'

'I'm so sorry for your loss …' Ruth leaned forward. 'I know this is a difficult time but could you tell us where you were this morning?'

Eryl frowned. 'Why do you need to know that?'

'We need to find out as much about what happened here this morning as we can,' Ruth explained in a calm voice. 'We're assuming that David was at home on his own?'

'Yes.' Eryl nodded as he took a breath. He blinked and rubbed away a tear as if he was embarrassed. 'I went to work just before nine.'

Georgie had taken out her notepad and began to scribble notes. 'Did you see David before you went?'

For a few seconds, Eryl didn't seem to have registered the question. 'Erm, yes. He was sitting at the kitchen table drinking coffee when I left.'

Ruth remembered the SOCO's remark that there had been two used coffee cups in the sink. 'Do you know if David was expecting anyone to pop round this morning?'

'No,' Eryl said. 'Not that I can think of.' Then something occurred to him. 'He mentioned something about talking to Brenda Williams or possibly having to go and see her.'

'Do you know why?' Georgie asked.

Eryl looked at them with a grave expression. 'David

said he thought he knew who was behind the fires at Brenda's barn and her car.'

Ruth glanced at Georgie. It was an interesting development.

Georgie stopped writing and looked over at him. 'But he didn't tell you who that was?'

'No unfortunately,' Eryl admitted. 'David wanted to talk to Brenda first.' He then rubbed his hand over his beard and sat forward. 'It seems obvious to me though.'

'How do you mean?' Ruth asked.

Eryl gave a sardonic snort. 'Eastland set fire to Brenda's car and her barn to frighten her into selling the land. They've been poisoning her sheep. And David had something that proved that.' Eryl took an emotional breath to steady himself. 'That's why they killed him. And that's why they killed that journalist.'

'Jake,' Georgie said.

Eryl fixed her with a stare. 'Jake,' he said sourly.

Ruth nodded. 'Whoever attacked David this morning was certainly looking for something because the annexe has been turned upside down.'

'You see?' Eryl said. 'There you go. Someone from Eastland came to our house this morning to find out what David had discovered. They killed him and then tried to find it. Why aren't you down there arresting the bloody lot of them?'

'I assure you that we are going to find out who killed your son and bring them to justice,' Ruth replied. 'There are a couple of loose ends that I'd like to tie up while we're here.'

Eryl shrugged and looked confused. 'Okay.'

'When we spoke to you the other day, you told us that you were fast asleep next to your wife at the time of Jake Neville's murder,' Ruth stated.

The Portmeirion Killings

'So what?' Eryl snapped aggressively.

Georgie looked at him. 'Your wife told us that you had taken the dogs out for a walk that morning at around 6am. She said you do that every morning.'

Eryl shrugged. 'I must have been mistaken then.'

Georgie frowned at him. 'You told us that the same day as Jake's murder. Are you telling me that you can't remember something that you did only ten hours before?'

'Actually ... no I can't,' Eryl said. He sounded embarrassed rather than angry.

Ruth narrowed her eyes. 'Can you explain?'

Eryl looked at them for a few seconds. 'I have a diagnosis of early onset dementia. I haven't told my wife Wendy yet as I don't want to worry her. But I can't remember what I've had for breakfast half the time.'

Chapter 42

Garrow and French were on their way over to the Matteo Haulage Company depot along the A5. The roads were winding and a light drizzle hung in the air and settled on the roofs of the houses and buildings they passed. Garrow could see that black clouds were rolling in from the west. They loomed ominously over the Snowdonia mountains in the distance.

Garrow knew that the Vale of Clwyd which stretched away to the north had been forged by an enormous sheet of ice, made from the Irish sea, that had cut through the area in the last ice age. The fields and meadows were now covered in heather and boasted red kites, black grouse and water voles.

His attention was broken as French clicked on the radio. *The Chain* by *Fleetwood Mac* was playing. 'Radio 2 okay?'

'Yeah, fine,' Garrow replied absentmindedly. He went back to gazing out at the countryside that swept away to the right. Behind that, the uneven ridges of the Clwydian

The Portmeirion Killings

Range which ran from Llandegla in the south all the way north to Prestatyn.

'We can put on Classic FM instead?' French said with a wry smile.

Garrow rolled his eyes – he knew French was teasing him. Garrow had been to public school and university so he was naturally known as *the Prof* in Llancastell CID.

'You do know that popular music exists both in public schools and universities, Dan?' Garrow sighed with a smile. 'The Who, Genesis, Coldplay, Florence and the Machine.'

French smirked. 'Just asking, mate.'

Garrow gestured to the view to the right. 'Actually, I'm just enjoying looking at the view. I'm normally driving so I don't get to just look.'

French glanced right. 'Offa's Dyke is over there isn't it? I'm pretty sure we went on a school trip there.'

Garrow smirked as he put on a fake, professor-ish voice. 'Yes. Built in the 8th century by King Offa of Mercia.'

French chortled as he indicated left to pull into the haulage yard. 'Thanks for that, Prof.'

They parked up, got out and headed towards the large blue Portakabin where they had spoken to Kevin Matteo the previous day.

A large articulated lorry trundled past, belching dark diesel fumes into the air before hitting its air brakes with a startling hiss as it slowed.

French knocked on the flimsy-looking wooden door and then opened it in one movement.

Looking inside, Garrow could see that Matteo wasn't sitting at his desk, as he had been yesterday.

'Can I help?' asked a female voice.

A woman in her early 30s wearing heavy make-up with dyed black hair looked over at them quizzically from the desk where she was sitting, reading a magazine and nursing a mug of tea.

They automatically fished out their warrant cards. 'DS French and DC Garrow, Llancastell CID. We're looking for Kevin Matteo.'

'Oh right, he's not here at the moment,' the woman replied with a forced smile. She had hooped earrings, a nose ring and a pierced eyebrow.

'Do you know where he might be?' Garrow asked.

The woman frowned as she put the magazine down on the desk. 'I think he might be down at the other depot.'

'Can you tell us where that is? French enquired.

'Just past Corwen,' the woman said, getting up from her seat. She then pointed to a large map of the area that was on the wall. 'I can show you on the map, if you like?'

'That would be great,' Garrow replied.

Garrow and French went over to the wall map of North West Wales. There were various coloured pins stuck in it.

'This is it,' the woman explained as she pointed to a red pin just off the A5, about three miles from where they were currently.

French looked at her. 'And Kevin is definitely down there?'

The woman pulled a face. 'Actually, I couldn't swear to it. I would give them a ring but their phone line is on the blink.' She then gestured outside. 'You could have a word with Maureen. She might know.'

'Maureen?' Garrow asked.

'Sorry. Mrs Matteo, Kev's wife,' the woman explained. 'She's in the cabin next door.'

'Thanks,' Garrow said with a half-smile as he and French headed for the door and went outside.

As they went down the steps, the wind seemed to rush

The Portmeirion Killings

in from the wooded area over to the left. Garrow brushed his hair out of his face with his hand as they made their way to the shabby cream-coloured cabin to their left.

French gave an authoritative knock on the door.

'Hello?' said a female voice. 'Come in.'

Opening the door, they saw that the cabin was only half the size of the one they had just been in. There was an old-fashioned, two-bar electric fire glowing in the corner, filling the air with a strange metallic smell.

An attractive woman in her 50s with a narrow face sat at a computer peering at them. 'Can I help?'

'Maureen Matteo?' French asked, showing his warrant card.

'Yes?' Maureen replied, looking confused.

'We're looking for your husband, Kevin,' Garrow explained. 'We understand you might know where he is?'

'Yeah,' she nodded. 'He's down at the other depot. You know where that is?'

'Yes, thanks,' French replied.

'Have you come about his car?' she asked.

Garrow exchanged a look with French. They didn't know what she was talking about.

French narrowed his eyes. 'His car?'

'Yeah. Well one of Kev's cars,' Maureen replied. 'Someone torched it this morning down at the other depot. That's why he's gone down there.'

Garrow pulled a face. 'Sorry, we weren't aware of the incident. We wanted to ask him a few routine questions regarding an ongoing investigation.'

'Oh, is it that journalist who got killed a few days ago?' Maureen asked.

Garrow looked at her. 'Why do you ask?'

'Just that it's been all over the news,' she explained with a shrug.

'Actually, there is something you can help us with,' French said. 'Can you tell us where Kevin was between 6am and 8am on Tuesday morning?'

Maureen frowned. 'I'm guessing he was downstairs working.'

'But you're not sure?' Garrow asked.

'No, sorry,' Maureen said with a smile. 'I'm not really a morning person, if I'm honest.'

'Okay, thank you,' French said as they turned to head back towards the door.

Garrow stopped. 'Just one more thing. Can you tell us what type of car was set fire to this morning?'

'Lexus,' Maureen said. 'I couldn't tell you what make or model, though. Think they're American, aren't they?'

Garrow couldn't remember where Lexus cars were manufactured.

'What colour was it?' French asked.

'Dark red,' Maureen replied.

Chapter 43

As Ruth and Georgie pulled up at Abbey Farm, they noticed that the black shell of Brenda Williams' barn on the field to the right was still smouldering a little and the air smelt of burnt wood.

Ruth got out of the car and spotted the uniformed patrol car that had been assigned to keep watch on Abbey Farm while their investigation continued. This kind of police work was incredibly tedious and she didn't envy the officers being stuck at the farm all day and night.

'God, I remember being stuck on a surveillance job like that in Clapham,' Ruth admitted. 'I was in a car with this dickhead called Harry O'Connor who had terrible body odour and insisted on eating his body weight in crisps every day. And Harry O'Connor was a big unit and took pride in belching the alphabet.'

Georgie laughed. 'Sounds lovely.'

Ruth's phone buzzed and she answered it. 'DI Hunter.'

'Hi there, it's Dylan Hunt at the forensics lab, ma'am,' said a male voice with a strong North Wales accent.

'Hi Dylan, what have you got for me?'

'We're going through the forensics from the Lang scene of crime,' Dylan explained. 'I've made a mould from the footprint we found at the scene.'

'That was quick,' Ruth said, sounding impressed.

'It was the first thing that arrived here. You're looking for a size 8 foot,' Dylan said, 'and a Nike Air trainer.'

'That's great, Dylan,' Ruth said.

'At a guess, they were brand new. There's virtually no wear on the soles at all.'

'Thanks,' Ruth said as she ended the call.

'Any joy?' Georgie asked.

Ruth looked at Georgie. 'David Lang's killer was possibly wearing a size 8 Nike Air trainer.'

'Which rules out our killer being a woman,' Georgie pointed out.

'It might do,' Ruth agreed, 'but obviously it's not conclusive. I once worked with a female DS who had size 8 feet and she was only 5ft 9in. To be fair, it did look like she was wearing flippers, though.'

Georgie grinned as they turned and then approached the patrol car as the young male constable buzzed down the driver's window. There was an older officer sitting next to him.

'How's it going, guys?' Ruth asked, flashing her warrant card. She was pretty sure she'd met the older officer.

'Not a peep, ma'am,' the younger officer replied.

The older officer, who had a greying, scruffy beard, looked over at Ruth with a smile of recognition. 'Detective Inspector Hunter, isn't it?'

Ruth nodded. 'That's right.'

'We worked together on the Andrew Gates case,' the older officer reminded her. However, it wasn't a case that she wanted reminding of. Gates had been a vile serial killer who had played a game of cat and mouse with Ruth a couple of years ago.

'That's right.' Ruth nodded. 'Sergeant Davies, isn't it?'

'That's right, ma'am,' he replied.

Ruth was keen to change the subject quickly. 'Have you seen much of Brenda Williams?'

Davies shook his head. 'Not much. To be fair, she's kept us topped up with so much tea, biscuits and cake, I'm going to have to go on a diet,' he chortled.

The younger officer gave them a darker look. 'We heard about David Lang.'

Ruth nodded with a serious expression.

'You think it's the same killer as the journalist?' Davies asked.

'We're going with that theory at the moment,' Georgie replied. 'His name was Jake Neville. The journalist.'

Ruth picked up on Georgie's slightly pointed tone but let it go.

As if on cue, Brenda appeared from the door of the farmhouse and looked over.

Georgie gestured. 'We'd better go and have a quick chat.'

'I've just spoken to Eryl Lang,' Brenda stuttered as they approached. Her face was ashen with shock. 'I just can't believe it.'

'I'm really sorry,' Ruth said gently. 'I know you and David were friends.'

Brenda blinked as her eyes roamed, trying to make sense of what she had just learned. 'David wouldn't harm a fly. I don't understand.'

Ruth gave her an empathetic look. 'We spoke to Eryl earlier. He seemed to think that you and David were due to meet up today?'

Brenda nodded. 'Yes, that's right. David said that he'd

uncovered something very shocking,' Brenda explained, 'but he didn't want to talk on the phone about it, so I agreed that I'd go round this evening.'

'Any idea why he didn't want to talk on the phone?' Ruth asked.

'David was convinced that Eastland were bugging his phone and mine,' Brenda explained. 'He said they'd go to any lengths to get me off the land. Apparently they'd done stuff like that before back in America.'

'Right,' Ruth said. Eastland bugging phones definitely wasn't beyond the realms of possibility given the amounts of money that were at stake. 'That's something we can look into.'

Brenda's eyes welled up as she shook her head. 'Poor, poor David. He was such a good man. He'd do anything for anyone.'

Georgie nodded in agreement.

'Any clue as to what David was going to talk to you about today?' Ruth asked.

Brenda took a deep breath as she wiped the tears from her face. 'Something to do with Eastland and that woman.'

'Claudia Berllucci?' Georgie asked.

'Yeah, evil bitch,' Brenda growled. 'David wouldn't tell me what it was but he said there was something in her past that explained Jake Neville's death.'

Ruth and Georgie exchanged a look – that fitted in with what they had seen on the memory stick they had found hidden in David's kitchen.

Chapter 44

Garrow and French arrived at the smaller depot of Matteo Haulage Company and parked up. As with the main depot, there were huge articulated lorries lined up in a row. To the left was a series of diesel pumps, a workshop and tyre inflators. Next to that, a line of half a dozen Portakabins. A small, white burger van sat over to the right with a few drivers milling about drinking coffee and eating an assortment of breakfast baps.

'Fancy a coffee?' French asked as he gestured over to the van.

Garrow hesitated.

'They probably won't have a skinny, double macchiato with soya, made with Fair Trade Nigerian coffee beans though,' French quipped as they wandered over.

'Very funny,' Garrow groaned. 'Go on then.'

'Two white coffees, please,' French said to the young woman serving. She had dark red dyed hair and piercing blue eyes.

'Sugar?' she asked.

'No, ta,' French said as he pulled out change from his pocket.

'You don't look like you belong here,' the woman observed as she busied herself making coffees in two large cups.

'Don't we?' Garrow asked.

'No,' she said with a little laugh. 'You're definitely not drivers. And if I was to guess, I'd say you were coppers.'

French handed her the money with a wry smile. 'That obvious is it?'

'Yes, love,' the woman said with a flirty smile as she plonked the two coffees down on the counter. 'Here you go, officer … I like your scarf, by the way. Suits you,' she said, gesturing to the stripey dark blue scarf that French was wearing.

'Thanks,' French replied.

Garrow smirked at French and then looked at the woman. 'Can you tell us where we'd find Kevin Matteo?'

'Been a naughty boy, has he?' she asked, raising an eyebrow. 'Yeah, Kev's over in that cabin at the end there.'

'Thanks,' French said. 'And thanks for the coffees.'

'Any time, officer,' she said with a flirty grin. 'You can handcuff me any day.'

As they wandered away, Garrow caught French's eye and smirked.

'Don't say a word,' French muttered under his breath.

'Hey, she was very attractive,' Garrow said. 'And you could have a lifetime's supply of burgers. What's not to like?'

'Jim?'

'Yes?'

'Shut up.'

They arrived at the far Portakabin that was a dark

green colour. It had a small set of steps leading up to a black door.

Garrow gave a knock and opened the door.

They immediately spotted Kevin Matteo sitting at a desk in the far corner. He looked over.

'You come about my car?' he asked.

'Actually, Mr Matteo, there are a few things we'd like to talk you about while we're here,' Garrow explained. 'But we can start with the car. Can you tell us what happened?'

'It's Kev, by the way,' Matteo said. 'I parked my car behind here this morning. One of the lads spotted that it was on fire. I tried to put it out but it's a right bloody mess. Total write off.'

'Did anyone see anything?' French asked.

Matteo shook his head. 'No. I asked around but no one saw a bloody thing.'

'Can you think of anyone who would want to do something like that?' Garrow asked as he took notes. 'Have you had any disputes with anyone that worked here, or anything like that?'

Matteo shrugged. 'I had to let a couple of the drivers go for drinking on the job but that was about a month ago.'

French looked at him. 'We're going to need details of those drivers.'

'Yeah,' Matteo said. 'I can do that.'

'What about CCTV?' Garrow asked.

Matteo pulled a face. 'Not out the back, I'm afraid. We've got it over where we keep the wagons.'

'Okay, we'll make a report of this. And we'll go and have a look in a minute and see if we need to get a forensics team down here,' French said. He then looked at him. 'Can you tell us where you were this morning, Kev?'

Matteo shrugged. 'I've been here all day.'

Garrow looked up from his notepad. 'What time did you arrive?'

Matteo thought for a second. 'Must have been just after eight.'

'And you've been here ever since?'

'Yeah,' Matteo replied. 'I haven't left the depot.'

French nodded. 'Okay. Thank you. We'll go around the back to see the car and file a report. I'll let you know if and when the forensic team will be arriving.'

Kev nodded.

French and Garrow got up, made their way over to the door and left. Going down the steps, they turned left and made their way round to the back of the cabins.

The darkened shell of Matteo's Lexus car honed into view.

'Setting a car on fire,' Garrow said as he frowned. 'It's the same MO as we had over at Brenda Williams' farm. But I can't see the link, can you?'

French shook his head. 'No. I had a suspicion that he might have torched the car himself.'

Garrow narrowed his eyes. 'How do you mean?'

'Kevin has motive to want both Jake Neville and David Lang dead. We know that David Lang was attacked, put into a car and then dumped. One way of removing any physical or forensic evidence from the inside of that car is to set it on fire.'

Garrow nodded. French had a good point. 'We need to check Kevin's alibi then, don't we?'

At that moment, a woman in her 30s came out of what looked like a nearby storage shed. She had a padlock in her hand and as she went to put it back on the door, Garrow approached.

'Hi there,' Garrow said, taking out his warrant card. 'DC Garrow and DS French from Llancastell CID.' He gave French a surreptitious look to indicate that he was about to tell a lie. 'I wonder if you can help. Can you tell me where I might find Kevin Matteo?'

The woman gestured to the end cabin. 'Yeah, Kev's working in there.' She then pointed to the burnt-out car. 'I can't believe someone's done that to his car. Nightmare.'

Garrow pointed to the cabin. 'And Kev's been in there all morning, has he?'

'I think so,' she replied with a frown. 'Actually, he must have popped out, because I went to take him a coffee around ten and he was out. I'm sure he can tell you if you go and ask him.'

'Thanks,' Garrow said, exchanging a look with French. Matteo had told them a blatant lie about his whereabouts that morning which was very suspicious.

As the woman went to close the door, Garrow spotted something over by the wall.

'Tell you what,' Garrow said to the woman. 'We're going to have a look around here for a while. If you give me that padlock, I'll make sure we lock the door and get it back to you in a bit.'

The woman frowned, then shrugged and handed him the padlock. 'Okay, no problem. I'm in the cabin at the far end.'

'Thank you,' Garrow said, noticing that French was giving him a confused look.

The woman turned and walked away, disappearing down a walkway between two of the cabins.

'What are you up to?' French asked with a bemused expression.

Garrow opened the door to the storage shed, took a

few steps towards the wall and then pointed. 'I spotted those while we were talking.'

Stacked against the wall were six white plastic containers marked *Premium Paraffin*. Next to those was a big red container with the words – *Super Rat and Mice Control Sachets*.

Chapter 45

Ruth and Georgie had just parked in a visitors' area of Eastland Energy. As they got out, an icy wind swirled around them. It was nearly April but there seemed to be no let-up in the cold weather.

As they wandered over towards the main entrance, Ruth spotted a reserved parking space with the name *Claudia Berllucci - Director*. A very new-looking black BMW 5 series was parked in the space.

Ruth gestured. 'At least we know she's in.'

Georgie nodded slowly. 'Do we really think she was unhinged enough to ram Jake off the road and then attack and kill David in his own home?'

'I'm not sure,' Ruth admitted. 'Before I saw that newspaper article about what she'd done in Chicago, I would definitely have said no. I guess we just need to hear what she has to say to us.'

At that moment, Claudia came out of the building and headed over towards her car, oblivious to their presence.

'Claudia?' Ruth called over.

The blood visibly drained from Claudia's face when

she saw them. She stopped in her tracks and looked around.

She definitely doesn't want to see us, does she? Ruth thought to herself.

'We were hoping to have a quick word with you?' Georgie explained.

'Really?' Claudia said, looking confused.

'Okay if we pop inside?' Ruth asked, gesturing to the main office. 'It won't take more than a few minutes.'

Claudia glanced at her watch. 'Actually I'm very late for a meeting. It'll have to wait.'

Ruth looked directly at her. She looked nervous and flustered. 'I'm afraid I'm going to have to insist. I'm running a murder investigation.'

'I think I've made it clear that no one from Eastland Energy would be involved in anything such as the death of that journalist,' Claudia snapped. 'I don't know what else to tell you.'

'We're actually investigating two murders,' Ruth explained calmly. 'And I'm going to need you to talk to us now, or arrange for you to come to the station.'

Claudia shook her head. 'Two murders? I don't understand.'

'David Lang was murdered this morning,' Georgie informed her.

Claudia's eyes widened. 'What?'

'Can you tell us where you were this morning between 9am and 11am, please?' Ruth asked in a stern tone.

Claudia shook her head slowly. 'David Lang's dead?'

'Yes,' Ruth replied.

'What happened?' Claudia asked.

Georgie looked at her. 'We're not at liberty to discuss that with you.'

'Could you please answer the question,' Ruth said, with a hint of irritation.

'Where was I?'

'Yes.'

'Don't be so ridiculous,' Claudia snapped. 'You can't possibly think that I'm somehow involved in David Lang's murder!'

Georgie fixed her with a stare. 'Just tell us where you were.'

'Am I under arrest?' Claudia asked.

'No,' Ruth replied. 'But your refusal to answer a simple question is suspicious.'

'Is it?' Claudia sneered. 'Well I've had encounters with law enforcement in the past and I don't trust anything you do or say.'

Georgie raised an eyebrow. 'We're well aware of your past. In fact, we'd like to ask you a few questions about that too.'

'Jesus Christ!' Claudia hissed. 'In that case, I *will* be bringing my lawyer with me.'

'That's your choice.' Ruth nodded slowly. 'I'd like you to be at Llancastell Police Station at 9.30am tomorrow morning.'

Claudia bristled. 'Fine.' She then waltzed away towards her car as the automatic locking bleeped.

Chapter 46

Looking at the mountain of paperwork in front of her, Ruth gave an audible sigh. There were witness statements, evidence logs and surveillance authorisations to check and sign off. To say it was tedious was an understatement.

Sitting back, she took a breath and sipped at her bottle of water that was now lukewarm. Garrow and French had fed back their discovery at the Matteo Haulage Company depot. Obviously there could be a perfectly rational explanation for why a haulage company was keeping paraffin and rat poison. However, Kevin Matteo had lied about his whereabouts that morning which was very suspicious. He had motive for both murders and his alibi for his whereabouts at the time that Jake Neville had been murdered was vague and sketchy.

Garrow knocked on the door and looked in. 'Boss, I've checked Kevin Matteo against the PNC and HOLMES database.'

'And?' she asked.

'Matteo was discharged from the army in 2009,' Garrow explained.

'What for?'

'You're going to love this,' Garrow said. 'He fell out with a staff sergeant so he tried to burn his house down.'

Ruth raised an eyebrow. 'Arson? Did he serve time?'

'Yes. One year of a two-year sentence in the Military Corrective Training Centre in Colchester.' Garrow then pointed to the file he was carrying. 'It gets better. Matteo has a string of arson convictions going back to when he was a teenager. Fines, suspended sentences and a couple of periods in a juvenile detention centre in Aylesbury.'

'Jesus,' Ruth said under her breath. 'Sounds like Kevin Matteo has a problem.'

'Pyromania,' Garrow suggested. 'It can be a psychological compulsion, boss.'

'Thanks, Prof,' Ruth said with a wry smile. 'It doesn't prove that he started the fires at Abbey Farm. Nor does it show that he burnt out his own car to hide evidence of murdering David Lang.'

'No, boss,' Garrow said in a frustrated tone.

'Thanks Jim,' Ruth said as she got up from her seat and followed him out into IR1. She walked over to the scene boards and looked at the assorted maps and photos. She looked at the photograph of David Lang sitting in his wheelchair, smiling up at the camera. 'Where's the bloody wheelchair?' she muttered almost to herself.

'Sorry, boss?' Georgie asked, looking up from her desk which was nearby.

'David Lang's wheelchair wasn't at his home,' Ruth said, thinking out loud. 'And it wasn't with him when his body was dumped. That means for some reason, our killer held on to it. Maybe they didn't want us to check it for forensics. Question is, where is it?'

'Think I've got something, boss,' French said, pointing to his computer screen.

'What is it?' Ruth asked as she went over.

There was CCTV footage on French's computer monitor.

'I ran Kevin Matteo's number plate through the ANPR and got a hit from the morning that Jake Neville was killed.'

Georgie looked over with an interested expression. 'What time?' she asked.

'That's the thing,' French said. 'This CCTV footage was taken at a retail park in Cheshire at 8.00am.'

Ruth frowned. 'His alibi for that morning was that he was working from home between 6am and 9am, so he was lying to us.' She then peered at the screen. 'What the hell was he doing in a retail park in Cheshire and why is he lying to us?'

French pointed to his monitor. 'The footage is too grainy for us to see if there's any damage to the front of his car.'

'But it is the right colour,' Georgie pointed out. 'Dark red.'

'Yeah, but I thought it was a paint only used on Toyota cars between 2009 and 2015?' Ruth asked, thinking out loud.

'Kevin Matteo has a Lexus, doesn't he?' Garrow said out loud with a frown.

'What are you thinking, Prof?' Georgie asked.

'Hang on a sec, I remember reading something …' Garrow said as he tapped quickly into his computer. 'I thought so.'

Ruth looked over at him. 'What is it?'

Garrow pointed to his screen and read, 'Founded in

The Portmeirion Killings

1989, Lexus is the luxury vehicle division of the Japanese automaker Toyota.'

'Brilliant,' Ruth said under her breath. The evidence against Matteo was starting to stack up.

'Boss,' French said. 'I've just played the footage forward and this woman gets out of the passenger side of Matteo's Lexus.'

Ruth moved closer and peered closely at the screen. 'Can you zoom in a bit?' she asked. There was something familiar about the woman standing beside Matteo's car.

'I'll give it a go but, as I said, the quality isn't great.' French tapped away and then the image got bigger but grainier.

Ruth squinted and then she recognised the woman. 'I'm pretty sure that's Wendy Lang.'

'What?' Georgie blurted out as she got up from her seat and headed over for a look.

'What do you think?' Ruth asked.

Georgie looked and immediately nodded. 'Yeah, that's definitely Wendy Lang. What the hell is she doing with Kevin Matteo?'

'Keep playing it,' Ruth said to French.

The CCTV footage played on. Kevin Matteo walked around the car, embraced Wendy Lang and they kissed.

'They're having a bloody affair,' Ruth said, her eyes widening.

Garrow looked over. 'And we suspect Matteo of killing her son?'

Ruth shrugged. 'Yeah, I know,' she said as the CCTV footage played on and Kevin Matteo and Wendy Lang walked away from the car hand in hand. She then spotted that they were heading into a large sports shop.

Something occurred to Ruth as she studied the CCTV footage. 'I know this is a long shot, but someone get me the phone number of the JD Sports shop at Cheshire Oaks Retail Park.'

'What are you thinking, boss?' Georgie asked with a frown.

'Humour me,' Ruth said as she marched over to the nearest phone and picked it up.

Garrow looked over. 'Boss, it's 0151 396 7474.'

Ruth dialled the numbers into the phone as the rest of the CID team gave each other blank looks.

'Hello, JD Sports,' said a polite female voice at the end of the phone.

'Hi there,' Ruth said calmly. 'This is Detective Inspector Ruth Hunter from Llancastell CID in North Wales. I need some information about a possible purchase made from your shop last Tuesday, the 23rd March.'

'Okay,' the shop assistant said uncertainly. 'If it was a cash purchase then it won't be on our system. But if the customer used a credit card or debit card, then we do normally take a name and email address in case they want to be added to our mailing list or want an invoice emailed to them.'

'Okay,' Ruth said. 'Thank you. The purchase would have been made at around 8.10am that morning. And the customer's name would have been Kevin Matteo.'

'Okay,' the assistant said. 'If you can give me a minute, I'll just check the sales log for Tuesday morning.'

'Thank you,' Ruth said. 'That's really helpful.'

Georgie looked over and nodded slowly. 'The trainers.'

'Hello,' the sales assistant said. 'Yes. That customer did make a purchase at 8.15am.'

'Can you tell me what they bought from your shop?'

'A pair of Nike Air trainers.'

'Can you tell me the size?'

'Yes, size 8,' the assistant said. 'Does that help?'

'Yes it does,' Ruth said as her pulse quickened. 'Thank you so much.'

Ruth ended the call and looked at the room. 'Kevin Matteo purchased a pair of size 8 Nike Air trainers last Tuesday morning.'

'Bloody hell,' French said.

Ruth looked at her watch. 'Right, I'm going to get an arrest warrant for Kevin Matteo issued. I also want to execute a Section 18 Search warrant at his property at the crack of dawn. Jim and Dan, I want you to pick up Wendy Lang first thing tomorrow too and bring her in for questioning.' Ruth let out a sigh. 'I think we've found our killer.'

Chapter 47

It was late afternoon and Nick and Steve were walking in the cold of the outside recreation yard. Technically, the yard and the showers were the places where you were most likely to get attacked. The showers had no cameras and there were just too many prisoners in the yard at any one time for the prison officers to intervene before things got out of hand.

Nick wandered over to the perimeter fence which loomed nearly 20 feet above them. An officer was doing a patrol with a huge German Shepherd. The dog gave a thunderous bark which seemed to reverberate around the whole prison.

Steve approached with a wry smile as he gestured to some of the gym-head prisoners. 'Funny isn't it?'

'What's that?' Nick asked, but he was still scanning the yard in case anyone fancied having a pop at him.

'All them there with the skinny legs,' Steve chortled. 'It's all very well building yer bloody biceps and pecs, but they look like pricks with them twiglet legs.'

Nick smiled. He could see what Steve meant.

The Portmeirion Killings

Steve gave him a more serious look. 'You know where you're going when you get out?'

Nick shrugged. 'Not really.' If he was honest, Nick wasn't sure.

'My advice, for what it's worth,' Steve said quietly, 'is to lay low for 48 to 72 hours. Let the dust settle before you do anything.'

'Yeah,' Nick nodded.

'Your money's cleared, so we're on for tomorrow,' Steve said under his breath. 'We go out of the gym at 7pm, just as they're locking it up. Out to the visitors' car park. Lad I know called Robbo is picking us up there. He said he can drop you anywhere between here and Llancastell. Then you're on your own. Head count is at bang up at 7.40pm.' Steve gave him a wry smile. 'And that's when all hell breaks loose when they realise we're gone.'

Chapter 48

It was dark by the time Ruth had settled herself in a comfy chair on the patio of her garden. She had put Daniel to bed, leaving him to read yet another football magazine. It was better than sitting on computer games, like most boys his age. In fact, Daniel hadn't really ever mentioned computer games to her. Maybe travelling around with his father, and even sometimes living in a campervan, meant that he'd never owned a games console.

Leaning over to the table, Ruth clicked her lighter and lit the wick on a candle that was inside a small, glass lantern. She then fished a cigarette out of the packet, lit it, took a deep drag and sat back in the padded garden chair. After a few seconds, she blew the smoke out in a long, bluish plume and watched it hang in the still air. It was getting cold so she pulled her blanket up over her shoulders.

Jesus, I look like some old granny out here like this, she thought to herself.

Gazing skyward, she spotted a large raven passing overhead – a black-shaped portent. The moon was pale. Only

The Portmeirion Killings

ten minutes earlier it had been crumbly-looking but now it had gained a hard-edged brilliance as the night drew in. The cluster of stars over to the south seemed to sparkle in silvery twinkles.

She spotted a tiny silver dot moving incredibly slowly from right to left in a great arc. She assumed it was some kind of satellite or maybe an aeroplane. A man-made star, traversing the globe as she sat on her chair in the middle of North Wales. In the corner of her eye, something bright zipped across the blackness. *Was that a shooting star?* she wondered. It seemed strange that something so powerful and fast as a shooting star was also so incredibly silent in the night sky.

'Why do you smoke?' called a voice, breaking her train of thought unexpectedly.

It was Daniel.

Turning around with a smile, she saw Daniel looking down at her from his bedroom window.

'You're meant to be going to sleep, sunshine,' she chortled.

'It's really bad for you,' Daniel said in a concerned voice.

'I know,' Ruth said with a shrug as she looked at her cigarette. 'I'm sorry.'

Daniel nodded. 'I don't want you to get ill.'

'Okay,' Ruth said, touched by his concern. 'I'll put this cigarette out if you close the window and go to sleep. Deal?'

Daniel nodded. 'Deal'. He gave her a grin as he closed the window.

Sarah appeared with two glasses of wine in her hand. 'He's got a point, you know?'

'Jesus,' Ruth groaned. 'Don't you start as well.'

'You're kicking on a bit,' Sarah joked, but Ruth could

see that there was also an element of worry in her comment. 'Look at my mum. Smoked all her life and now …'

Ruth nodded as she stubbed out her cigarette. 'Okay. I'll try and cut down.'

'Thank you,' Sarah said, handing her a glass of wine. 'Any word from Nick?'

Ruth shook her head. 'I've put out some feelers but I'm getting nothing back. For some reason, no one seems to want to believe that he's been set up.'

It wasn't the time to go into Nick's concerns that Blake was going to blackmail him into working for him.

'What's he going to do then?' Sarah asked. 'Will he go to appeal over his application for bail?'

Ruth gave an audible sigh. 'I just don't know.'

'Poor Amanda and Megan,' Sarah said. 'They must be lost without him.'

Ruth nodded. 'This investigation looks like it might be drawing to a close, so I'll be able to spend some time with them.'

'You've found out who killed that journalist?' Sarah asked.

'Possibly.' Ruth nodded. 'We don't have enough evidence to charge him yet but he's told us a pack of lies so far.'

Sarah held up her glass of wine and chinked it against Ruth's. 'Good for you.'

'Thanks,' Ruth said before taking a large mouthful. It had been one of those days. Then again, it always seemed to be *one of those days*.

Chapter 49

'Here you go, dear,' Pam said as she placed a mug of tea down in front of where Georgie was sitting.

'Thanks, Pam,' Georgie said with a kind smile.

Pam went over and sat down next to Bill on their large, beige sofa. They both looked tired and drawn.

Georgie took a breath, sat forward and looked at them. 'I wanted to let you know that we are going to arrest someone in the morning in connection with Jake's murder.'

Pam let out a gasp and then broke down in tears. Bill put his arm around her, his face full of pain.

'Hey, hey,' Bill said, his voice breaking with emotion.

Georgie pursed her lips together to stop herself from crying too. 'Obviously, it's going to be on the TV and radio tomorrow.'

'Can you tell us who it is?' Bill asked.

Georgie shook her head. 'I really wish I could, Bill. But until we actually charge him, we can't release any details.'

Pam dabbed her eyes with a tissue. 'But you do think it's him?'

'Yes,' Georgie said quietly with a nod. 'I'll have more information for you tomorrow.'

'Thank you for coming to tell us,' Pam said as she visibly took a deep breath.

Bill looked over with a poignant smile. 'It's funny when you told us that you'd been with Jake the night before, you know? We always said you were the one that got away.'

Georgie felt a twinge of guilt. Even though it had been a long time ago, her decision to sleep with someone else had effectively ended her and Jake's relationship. She was pretty sure that Pam and Bill weren't aware that was the reason, which made her feel even more guilty.

'You really were,' Pam whispered gently. 'I suppose with Jake being in London and everything, you just drifted apart. But I don't think he ever met anyone else like you after that.'

Georgie sipped her tea. 'Do you remember when I had to bring Jake home from the pub on his 18th birthday? He was so drunk he could hardly walk.'

Pam and Bill smiled at the memory of it.

'He'd been sick on his new shirt,' Pam said, shaking her head and looking at Georgie. 'And then the two of us had to put him in the bath to shower him off.'

'That's right.' Georgie laughed. 'And then he fell asleep, so we just left him there.'

'Bill went in the next morning,' Pam laughed, 'and put on the shower to warm it up without looking. Jake screamed with all the cold water and then Bill screamed because he didn't know Jake was in there!'

They all dissolved in laughter.

Chapter 50

It had been half an hour since Kevin Matteo's solicitor, Patricia Blain, had arrived and had been briefed on his arrest. Matteo was now dressed in a regulation grey tracksuit as his clothes had been taken for forensics. He had also been swabbed for traces of DNA. Georgie leaned across the table to start the recording machine. A long electronic beep sounded as Ruth opened one of her files.

'Interview conducted with Kevin Matteo, Llancastell Police Station. Present are Detective Constable Georgina Wild, Solicitor Patricia Blain and myself, Detective Inspector Ruth Hunter,' Ruth stated and then glanced over at Matteo. 'Kevin, do you understand you are still under caution and that we are going to be questioning you in connection with the murders of Jake Neville and David Lang?'

'Yes,' Matteo replied, sounding annoyed. However, Ruth could see from the way he was fidgeting and jigging his foot, that he was nervous.

'For the purposes of the tape, I am showing the suspect

a photograph, Item Reference 7WT. Kevin, can you look at this photograph please?' Ruth said.

Matteo leaned forward and looked at the photograph and then gave her a nonchalant shrug. 'Okay.'

'The photograph is from a CCTV camera at Cheshire Oaks Retail Park,' Ruth said. 'As you can see, the time stamp on this footage is 8.00am on Tuesday 23rd March. Can you confirm that is you and your car in that image, Kevin?'

Matteo snorted. 'Yes, I suppose so.'

Georgie looked at him with a frown. 'Which is strange, because I have here notes from a conversation you had with DS French and DC Garrow where you claimed to have been at home working at that time. Have you anything you'd like to say about that?'

'Not really.' Matteo shifted awkwardly on his seat. 'I must have forgotten.'

Ruth raised an eyebrow. 'Come on, Kevin. Two police officers ask you for your whereabouts at the time of a murder which happened the day before, and you forgot that you drove over to Cheshire?'

'Can you tell us why you lied about that, Kevin?' Georgie asked.

'I just told you,' he growled. 'I forgot.'

Ruth sat forward. 'You see, that does mean that you don't have an alibi for the time of Jake Neville's murder, Kevin. Can you see that the fact that you lied to us is going to make us suspicious?'

Matteo gave an audible huff. 'You know why I lied about my whereabouts. You've seen the CCTV.'

'Sorry,' Ruth shrugged. 'I don't follow.'

'Come on,' Matteo said, rolling his eyes. 'You've seen that I'm with another woman that morning, who's not my wife. That's why I lied to you.'

The Portmeirion Killings

'We believe that the woman in the CCTV is Wendy Lang,' Georgie said. 'Is that correct?'

Matteo nodded but didn't reply.

'For the purposes of the tape, the suspect confirmed that the woman in the CCTV with him is Wendy Lang,' Ruth said.

'And Wendy Lang will confirm that you were with her between 6am and 9am on Tuesday morning?' Georgie asked.

'Yes,' Matteo replied.

Ruth looked over at Georgie. She wondered if Matteo had primed Wendy Lang to provide him with an alibi for that time? Or was he just taking a chance that she would lie to give him an alibi when questioned?

'Did you buy anything while you and Wendy Lang were at the retail park?' Ruth enquired.

Matteo frowned as if trying to remember. 'No, I don't think so. We were just browsing.'

'For the purposes of the tape, I'm going to show you Item Reference SFG3, which is a digital receipt for a pair of size 8 Nike Air trainers that you purchased at 8.15am that morning,' Ruth said as she turned the image for Matteo to look at. 'Is there anything you want to tell us about that, Kevin?'

Matteo peered at the image, frowned and then shrugged. 'Oh that? Yeah, now I think about it, I needed some new trainers so we popped in and bought some while we were there.'

Ruth raised an eyebrow. 'But you forgot about that too?'

'I suppose I did,' Matteo sneered at her.

'Wendy Lang lives at 34 Princes Drive, Pentredwr, Llangollen,' Ruth said, looking down at her notes. 'Have you ever visited Wendy at that property, Kevin?'

Matteo shook his head emphatically. 'No, of course not.'

Georgie raised an eyebrow. 'Have you ever been to that property?'

'No,' Matteo replied sharply.

'For the purposes of the tape, I'm going to show you Item Reference 798F,' Ruth said as she slid over yet another image. 'Kevin, can you tell me what you can see in that image please?'

Matteo looked annoyed but leaned forward for a look. 'I don't know. It looks like a footprint to me.'

'Would it surprise you to know that it's a footprint belonging to a new size 8 Nike Air trainer?' Ruth asked.

Matteo visibly took a breath. 'Okay,' he mumbled.

'Would it surprise you to know that we found that footprint in a flowerbed at 34 Princes Drive, Pentredwr, a property that you've just told us that you've never visited. And that footprint was discovered a few hours after David Lang was murdered at that property. Is there anything you'd like to say about that, Kevin?'

Matteo shrugged. 'I don't think I'm the only person to own size 8 Nike Air trainers.'

'That is true,' Ruth agreed. 'But we have searched your house this morning and we've retrieved a pair of size 8 Nike Air trainers which are now undergoing forensic tests. I'm pretty sure that the soil we find on the soles of your trainers are going to match the soil at the Langs' home.'

The blood visibly drained from Matteo's face.

Georgie looked at him. 'Come on Kevin, you need to stop lying to us.'

Matteo was now looking at the floor. He was rattled and his leg was jigging more than ever.

'You're tying yourself in knots here,' Ruth said.

'Okay, okay,' Matteo blurted out, holding up his hands. 'I was there. A few days ago.'

'Why did you lie to us?' Ruth asked.

'Why do you think?' Matteo replied. 'David Lang had been murdered there so I panicked.'

'When did you go to the Langs' home?'

'I don't know. Two ... or three days ago,' Matteo stammered.

'Did you go to see Wendy?'

'No, of course not.' Matteo shook his head emphatically. 'I went to see David. I wanted to talk to him about the campaign he and Eryl were running against the nuclear plant. I knocked on the door but there was no answer, so I went around the back. I guess I must have stood on that flowerbed when I was looking through a window to see if anyone was in.'

'And you expect us to believe that?' Georgie snorted.

'It's the truth,' Matteo said, starting to sound desperate.

'Come on, Kevin. You and your haulage firm stood to make millions of pounds once Eastland Energy built and ran that nuclear plant,' Ruth stated. 'Eryl and David Lang were standing in the way of that. And so was Jake Neville, if he managed to expose any corruption or malpractice during the bidding process. You must have hated what they were doing?'

Matteo shook his head and looked at the floor. 'No, you've got it all wrong.'

'You were furious that Jake Neville was going to expose Eastland Energy for what they were, so you rammed him off the road,' Georgie snapped. 'And then you went to the Langs' home. Maybe you intended to reason with David Lang about the campaign he and his father were running. And maybe things got heated and out of control. And then you lost your temper, you killed David Lang and then dumped his body.'

'No,' Matteo said in a whisper.

'You panicked that David's blood and DNA were going to be all over the inside of the car, so you drove it to your depot,' Ruth said, keeping the pressure on. 'You parked it out of sight, set it alight and then rang the police, claiming there had been an arson attack.'

There were a few seconds of silence.

Ruth leaned forward. 'Kevin,' she said in a soft voice, 'you need to do the right thing here. Jake and David's families are devastated by their deaths. Don't make them go through the whole ordeal of a trial. Just tell us the truth.'

Matteo slowly raised his head and looked at them both. He now looked broken. They had him on the ropes and Ruth wondered if this was the moment when he was going to confess.

'I didn't kill anyone,' he murmured.

'Come on, Kevin,' Georgie said. 'Plead guilty now and you'll get a reduced sentence.'

Matteo gritted his teeth as he twisted his face in anger. 'Why don't you understand what I'm saying? I didn't kill anyone!'

Chapter 51

Garrow and French were sitting opposite Claudia Berllucci and her solicitor, James Creed, who was also American, in Interview Room 3.

'Miss Berllucci,' French said.

'Claudia, please,' Claudia said with a forced smile.

French nodded politely. 'Thank you for attending a voluntary interview this morning. Unless you have any objections, we will be making an audio recording of this interview should we need to use any of what you tell us at a later date.'

Claudia leaned over, whispered to Creed and then nodded. 'Yes, that's fine.'

Garrow leaned across the table to start the recording machine. A long electronic beep sounded as French opened one of his files.

'Voluntary interview conducted with Claudia Berllucci, Llancastell Police Station. Present are Detective Constable James Garrow, solicitor James Creed and myself, Detective Sergeant Daniel French.' French then glanced over the table. 'Claudia, you understand that we are going to be questioning you in connection with the murders of Jake Neville and David Lang?'

'Yes,' Claudia replied, sounding annoyed. It was clear that she felt it was a total waste of her time.

'We'd like to check your whereabouts yesterday morning between 9am and 11am,' French said.

'I arrived at the Eastland Energy building around eight, and I stayed there until around ten,' Claudia explained.

Garrow looked over. 'Can you tell us where you went at 10am?'

'I travelled over to Llangollen to talk to the local MP, Sally McGrath.'

'And what time was that meeting?' French asked.

Claudia shrugged. 'Eleven thirty.'

'That's a thirty-minute drive,' Garrow said as he narrowed his eyes, 'which leaves an hour unaccounted for.' By Garrow's calculations, Claudia could have driven from her offices, via the Langs' home, murdered David Lang, dumped his body and then parked in Llangollen in time for her meeting.

'What?' Claudia pulled a face as if this was the most ridiculous thing she had ever heard. 'I parked in Llangollen. I walked around a few shops and then down by the river. And then I went to my meeting. Are you trying to suggest that I had something to do with David Lang's murder yesterday?'

French looked at her with no expression. 'Did you?'

'No,' Claudia said, looking aghast. She then turned to Creed. 'Can they actually ask me all this?'

'We're just trying to establish where you were at the time of David Lang's murder,' Garrow explained calmly.

Creed gave them a supercilious look. 'I think my client

has given you an adequate explanation of where she was between those times.'

French moved a document in front of him and then looked up. 'How did you feel about David Lang?'

'How did I feel?' Claudia frowned. 'I didn't know David Lang, so I don't even know how to respond to that question.'

Garrow shifted his chair forward. 'You must have been pretty angry with Eryl and David Lang and their *Stop The Nuclear Plant* campaign group? I mean they were threatening to tie up your proposed construction in a series of appeals and legal challenges.'

'It goes with the job,' Claudia replied with a nonchalant shrug.

'Except if this dragged on for years, or if the plans were shelved, you would have been out of a job,' Garrow suggested.

Claudia gave a snort. 'That's just supposition.' She fixed Garrow with an icy stare. 'I've worked in the nuclear energy industry for some time now, and dealing with local protests, legal challenges and investigations is just part of the process. And the idea that I, or any other employee of Eastland Energy is somehow mixed up in the murders of either of these men is insulting and probably slanderous.'

Chapter 52

'For the purposes of the tape, I am showing the suspect a photograph, Item Reference 8FN. Kevin, can you look at this photograph please?' Ruth said.

Matteo leaned forward and looked at the photograph.

There was a knock at the door and French poked his head in. 'Boss, can I have a word? It's urgent.'

Ruth nodded.

Georgie looked over at Matteo. 'For the purposes of the tape, DI Hunter is leaving the interview room.'

Ruth got up from the table and made her way into the corridor with French.

'What happened with Claudia Berllucci?' Ruth asked, wondering if that's why French had pulled her out of the interview room.

'Not a lot. She denied everything,' French explained. 'But I got the feeling she was hiding something. And she doesn't have a decent alibi for the time of David's murder yesterday.'

'Right.' Ruth raised an eyebrow. 'Couldn't that have waited?'

'That's not why I need to talk to you,' French said. 'Forensics analysed the paraffin and rat poison we found over at Matteo's haulage yard. They are chemically identical to the poison that killed Brenda Williams' sheep and the paraffin that started the fire at the barn.'

'Is that significant?' she asked.

'Very,' French nodded. 'The poison can be identified by the waxy capsules, so it's exactly the same brand. And there are over seventy brands for sale in the UK. The same is true of the chemical make-up of the paraffin. It's not definitive, but the chances of both being coincidental are a million to one.'

'Interesting,' Ruth said. 'So, we can be certain that Kevin Matteo committed both crimes. At the moment, he's maintaining that he had nothing to do with Jake or David's murders.'

'If you confront him with these forensics, maybe he'll fold and confess to the murders?' French suggested.

'It's worth a try,' Ruth agreed. 'Thanks Dan.'

Opening the door, Ruth entered the interview room and returned to her seat.

Georgie shifted on her chair. 'For the purposes of the tape, DI Hunter has re-entered the room.'

Ruth looked over at Matteo and pointed again at the photograph. 'Kevin, this is a photograph of the paraffin and rat poison that we found at your haulage depot. Is there anything you can tell us about that?'

Matteo blinked nervously. 'It's not illegal to have rat poison or paraffin is it? We get rats at the depot and we have paraffin heaters in the Portakabins.'

Ruth tapped the photograph. 'Would it surprise you to know that the rat poison we found is an identical match to the poison used to kill sheep on Brenda Williams' farm?'

'So what?' Matteo replied defensively.

'Well, Kevin, we can identify that poison by the unique wax pellets that it comes in,' Ruth explained. 'And those are the same as the ones we found at your depot.'

'That still doesn't prove anything,' Matteo muttered.

'Come on, Kevin. There are over seventy brands of rat poison on the market. You poisoned the sheep on Brenda Williams' farm to try and put her out of business so she would sell her land to Eastland. And so you would make a fortune.'

'No,' Kevin said, shaking his head anxiously.

'And you burnt out her car and set her barn on fire to do the same,' Georgie snapped.

'No, that's not true.'

'And you murdered Jake Neville and David Lang because they were standing in the way of the plant being built,' Georgie growled.

Matteo shook his head. 'I didn't murder anyone.'

Ruth fixed him with a stare. 'Kevin, look at me.'

After a few tense seconds, Matteo gingerly looked over at her. He was visibly jittery and definitely hiding something.

'Did you poison Brenda Williams' sheep and set fire to her car and barn?' Ruth asked very quietly.

Matteo gave a very slow nod. 'Yes,' he whispered. 'But I didn't have anything to do with killing anyone.'

Ruth looked over at Georgie. Matteo's confession wasn't what they'd hoped for and now Ruth was having her doubts about his guilt in Jake and David's deaths. Her instinct was that if he was responsible, he would have cracked in the past half hour.

'Kevin Matteo, I am charging you with two counts of arson and the offence of killing livestock under the Animal Welfare Act. You do not have to say anything, but it may harm your defence if you do not mention, when questioned, something you later rely on in court. Anything you do say may be given in evidence.'

Chapter 53

After a frustrating morning, Ruth wandered amongst the CID team who were hard at work on their computers or making phone calls. She went over to the scene boards and studied them. She looked at the photograph of Kevin Matteo. Was this really their prime suspect? Despite her earlier certainty that Matteo was their killer, she was beginning to have her doubts.

'Georgie?' Ruth said as she approached her desk. 'You still think Kevin Matteo is guilty, don't you?'

'Yes, boss.' Georgie frowned as if this was a strange question. 'Don't you?'

'If I go with my gut, then no,' Ruth admitted.

French looked over. 'That leaves us with Claudia Berllucci, doesn't it?'

'I guess,' Ruth said, deep in thought. 'Has anyone managed to speak to Wendy Lang yet?'

Garrow looked over. 'Eryl Lang told me that she's too upset to return home so she's continuing to stay with relatives in Chester.'

Ruth raised an eyebrow. 'Rather than be with her husband the day after their son has been murdered. That doesn't seem right does it?'

Georgie shrugged. 'Unless he knew about her affair with Matteo. Maybe their marriage was on the rocks and the last person she wants to be with is Eryl,' she suggested.

Ruth thought for a second. 'Jim, can you see if you can make contact and speak to Wendy Lang? I'd still like us to talk to her about her affair with Kevin Matteo and her whereabouts last Tuesday morning.'

'Yes, boss,' Garrow replied.

As Ruth turned to head back to her office, Georgie signalled to her. 'Boss, something weird here.'

Ruth went over. 'What are you looking at?'

'I'm still going through those encrypted files on David Lang's memory stick,' Georgie explained, pointing to a document on her screen.

'Okay,' Ruth said. 'What's the issue?'

'This is the land registry document for Abbey Farm,' Georgie replied. 'The registered owner of the farm is a Frank Williams.'

Ruth frowned. 'What about Brenda?'

'No.' Georgie shook her head. 'She's not on there. It's just her brother Frank.'

'That's weird.' Ruth processed the information. 'If Brenda doesn't own any of the farm, she can't make a decision whether or not any of the land is sold to Eastland Energy. That's a decision that can only be made by Frank. We're going to need to speak to him as soon as possible.'

Georgie gave her a dark look. 'That's the problem, boss. I can't find any contact details for him. So, I looked up his National Insurance and phoned HMRC. The last tax that Frank Williams paid was in 2004. That was the year that Aled Williams died and when Brenda told David

Lang that Frank had moved to Cornwall to work as an art teacher.'

'Except Frank Williams hasn't worked since then?' Ruth stated, getting a very uneasy feeling. 'What about council tax?'

Georgie shook her head. 'He's not registered for council tax anywhere in Cornwall.'

'Right,' Ruth said, starting to wonder why Brenda had lied about her brother and where he was now. 'Let's get down to Abbey Farm and talk to Brenda now.'

Chapter 54

As Ruth and Georgie pulled into Abbey Farm, dark clouds had started to roll in from the west. The sun had disappeared behind a bank of blackness.

They parked up beside the uniformed patrol car and got out. The wind was strong as it battered noisily through nearby trees. It felt like a storm was imminent.

Sergeant Davies buzzed down the window as they approached. 'You've just missed her, ma'am.'

Ruth frowned. 'Brenda Williams?'

Davies nodded. 'Yeah. She's going to her sister's for a couple of days for a change of scene and a rest.'

Georgie frowned at Ruth. 'She hasn't got a sister.'

'I don't understand.' Davies looked perplexed. 'She told me she'd spoken to you this morning to okay it all. It's not like she's a suspect or anything. We were about to go.'

'Shit,' Ruth muttered.

'Sorry if that's caused a problem,' Davies said, pulling a face.

'When did she leave?' Georgie asked.

'Literally five minutes ago,' Davies replied and then pointed. 'She went left out of here, towards Llangollen.'

'What is she driving?'

'A red pickup truck,' Davies replied.

Ruth gestured to their car. 'Right, follow us. We're going to try and catch her up and pull her over. Something's not right.'

'Yes, ma'am,' Davies said as he started the engine and immediately switched on the blue lights.

Ruth and Georgie dashed back to their car. They jumped in, Georgie started the engine and they sped away.

'I can't believe they let her go,' Georgie growled.

Ruth shrugged as the car bounced over some potholes on the track. 'They were there to protect her. Up until now, Brenda Williams has been a victim in all this.'

'Where do you think she's going?' Georgie asked as they sped out of the farm towards the main road.

'No idea,' Ruth replied as she peered at the road ahead.

Georgie turned left with a squeal of the Astra's tyres.

'You think she could have killed Jake and David?' Georgie asked.

Ruth looked over at her. 'The land didn't belong to her. It belonged to her brother Frank. And we know that David had discovered that because there's a copy of the Land Registry document on his memory stick. If he confronted her with what he'd found, then maybe she killed him.'

'What about Jake?' Georgie asked.

'He was an investigative journalist,' Ruth said. 'If he had checked the local land records to see what the planning status of Abbey Farm was, then he would have seen that the land was registered to Frank Williams too. Maybe

The Portmeirion Killings

Jake called Brenda to find out why it wasn't Frank who was dealing with Eastland Energy.'

Georgie nodded and then gave Ruth a dark look. 'And we think that Frank wasn't dealing with Eastland Energy because he's dead?'

Ruth nodded. 'Yes. I think that Aled Williams was an old-fashioned North Wales sheep farmer. It wouldn't be beyond possibility that he left the farm to Frank as his only son and heir. I'm guessing that didn't sit very well with Brenda. Maybe they fought about it. But Frank Williams disappeared off the face of the earth in 2004 and Brenda was desperate to make sure that no one found out why.'

'Because she killed him,' Georgie said under her breath.

'Possibly.'

Georgie nodded slowly but she looked upset.

Ruth reached over and placed a hand on her shoulder. 'I know the past few days have been really difficult for you, but at least we might have got to the bottom of why Jake and David were killed.'

'Yeah,' Georgie said sadly. 'I did promise Pam and Bill that I'd find out what had happened to Jake.' Georgie then pointed up ahead. 'Boss, look!'

A mud-splattered, dark red Toyota Helux pickup truck had pulled over to the side of the road and was parked.

'I'm guessing that's Brenda Williams,' Ruth said as Georgie started to slow the car a little.

'What's she doing?' Georgie said under her breath.

Ruth frowned. There was something about the stillness of the pickup truck just parked there that unsettled her. 'I'm not sure,' she said quietly.

Georgie pulled the Astra over slowly so that it was parked up behind the truck. Davies pulled in behind them.

Ruth got out of the car and signalled for Davies and his partner to stay put for the time being.

Slowly they approached the vehicle.

Ruth could see the back of Brenda's head sitting in the driver's seat. She was motionless.

As they walked past the back of the pickup, Ruth glanced down inside. At first she thought there was just a dark green tarpaulin lying in the back. Then she realised that a wheel was jutting out from underneath.

As she reached in to pull back the sheet, she had a pretty good idea what was going to be underneath.

It was David Lang's wheelchair.

The leather armrest had a couple of spots of dry blood on it. There was no doubting Brenda's guilt now.

Ruth and Georgie looked at each other before moving towards the driver's door.

The driver's window was fully down.

'Brenda?' Ruth said gently.

There was no response.

Moving so that she was now parallel to the driver's door, she could see that Brenda was sitting motionless, staring ahead.

At first, Ruth thought Brenda was dead. And then she blinked.

'Brenda?' Ruth said again.

After a few seconds, Brenda seemed to register Ruth's presence. She turned very slowly to look at her with a strange, haunted expression.

'What have I done?' Brenda whispered with a confused look.

'It's okay, Brenda,' Ruth reassured her.

'I can't do this anymore,' she said shaking her head.

Ruth went to the driver's door and opened it very slowly. 'Do you want to step out here for me?'

'Yes,' Brenda nodded with an almost childish expression. She climbed down out of the pickup truck.

'There you go,' Ruth said.

Brenda then looked directly at her. 'I need to show you where he is … Is that okay?'

Ruth nodded. 'Yes, I think that's a good idea.'

Chapter 55

It was an hour later and Ruth, Georgie, Brenda and the two uniformed officers had returned to Abbey Farm. Brenda had led them along a pot-holed track that led north from the farmhouse about half a mile from where they had parked.

Looking over to her left, Ruth could see the last glow of daylight slipping imperceptibly below the horizon. The storm clouds that had threatened earlier were gone and a small string of apricot-coloured clouds now lay in a wispy thread in their place. High up, a smoky outline of the moon had started to appear.

To the left, wind-shrunken trees, darkened and covered in grey-green moss. Beyond that, an expanse of wild flowers and then beechwood trees.

'It's just up here,' Brenda said as she stopped and pointed. 'He's just up here.'

Ruth nodded and then looked at Georgie as they trudged on.

After five minutes, they got to a long aluminium gate which Brenda opened. She walked over to an enormous oak tree that towered over the meadow. Brenda pointed to the earth beside its vast trunk which was now covered in grass.

'I buried Frank here,' she said, her voice breaking with emotion. 'He liked it here. We used to play in this meadow when we were kids.' Brenda squatted down on her haunches and patted the ground gently. 'I thought it was peaceful for him. I thought he'd like to be here.'

Ruth looked down at her. 'What happened, Brenda?'

Brenda looked up at her and then sat on the ground. 'I don't even know where to start ...'

'Your father left the farm to Frank but not you, didn't he?' Ruth said in an attempt to prompt her.

'My father was a cold, violent man,' Brenda said, looking away over the fields. 'He made me and my mum's life hell. Never laid a finger on Frank mind. Not once.' Brenda shook her head slowly. 'My mum died from cancer in 1996 and he didn't even shed a tear at her funeral. Bastard.'

Georgie nodded. 'And your father died in 2004, is that right?'

'Yeah,' Brenda replied with an ironic snort. 'Best day of my life, that was. I'd always assumed the farm was coming to me and Frank, as it was just the two of us. But that bastard didn't leave me anything in his will. Everything went to Frank.'

Ruth looked at her. 'That must have made you very angry?'

'Yes, it did.' Brenda nodded. 'Me and Frank were very close, so I assumed that he'd do the right thing and share out my dad's estate.'

There were a few seconds of silence as Brenda gathered her thoughts.

'But he didn't?' Ruth asked.

'No, he didn't,' Brenda whispered. 'He said he wanted everything. There was nothing I could do. And one night, when we'd had too much to drink, we had this huge row. And I pushed him over and he hit his head on the AGA. He just didn't move. At first, I thought he was messing around. Then I saw the blood coming from the back of his head.'

Georgie looked at her. 'You'd killed him?'

'Yes. I killed my own brother.' Brenda blinked away the tears. 'Can you believe that? I was so ashamed … I buried him here a few nights later. I told people that he'd moved down to Cornwall for a fresh start.'

'Did no one try to contact him or get suspicious?' Ruth asked.

'Not really,' Brenda replied, shaking her head. 'Frank had always kept himself to himself. But then Eastland Energy started to poke their noses into everything. They came to me, offering to buy the land over there, up by the lake.' She pointed to the left. 'It wasn't mine to sell but I couldn't tell anyone why or what had happened.'

'What about Jake?' Georgie asked.

'He'd looked at the planning applications,' Brenda explained. 'Then he got copies of the land registry. He came up here and asked why I had been dealing with Eastland as it was Frank's name on the deeds.'

'So, you ran him off the road?' Georgie said coldly.

Brenda nodded and began to weep. 'I'm so … sorry.'

'And then David found out the same,' Ruth said. 'So you murdered him too?'

Brenda closed her eyes and nodded. 'I'm so, so sorry.'

Ruth looked down at her. 'You're going to need to come with us now, Brenda.'

Chapter 56

It was the following morning and Ruth looked around at the tiny DI's office in IR1 as she started to tidy up her stuff. They would be moving back to the main CID office within 24 hours. She was looking forward to getting back there as soon as possible.

'Boss?' said a voice. It was Georgie.

'You don't look well,' Ruth observed.

'Don't I?' Georgie asked with a shrug.

'Just a bit green around the gills,' Ruth said. 'You've been through a lot in the last week, so it's not surprising. How can I help?'

Georgie brought a large cup from behind her back. 'Extra-large flat white.' She handed it to Ruth. 'I just wanted to say thank you.'

'For what?' Ruth asked.

'I think you know what, boss,' Georgie said with a raised eyebrow. 'Lots of SIOs wouldn't have allowed me anywhere near this case because of my personal involvement. But you could see how important it was to me to find justice for Jake and his parents.'

'I needed you on the case. You're an excellent copper, Georgie,' Ruth pointed out. 'And I know from experience what it feels like.'

'I'm just glad we found out what happened to him,' Georgie said.

Ruth got up, put a reassuring hand on her arm and gestured to her coffee. 'Thanks for the coffee,' she said with a warm smile. 'Come on, I'd better get out there.'

Ruth wandered out into IR1 where the CID team were assembled. There was some applause and shouts of *Well done*.

'Right guys,' Ruth said with a relieved expression. 'We got the result we wanted. And I need to thank you all for your hard work on this investigation. As you know, it felt like it was more personal.' She looked over to Georgie. 'But we got justice for Jake and for David and their families. We also got justice for Frank Williams.'

French put down the phone and looked over. 'Boss, that was the CPS. Brenda Williams' solicitor has confirmed that she will be entering a guilty plea for all charges.'

'Thank God,' Ruth sighed with relief. The amount of work and stress that a long murder trial brought was exhausting. Instead, Brenda Williams would be appearing before a judge in a Crown Court for sentencing – and that was that.

There were mutters and general sounds of relief from the CID team.

Garrow looked over. 'We've had a call to say that uniform have arrested a former driver of Matteo Haulage and he's confessed to torching Kevin Matteo's car the day before yesterday.'

'Anything else?' Ruth asked. She wanted to tie up any loose ends of the investigation as soon as possible.

There were a few shakes of heads – they were all exhausted.

'Okay,' Ruth said with a smile, 'in that case, I'll be in the pub at 6pm and the first round is on me.'

The CID team cheered and began to chatter.

Ruth approached Georgie. 'Coming to the pub later?'

Georgie shook her head. 'Actually, there's somewhere else I've got to be.'

Chapter 57

Georgie parked outside St Mary's, a hexagonal-domed church a few miles south of Llangollen. Pam and Bill had sent her a text to say that even though they had never been a religious family, they were having a service of remembrance for Jake's life with a small number of friends and relatives. They would like her to be there but understood if she couldn't make it.

Checking her watch, Georgie could see that she was nearly an hour late. She had debated as to whether she felt up to going. The church and graveyard were quiet and she assumed that she may be too late. Then she spotted a couple sitting on a bench in the distance. Even from where she was standing, she could see that it was Bill and Pam.

She walked slowly along the gravel path through the graveyard to where they were sitting. Thick, small-leaved ivy had grown over the older graves, and those that she could see were covered in lime green lichen. The sound of a distant aeroplane high above drew her eyes skyward. The church's tower and its thin grey spire loomed over her.

Pam and Bill looked up as she approached and gave

her a kind smile.

'I wasn't sure whether or not to come,' Georgie admitted. 'I think I've been holding it together this week until we found out what had happened to Jake. But I didn't know if I could hold it together this afternoon. I didn't want to spoil anything.'

Pam smiled and shook her head. 'It doesn't matter. You're here now.'

'I don't know if the FLO told you, but Brenda Williams is going to plead guilty,' Georgie said.

Bill nodded sadly. 'Yes, we had heard. And that is a relief, I suppose.'

'It doesn't bring him back though, does it?' Georgie said, feeling slightly overwhelmed.

'Do you want to come and sit down, dear?' Pam said. 'You look a bit washed out.'

'Yeah, you're the second person that's told me that today,' Georgie said. 'I think I'll go home and have a bath and an early night.' She then looked at them. 'Of course, I will be at the funeral.'

Bill nodded slowly. 'We were going to ask you something.'

'Okay,' Georgie said with a quizzical expression. 'What is it?'

Pam looked at her. 'Would you say a few words about Jake for us? We've asked a couple of people. But you two were so close when you were younger.'

'It would mean a lot to us,' Bill said quietly.

'Of course,' Georgie said as she went over and gave them both a hug. 'Of course I will.'

She became aware that a figure was approaching along the footpath.

Looking over, she saw that it was Eryl Lang.

I wonder what he's doing here, she wondered. She hoped

that he hadn't come to cause any trouble.

Eryl walked to the end of the path, stopped, and looked at them with an awkward expression. 'Bill, Pam … I felt that I wanted to say something to you. It didn't seem appropriate that I come this afternoon so …'

It was clear that Eryl was struggling with his emotions – he certainly didn't have the air of a man who was going to be confrontational.

Bill gestured to another bench that was opposite. 'Why don't you sit down for a minute, Eryl.'

'Yes,' Eryl nodded, looking a little relieved. 'I think I will.'

'We were so sorry to hear about David,' Pam said gently.

'Thank you.' Eryl looked at them. 'I need to apologise to you. I said some terrible things about Jake in the past. And I'm ashamed of myself. I know that Jake was a good man and he was a good friend to David. And now we've lost them both.'

Georgie looked at them and gestured towards her car. 'I'm going to leave you to it and get going.'

Pam gave her a smile. 'Thank you.'

Eryl looked over at her. 'And thank you for getting justice for David.'

Georgie nodded, turned, and made her way back through the graveyard, her shoes crunching softly on the gravel.

Opening the car door, she got in and settled in the driver's seat. She pulled the seatbelt across her and put the key in the ignition.

Looking over to the passenger seat, she just stared at the three packets that she had bought earlier from a chemists.

Three home pregnancy tests.

Chapter 58

It was late afternoon and 'Association' time at HMP Rhoswen was drawing to a close. Nick and Steve were in the VP wing gym pretending to work out and train but doing very little. Instead, Nick was actually starting to feel sick with fear. The nerves in his stomach swirled and gripped. His pulse was quickening as the time for them to escape fast approached. He knew that if he got caught, it would add years to his sentence. He also knew it was still technically a criminal offence to escape from prison to clear your name. He just hoped that the CPS and a judge would be lenient, but he could still serve some time in prison.

In his head, Nick had run through his plans for when he escaped about a hundred times. However, he couldn't seem to formulate a plan that he wanted to stick with. He knew that he couldn't go anywhere near his home that he shared with Amanda and Megan. Nor could he contact any old friends or those he knew in AA. The police would be monitoring everyone he knew and places that he was familiar with.

What Nick did know is that he needed to change his appearance almost immediately, get hold of cash and travel to Merseyside.

The prison officer, who was sitting at a desk, looked over at them. 'Right lads, time to finish up now.'

Nick put down a 10kg dumbbell that he'd been holding, placed it in the rack and approached Steve.

'What's going on?' Nick asked under his breath.

Steve glanced over at the officer. 'Just keep calm mate.'

The prison officer got up from his desk, stretched his arms and then looked over.

'Come on lads,' he growled. 'Time to go.'

Steve looked confused.

'Where's your contact?' Nick hissed.

Steve's eyes roamed around the room nervously. 'Just be patient.'

Nick's pulse was racing.

Are we escaping or not? he wondered uneasily.

'Oi, are you two deaf?' the prison officer snapped. 'I want you out of here now or I'll put you on a charge.'

'Sorry, boss,' Steve said.

Nick fixed Steve with a stare. 'Are you kidding me?' he murmured angrily.

What the hell is going on?

A figure appeared at the doorway.

It was another prison officer. He was young with cropped blond hair and was pushing a trolley with a large stainless steel tea urn on it.

'That's him,' Steve whispered to Nick. They were on.

'Trev,' the blond officer said with a grin. 'Chaplain is looking for you. Reckons you've locked him out of the chapel.'

'Shit!' Trev said, looking panicked as he got up.

The blond officer gestured to the gym. 'Don't worry

mate. I've got the master with me. I'll lock this up and make sure these two get out of here.'

'Thanks mate,' Trev said as he hurried out and disappeared.

Glancing around, the blond officer quickly wheeled the trolley into the gym and closed the doors behind him.

'Over here now!' he barked at them.

As Steve and Nick scurried over, the blond officer took the lid off the top of the tea urn and reached inside. There clearly wasn't boiling hot tea in there.

'Put these on quickly,' he snapped as he threw them both a hoodie with a bright logo on and a baseball cap.

Nick pulled the hoodie over his head as his heart pounded against his chest.

'And these,' the blond officer said as he threw over two blue visitor lanyards with badges.

The blond officer motioned to them. 'Right, follow me. Keep your heads down, don't make eye contact with anyone and do not break your stride at any point. Understood?'

'Yes,' Steve replied.

Marching across the gym to the far corner, the blond officer pulled out a huge bunch of keys. He unlocked a fire exit door that led to an outside metal staircase that led down to the ground.

Jesus, I can't believe this is actually happening.

The three of them descended down the staircase, their shoes making metallic clangs as they went.

Getting to the ground, Nick glanced around. They were surrounded by the towering perimeter fence.

The officer turned left and marched them to a gate which he unlocked using his security pass.

'Come on, keep moving,' he hissed.

Keeping his head down, Nick was aware of other prisoners out in the recreation yard to the right of them. It would only take one of them to see him and Steve and the alarm would be raised.

Looking ahead, he saw what looked like the final gate before the visitors' car park.

However, there was another prison officer standing there with a clipboard and a walkie talkie.

Shit! How the hell are we getting past him?

'Roy!' the blond officer said, greeting him cheerily as they approached. 'See United lost again last night, eh?'

'They're fucking shit!'

The blond officer pointed to Steve and Nick. 'These guys are part of the Substance Misuse Team. I've checked and they've both been vetted.'

'Right you are,' Roy said as he opened the gate to let them walk through. 'Have a grand day, fellas.'

The blond officer stopped, engaging Roy in more talk about football as Steve and Nick walked down a footpath and found themselves in the visitors' car park.

'Jesus Christ!' Nick gasped.

'Don't drop your guard yet, mate,' Steve growled. 'There are cameras everywhere.'

From the right, a white Audi 4x4 pulled up slowly.

'This is us,' Steve said, gesturing to the car as he went over and opened the passenger door.

Keeping his head down, Nick walked casually to one of the rear doors, opened it and got in.

The car pulled away and out of the prison car park.

Chapter 59

Ruth had been at Sarah's house for about an hour with Daniel. Sarah had made Daniel a fishfinger sandwich – his favourite – and he was now watching TV. Climbing the stairs, Ruth wanted to pop in to see Doreen. She wondered if Doreen had thought any more about when and if she was going to talk to Sarah about not being her biological mother.

Poking her head in through the door, Ruth spotted that Doreen was engrossed in reading her Kindle.

'How is the crime wave in Norfolk?' Ruth asked quietly.

Lifting up her reading glasses, Doreen peered up at her. 'Oh hiya.' She then gestured to her Kindle. 'I finished that series. I'm on to Cornwall now. This time the main detective is gay.'

Ruth gave an ironic laugh. 'Well that's not very realistic.'

Doreen chortled as she realised Ruth's joke. 'No. As if that ever happens, eh?'

'Is she happy?' Ruth asked.

'It's a *he* and he's married with kids,' Doreen said, raising an eyebrow. 'His life is a bit of a mess.'

'No serial killers though?' Ruth asked.

'No.' Doreen shook her head. 'Although someone has just sacrificed the new vicar on a tombstone in the graveyard.'

'Gosh,' Ruth laughed. 'Welcome to Cornwall, eh?'

Doreen put down the Kindle and gave Ruth a meaningful look. 'Can you sit down for a second dear? It's hurting my neck looking up at you from here.'

'Of course.' Ruth went over and sat on the edge of the bed. 'Everything okay?'

Doreen looked nervously towards the door, so Ruth got up, pushed it shut and went and sat down again.

'I've made a decision,' Doreen said quietly.

'Okay,' Ruth said with an empathetic look.

'I'm not going to tell Sarah about what we talked about the other day,' Doreen said shaking her head, deep in thought. 'About my sister Alice. I don't see what it would achieve. And I don't know how long I've got left.'

'Don't say that,' Ruth said, pulling a face. 'You'll outlive us all. I had to run after someone a couple of nights ago and I nearly had a heart attack.'

Doreen gave her a smile. 'I just don't want anything to come between us now that I've got Sarah back in my life. Every day is precious, isn't it?'

'Yes, it is,' Ruth agreed. 'And, for what it's worth, I think that's a very wise decision. I don't think Sarah or you have anything to gain from this coming out now. And it could really damage your relationship.'

Doreen looked a bit teary as she reached over and patted Ruth's hand. 'Thank you, dear. You don't know how much it means to me to have talked this through with you.'

'Any time,' Ruth said, taking her hand and holding it.

The Portmeirion Killings

There was a knock at the door.

Ruth and Doreen looked at each other but before either of them could answer, the door opened and Daniel poked his head around it.

'There he is,' Doreen said with a beaming smile.

Daniel frowned at Ruth. 'I thought you'd be outside, you know ...' Daniel mimed someone smoking a cigarette.

Ruth patted her jacket and smiled at him. 'I've got something to show you.'

'What is it?' he asked with a curious expression.

Ruth fished a packet out of her jacket pocket. It was nicotine chewing gum. She handed it to him to look at. 'I'm using this to give up smoking.'

'Really?' Daniel smiled as he read the packet.

'Otherwise you'll end up like me,' Doreen pointed out.

'Cool,' Daniel said, handing her back the packet – he looked pleased.

Ruth ruffled his hair. 'Right, sunshine, I've got to get you home. Big day tomorrow.'

Doreen nodded. 'That's right. You're going to meet the headmaster at your new school, aren't you?'

'Apparently we have to call them headteachers these days,' Ruth said. 'Mr Roberts.'

Daniel frowned. 'I don't want to go. I want to stay with you.'

Doreen snorted. 'You can't stay with Ruth all day. She's got to go out and catch all the baddies.'

Daniel nodded as if this made perfect sense. 'Oh yes. Of course.'

Doreen looked over at Ruth and gave her a wink.

Chapter 60

Looking at her watch, Georgie saw it was 8pm. She had just finished tidying up her living room. She always tidied when she was feeling anxious. Now she was wearing a t-shirt, she could see that the bruise on her forearm where she had been hit earlier was developing a purple and green colour. The throbbing had stopped but it was very sore to the touch.

Slumping down onto the sofa, she checked her watch again. 8.01pm. She would wait another five minutes to be on the safe side. She let out a nervous breath and wondered if she should fix herself a strong drink. Maybe not quite yet.

Something caught her eye. A tiny fringe of dark wool was stuck between the sofa and the back of the wall. She couldn't work out what it was. Moving the sofa back an inch, she reached down, pulled at it and realised that it was actually the fringe to a black and blue scarf that had fallen down the back of the sofa. It was Jake's scarf. It must have got stuck there when they had undressed and made love a few nights earlier.

A wave of emotion swept over her and made her catch her breath. She held the scarf in both hands, feeling its soft texture. Her eyes filled with tears as she put the scarf to her face and smelt it. It was permeated with Jake's aftershave and she was instantly transported back to the night they had spent together. The touch of his skin, his lips, his breath. His long eyelashes and dark chestnut eyes.

Pushing the scarf into her face, she let herself be crushed by her grief. She sobbed uncontrollably, gasping for breath and shaking. She wanted him to be sitting next to her there on the sofa. It was so bloody unfair. Her feelings of loss became tinged with anger. If Brenda Williams had been standing there right now, Georgie would have happily stabbed her to death. She didn't care if that was a crazy thought. She would have stabbed her to death and enjoyed it.

Taking the scarf from her face, Georgie rocked back on the sofa and took a deep, long breath. She wiped her eyes and tried to compose herself. Blowing out her cheeks, she knew what she needed to do.

She got up from the sofa with the scarf still clutched in her hands and walked very slowly from the living room into the hallway. As she turned towards the downstairs toilet, she caught her reflection in the mirror. Her face was red and puffy. Her mascara had streaked a little on her cheeks.

The next two minutes might define the rest of her life. She looked into her own eyes, looking and wondering about the person that peered back at her. What would she do? What sort of person was she? She knew the choices she might make could define her.

She ran her hand through her hair and gave it a little shake to tidy it. Rubbing the moisture and smeared make-up from her face, she got another waft of Jake's aftershave.

Turning cautiously, she took the final steps along the hall and entered the small toilet cubicle.

There they were.

Three pregnancy tests were lined up on the closed lid of the toilet.

Taking a deep breath, she went over to take a look.

In that moment, she still wasn't sure what she wanted to see.

All three pregnancy tests had the tell-tale two red lines of a positive test.

Georgie blinked as she looked at them.

She was pregnant with Jake's baby.

Chapter 61

It was dark by the time Ruth pulled away from Sarah's remote house. She glanced over at Daniel in the passenger seat. He was clearly deep in thought.

'You thinking about tomorrow?' she asked him.

'Sort of,' he said with a shrug.

'You don't need to worry,' she said, trying to reassure him. 'It's a really nice school. And you're going to make lots of new friends.'

Daniel frowned. 'Everyone's a Liverpool fan round here.'

'Yeah, I know,' Ruth said with a smile, 'but you learn to tolerate them. Sometimes.'

A moment later, Daniel looked over. 'I was also thinking about my dad.'

'Were you?' Ruth asked.

'Yeah.'

'You must miss him a lot?' she asked gently.

Daniel nodded but didn't reply. He looked out of the window as they made their way down the bumpy track that led away from Sarah's house. There were thick woods either side that seemed impenetrable in the darkness.

'Can we go and see him?' Daniel said, still looking out of the window.

'See who?'

'My dad. Where he's buried. Can we go there?'

'Of course we can,' Ruth said. 'I can take you there at the weekend if you like.'

'Yeah.' Daniel nodded. 'I'd like to tell him about me going to a new school. He said I was very bright for my age.'

Ruth smiled. 'You are very bright for your age.'

As she turned the corner, she was filled with the delight that only that type of conversation with a child can bring.

Suddenly, a figure in a hoodie stepped out across the track.

'Jesus!' Ruth cried, slamming on her brakes.

The figure didn't move for a second.

Ruth hit the automatic locks to keep them safe as her heart pounded.

The figure then moved quickly towards them.

For a second, she wondered if it had anything to do with the man she and Georgie had encountered at the warehouse.

'Who's that?' Daniel asked, sounding scared.

'I don't know,' she admitted as she put the car into reverse. 'And I don't want to find out.'

From out of nowhere, a face appeared at the window of the driver's door.

'Bloody hell!' Ruth yelled, jumping out of her skin.

As she stamped on the accelerator, she caught a glimpse of the man's face.

The car had shot back over twenty yards before she realised that she knew who the man was.

It was Nick.

'Oh my God,' she muttered, stopping the car.

Unclipping her seatbelt, she leapt from the car as Nick walked towards her.

'What the hell are you doing?' she asked in a panic.

'Long story,' Nick said as he reached the car.

'Erm, aren't you meant to be in prison?' she asked in utter disbelief.

'Yes,' he replied.

Her eyes widened. 'You've escaped?'

'I didn't have a choice,' Nick explained. 'And I couldn't go to your house as they'd be watching it.'

'Jesus Christ, Nick!' Ruth gasped as she went and gave him a hug. 'Are you all right?'

'I've been better,' he admitted. 'I don't want to drag you into the middle of this, but I do need help.'

'Don't worry. Get in the car,' she said, looking around nervously.

They jumped back in the car.

Daniel spun around to look at Nick. 'You're that policeman that Ruth works with, aren't you?'

Nick put down his hood and nodded. 'Yeah, I am.'

Ruth took a deep breath as she put the car back into gear and they sped away.

Enjoy this book?
Get the next book in the series
'The Llandudno Pier Killings'
on pre-order on Amazon
Publication date February 2023

https://www.amazon.co.uk/dp/B0B4X2SMCG
Https://www.amazon.com/dp/B0B4X2SMCG

The Llandudno Pier Killings
A Ruth Hunter Crime Thriller #Book 14

Your FREE book is waiting for you now

Get your FREE copy of the prequel to
the DI Ruth Hunter Series NOW
http://www.simonmccleave.com/vip-email-club
and join my VIP Email Club

DC RUTH HUNTER SERIES

London, 1997. A series of baffling murders. A web of political corruption. DC Ruth Hunter thinks she has the brutal killer in her sights, but there's one problem. He's a Serbian War criminal who died five years earlier and lies buried in Bosnia.

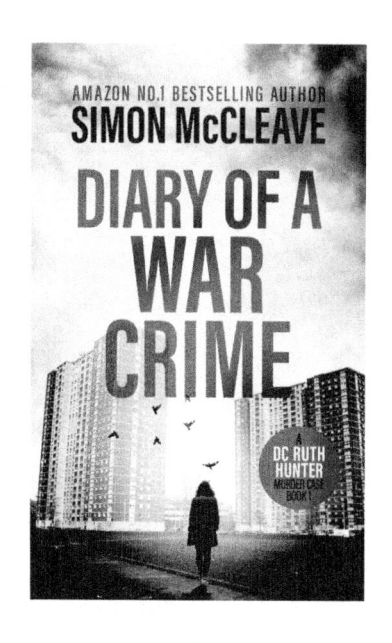

My Book
My Book

AUTHOR'S NOTE

Although this book is very much a work of fiction, it is located in Snowdonia, a spectacular area of North Wales. It is steeped in history and folklore that spans over two thousand years. It is worth mentioning that Llancastell is a fictional town on the eastern edges of Snowdonia. I have made liberal use of artistic licence, names and places have been changed to enhance the pace and substance of the story.

Acknowledgments

I will always be indebted to the people who have made this novel possible.

My mum, Pam, and my stronger half, Nicola, whose initial reaction, ideas and notes on my work I trust implicitly. And Dad, for his overwhelming enthusiasm. Carole Kendal for her meticulous proofreading. My excellent publicists, Emma Draude and Emma Dowson at EDPR. My designer Stuart Bache for yet another incredible cover design. My superb agent, Millie Hoskins at United Agents, and Dave Gaughran and Nick Erick for invaluable support and advice.

Printed in Dunstable, United Kingdom